THE HOUSEKEEPER

VALERIE KEOGH

First published in Great Britain in 2023 by Boldwood Books Ltd.

Cover Design by Head Design Ltd

Cover Photography: Shutterstock

A CIP catalogue record for this book is available from the British Library.

Paperback ISBN 978-1-80549-413-3

Large Print ISBN 978-1-80549-409-6

Hardback ISBN 978-1-80549-408-9

Ebook ISBN 978-1-80549-406-5

Kindle ISBN 978-1-80549-407-2

Audio CD ISBN 978-1-80549-414-0

MP3 CD ISBN 978-1-80549-411-9

Digital audio download ISBN 978-1-80549-405-8

Boldwood Books Ltd
23 Bowerdean Street
London SW6 3TN
www.boldwoodbooks.com

For my niece, Jean Fearon
With love

PROLOGUE

The wrought-iron gates, set several feet back from the narrow country road, had seen better days, their once lustrous black corroded in places as if the gate was edged in rot. Ivy and bramble crawled from the hedgerow on both sides, slithering and twisting around the upright and cross bars. The vicious tangle of greenery filled the gaps and hid what lay behind from curious eyes.

The gates were locked. A chain, far heavier than was surely necessary, bound them together, winding around and around as if to be sure, as if to be absolutely certain, they'd hold it tight. The ends were secured with an incongruously large padlock. It was oddly shiny and, at first glance, seeing it nestled among the ivy, a passer-by might be reminded of a long-forgotten Christmas decoration on an abandoned tree. It was only on a second glance, when they'd reached for it and had their skin pierced by bramble thorns, when they'd pulled their hand back to suck the bubble of blood, that they'd look again and see that the metal didn't shine as much as glint with almost malevolent intent.

If they weren't warned away, if they were still consumed with curiosity to know what lay behind, they'd look up and shake their heads. The gates may have seen better days, but the finials that edged the concave curve at the top of each still appeared pointed as if they'd been honed razor sharp.

They were enough to deter the adventurous, the curious, or the merely stupid from climbing over.

Nobody was getting into the grounds of the old house.

But perhaps that wasn't the idea.

Maybe it was to stop anything – all the secrets – from getting out.

1

Cassie Macreddin had left her London home early to make her nine o'clock appointment with the estate agent in Hindon. She'd made allowances for rush-hour traffic and added extra time to negotiate the unknown winding country roads in Wiltshire. The journey had gone without mishap, and as a result, she'd arrived far too early.

Passing a small garage on the outskirts of the village, a sign advertising takeaway coffee caught her eye and she hurriedly indicated and pulled in. Inside, she resisted the sad selection of pastries and ordered a large cappuccino. She sat in her car to sip it and watch the time click by.

When the disposable cup was empty, she got out and tossed it into a nearby bin. It was still too early but there was no point in hanging around the garage when she could be investigating the village she might soon be calling home. Feeling a mix of anxiety and excitement, she drove on. She'd looked at Street View on Google Maps. The reality, as was often the way, was prettier. Honey-coloured houses, pollarded lime trees, a church steeple. All picture-book perfect.

There was a parking space directly outside the estate agent's office. She pulled into it, turned off the engine and sat for a moment looking around before climbing out. Shivering a little in the early morning breeze that drifted along the wide street, she glanced at the back seat where she'd thrown her jacket a few hours earlier. Instead of reaching for it, she wrapped her arms across her chest and crossed to the window to examine the property photographs on display. It was a relief to see that the house she was interested in wasn't among them. Since she'd found it on the internet two weeks previously, she'd been terrified in case someone else might see it, fall in love with it as she had done, and outbid her.

It was *the one*. She'd looked at the details of so many properties over the previous two months and was beginning to think she'd never find what she was looking for, and then, there it was. An old house – tick. Detached – tick. In need of extensive repair and redecoration – tick, tick. She'd pored over the photographs, enlarged the floor plans, pored over them, imagined knocking down walls, extending the kitchen. She'd almost been tempted to put in an offer based on the extensive details she'd read on the website. Almost tempted, but although Cassie was a lot of things, she wasn't stupid. Or at least, she qualified with a smile, not about property.

Her appointment with the agent was for nine. At five to, she looked up the street and saw a besuited thin man hurrying towards her.

'Cassie Macreddin?' he said, extending his hand as he reached her side.

'Yes, good morning,' she said, shuffling the bag and the papers she held, to take the hand that was hovering between them. 'Sorry, I wanted to make sure I was bringing everything I needed.'

'I'm not who you were expecting to meet,' he said, surprising her. He pulled a huge bunch of keys from his jacket pocket, inserted one into the office door and pushed it open. Immediately there was the beep beep of a security alarm. 'Hang on a sec.' Two long strides took him to the control panel. He tapped in a series of numbers, turning to wave her in as the beeping stopped. 'Come in, please.' He indicated a chair for her to take and took the one on the other side of the desk. 'I'm Chris Baker. You were expecting my partner, Joe Major. Unfortunately, he won't be in today.'

Disappointment hit Cassie like a physical blow. She could feel her hopes and dreams bounce away.

'I should explain,' Baker said, running a hand over his face. 'You'll have to excuse me; it's been a bit of a shock. Joe had a heart attack. Early this morning. He's in hospital in Bath. His wife says he's going to be okay.'

'Good, that's good.' Cassie tried to sound sympathetic. It was hard. She didn't know the man. She was glad he was doing well, obviously, but she was more concerned with how his condition was going to impact on her plans. She wasn't a selfish woman, but she had her heart set on getting this house, and any delay might capsize that dream. All she wanted was for one thing, one damn thing to go her way. Was it too much to ask for?

'Unfortunately, by the time I'd gathered my thoughts, it was too late to contact you to let you know,' Baker said. 'I knew you were coming from London, so I thought it was best to meet you here.'

Cassie relaxed a little. Maybe the day wasn't going to be a disaster after all. 'Okay, so you're going to show me around the property, yes?'

Baker huffed a frustrated sigh. 'I wish I could, I really do. Unfortunately, I'm tied up all morning. If you could wait, I do have time late afternoon.'

Late afternoon? She only had the one day off work so she

needed to get home, but leaving Hindon that late would bring her back to London in the thick of rush hour. Always a nervous driver, after the accident she'd been worse. That morning, a crippling fear had her clenching the steering wheel with such painful intensity that her fingers had been cramped by the time she'd arrived. This had been her first long journey in months. Maybe it would get easier.

'That's not going to work for me, I'm afraid. I need to get back to the city this afternoon.' A ripple of annoyance slid over her when she saw his lips narrow. She knew before he spoke that he was going to apologise and ask her to come another day. She held up a hand to stop him. 'I really need to see the property today. I have another few that I'm looking at and I've promised to let the other vendors know before the end of the week.' It was a lie, but he wouldn't know that.

'I'm really sorry,' he said, and did manage to look suitably apologetic. 'There is nothing I can do, I'm afraid.'

Cassie wanted to reach across the desk, grab his shiny blue tie, and strangle him with it. 'It's been on the market for a long time, I'm sure the vendors would like to get it sold.'

He shrugged off her comment. 'It's a repossession. The previous owners bought it almost two years ago. They did some work on it, then went bust before finishing. The bank isn't in any great rush to sell.'

But she was in a rush to buy. 'I've come all this way; I really don't want to leave without seeing it. Could I go on my own? I've seen all the details on your website; I just need to get a feel for the place to see if it would suit.'

'You told Joe you were thinking of starting up a B&B. Is that right?'

'Yes. The property is in the right location; it'd be ideal.' It had been a dream for a long time. Chuck the stultifyingly boring job in the civil service. Get out of London. Start afresh. It was ironic how the circumstances that had almost ended her life were responsible for making the dream possible.

'We don't usually allow clients to go alone,' he said.

His expression was giving nothing away, but Cassie took heart from the *usually* and held her breath.

'The last owners left it in a bit of a mess,' he said. One of his thin hands was resting flat on the desk – he tapped the middle finger rhythmically as he stared at her.

Perhaps it helped his thought processes. She tried to portray herself as the solid dependable type. The kind of person you could trust to look around a house unescorted.

'There are floorboards up in some of the rooms.'

She sensed he was giving way, but she wasn't there yet. 'I'll be very careful, I promise. I don't need to go into the rooms really. It's the outside of the house that I'm keen to see. The condition and size of the gardens, where the outhouses sit, etcetera.'

Baker nodded. 'It is difficult to see how extensive it is from the photos.'

It seemed best to say nothing, let the pros and cons tick in the estate agent's head. Cassie's hand was resting on her lap, she crossed her middle and first fingers, making a wish like a child.

'It's an exceptional circumstance,' Baker said. Abruptly, almost as if he was afraid he'd change his mind, he got to his feet and crossed to a desk on the other side of the office. He pulled open a drawer and fumbled in it, pulling out various bunches of keys to peer at the labels attached. Finally, he gave a grunt of satisfaction and returned to his desk. He held the bunch out, then hesitated as it dangled over Cassie's outstretched hand. 'It's just unfortunate that you can't wait till this afternoon. I'd be happy to show you around then.'

Cassie's fingers closed around the cold metal and tugged

slightly till he had no option but to release them. 'I'll be fine, honestly.'

Baker didn't appear convinced. He nodded towards the keys. 'They're all labelled. The smaller one is for the padlock on the main gate. I haven't been out for a while; it might need a bit of jigging to get it to open.

'The road to Hindon House is straightforward.' He pointed to where her car was parked outside. 'You're facing the right direction. Follow the High Street from the village. I will warn you,' he said with his first smile, 'that it's quite narrow. When you pass the national speed limit sign, take the next turn right. The property is about half a mile down that narrow road. Keep an eye for the gate. It'll be on your left. You can't miss it.'

Cassie hated when people said that. Invariably she did miss whatever it was, and it made her feel twice as stupid, as if everyone but her wouldn't have done. Her fingers closed over the keys. It didn't matter. She would find it, and it'd be perfect, and everything would go to plan.

And everything that had happened. Everything she'd done. None of it would matter any more. Her fingers tightened painfully on the keys. She had to believe that.

2

Cassie leaned forward as she drove, hands clutching the steering wheel. She drove slowly, slower still when she reached the speed limit sign until she saw the road to the right. Indicating, she turned down a road so narrow she hoped not to meet something coming in the opposite direction.

Half a mile, the agent had said. She checked her milometer and crawled along, eyes straining to see a gap in the high hedge that edged the road. She didn't precisely miss the gate but had passed it by before realising. It wasn't surprising. It was set several feet back from the road and had been almost swallowed by the hedgerow on either side.

On the narrow country road there was no space to turn. Putting the car into reverse, she slowly backed up and pulled into the semicircle in front of the gate. The ground was carpeted in daisies, dandelions and a mix of grasses that were probably from seed blown in on the wind from nearby farms. The grasses swayed gently in the breeze, daisies nodded, and downy white parachutes sailed upward from the gone-to-seed dandelions.

Cassie lowered her window. Her first thought was how idyllic it was; her second that it looked as if the wrought-iron gate hadn't been opened in a long, long time. She was struck by the idea that the encroaching ivy and bramble was trying to drag the iron back into the ground from whence it had come. Prone to flights of fancy as she was, this one made her smile.

The ivy might not have succeeded in dragging the gate downward, but it did make it impossible to see through to the house and land that lay behind. She switched off the engine and climbed out. The silence was broken only by the twittering of birds. It sounded as if the hedgerow was filled with them. Her plan was to run a country house B&B. A retreat. Birdsong was the ideal soundtrack for it. So far, she thought, so absolutely perfect.

Ivy had coiled around the padlock and chain. She tore it away, grimacing when woodlice scampered over the metal. The bunch of keys was in her pocket. She pulled it out and searched through it for the smallest one. When the woodlice appeared reluctant to vacate their home, she pulled a leaf from the ivy to sweep them away and inserted the key into the lock before they'd a chance to return.

She'd expected to have to struggle so was surprised when the key turned smoothly in the lock, the click as it opened loud enough to startle birds on both sides, a flurry of sparrows rising and moving in a noisy twitter to vanish into a spot further along the hedge. Tossing the padlock to the ground, Cassie tugged at the chain to separate it from the tendrils of ivy and other plants that had wound round it. When finally, it was free, she dropped it on the ground beside the lock.

It quickly dawned on Cassie that getting the lock and chain off had been the easy bit. Between the ivy and brambles that had wrapped themselves around the bars, and the weeds that had grown at the base on both sides, the gates were stuck fast. Cassie used her feet to flatten sycamore saplings and seedlings and was grateful she was wearing trousers as she kicked down tall stinging nettles. The edge of one of the bigger keys proved to be a useful tool to split the ivy stems that seemed determined to prevent her entry. The brambles were more difficult, their thorns piercing her skin as she tried to lever them away.

It was hard dirty work. By the time she felt one of the two gates give a little, she was hot and sweaty and multiple scratches and thorn pricks decorated her hands and arms. She refused to give up though. Digging her heels in, she gripped the edge of the gate, put her weight behind it and pulled.

As soon as the gap was wide enough, she squeezed sideways through it. 'Damn it,' she said, when her T-shirt caught on a bramble. It took a few seconds, and more thorn damage to her fingers, before she was able to release it.

She was sucking a drop of blood from her thumb when she finally turned to look towards the house. Despite the metallic taste of blood in her mouth and the stinging pain from the punctures and scratches, her lips curved in a relieved smile.

Overgrown bushes lined the weed-strewn driveway as it snaked its way to the house a quarter of a mile ahead. Between the bushes, and the hedgerow that made up the boundary to the land, saplings and tall weeds flourished. It didn't look as if the people who'd bought it two years before had done any work on the grounds. According to the estate agent's details, the last time the house had been occupied for more than a couple of years at a time had been ten years before that. In the absence of care, the grounds had reverted to wilderness.

As she walked along, her footsteps quiet on the moss and weeds that carpeted the gravel drive, her mind was whirring with ideas. She was giving herself six months to do the necessary renovations and decorating. By that time, she'd need to start earning money. The gardens would take forever. Perhaps she could use it as a selling point, in a similar way to the Lost Gardens of Heligan in Cornwall. On a far smaller scale, of course, but it might be worth considering.

It would be good to have things to think about. It would help to chase the demons away.

She needed to keep them away if she'd any hope of making a new life.

3

Because of the overgrown trees surrounding the house, Cassie didn't get a good view until she was almost upon it. The driveway ended in a semicircle, the house lying along its flat edge. Some attempt had obviously been made by the previous purchasers to clear the weeds. It made it easier to imagine how it must have looked in its heyday. More importantly, how it could look again.

Early Victorian, the three-storey mansion had been built for a wealthy social-climbing wool merchant. He'd obviously been determined to make a statement. From the stone steps that led up to a very grand imposing front door, to the two elegant bay windows on each side and the row of windows on the upper floor, everything screamed *look at me*.

She stood staring. This could be it. This could work. Wasn't this exactly what she'd wanted, what she'd dreamt about for so long? But she'd never expected to be doing it alone. Richie should be here with her. They should be standing hand and hand, facing their future together. She swallowed the lump in her throat, pushed back the guilt, forced herself to concentrate on the grand house in front of her.

The idea that there was less work to do than she'd expected faded as she crossed the semicircle to the steps leading to the front door. Close to, she could see the window frames on each side were badly rotten, the glass in most of them intact but cracked. All the windows had shutters. And when she peered from the steps down to the lower ground-floor level, she could see that the windows there were barred. Such security seemed excessive in such a rural setting. She'd read about the history of the house. Over the years it had gone from being a private home to, at various times, a convent, a school, a rehabilitation centre during the last war, and then back to a private home. It had changed hands several times over the last few decades.

She wondered which of its owners was so afraid of being burgled that they'd felt the need to put bars on the windows.

Removing them would be added to her list of things to do.

Continuing up the steps to the front door, she was pleased to see this was in good repair. It possibly wasn't the original, but it was in keeping with the house. It wouldn't need to be replaced and every penny would need to count.

Taking out the bunch of keys, she shuffled them to find the one labelled *front door*. The lock too was in good condition and the key turned with ease. Cassie took a deep breath and pushed the door open.

Despite not being original, it was old, and she wouldn't have been surprised if it had squeaked or creaked. Neither sound would have startled her or have sent goosebumps running over her skin. What did unsettle her though was the soft sibilant shush the door made as it slid over the floor behind. A whisper, as if to warn her of something. It brought Cassie to a halt with her hand on the door, her body half-turned as if to flee. Fear seemed to be her instant reaction to everything these days. She shook her head in part acknowledgement of how silly she was being, part recognition of how damaged she still was by what had happened.

It had been six months since the accident that had killed her husband. She'd walked free, without as much as a scratch. Her friends said she was suffering survivor's guilt, but then her friends didn't know the truth about what had happened that day. It wasn't something she could tell. Unfortunately, she couldn't let it go either, and it stayed inside, curdled and sour. Sometimes, she worried that it would taint everything she had planned. Could she really build a happy life based on such a shattered and shaky foundation?

Once again, Cassie forced her thoughts back to the present. There wasn't time for nonsense. Gritting her teeth, she pushed the door fully open and stepped inside.

The entrance hall was large and probably would have been very elegant and inviting. Time, and the previous owners, had taken a heavy toll. One wall was covered in fuzzy black mould, hinting at a leak from somewhere above. Either it hadn't been sorted last time, or it had occurred since. Since, she guessed, stepping closer. The wall was so wet, it almost glistened.

The agent had been right. It wasn't the safest of places. Floorboards had been taken up in several places, and not replaced. Possibly when they were doing the rewiring, or plumbing, or something. No doubt it would all become clear.

The cantilevered stairway that ran from the hall to the upper floor looked to be intact. Before heading up, she investigated the other rooms on this level. A huge one on the right, with windows to the front and to the rear was littered with broken furniture, piles of floorboards, tins of paint and other paraphernalia. But there wasn't, she was pleased to see, any sign of damp here.

The room on the other side wasn't so lucky. It was on the other side of the mouldy wall and shared the same problem. Otherwise, it was in a similar state as the other, all kinds of rubbish had been dumped in it. She'd have to hire a skip to get rid of it all.

Pound signs were flashing in front of her eyes as she climbed the stairs to the upper floor where there were five bedrooms and one bathroom. Her plan was to make all the rooms en suite. Although it would cost a hefty amount, it was necessary if she wanted to attract high-paying customers.

All the rooms were a mess, but structurally they were okay. It was in the last room, the bathroom, where she found the problem. And she'd been right. It was a new problem or at least it hadn't predated the previous owners. They'd caused it. The bathroom had been gutted; the fixtures disconnected. The house was connected to mains water, and it had been turned off, so she wasn't sure how one pipe was dripping. Only a drop every few seconds, it was enough, over the previous two years, to have caused chaos.

It was a case of shutting the stable door after the horse had vanished over the hills, but there was a bucket nearby with nothing else to do so she stuck it under the pipe.

Back on the ground floor, she opened a door under the stairway, and headed down to the lower ground floor. She found herself in a small dim hallway. To one side a corridor stretched ahead, disappearing into the darkness. She took a few steps along it, stopping to peer into the first room. A tiny space, jammed with all sorts of junk: tables, chairs, beds, suitcases and unidentifiable items. The rubbish of years. A grim little room. Dark too, the little light coming through the small windows further dulled by the security bars. Cassie folded her arms across her chest and shivered. Not even the recent good weather had managed to dispel the lingering damp dreary sadness that seemed to cling to the walls.

Back in the corridor, she looked along its length seeing pockets of light in the darkness that hinted at more rooms. She wasn't risking going further. If they were all the same as this one, there was no hurry to explore them.

Back in the small hallway, she pushed open the door opposite. It led to another corridor, but this time she nodded in satisfaction. According to the estate agent details, this part of the lower ground floor had been used for domestic staff accommodation. It was where Cassie planned to have her living quarters. All it took was to remove all the accumulated junk and knock down a few walls. Easy! She was smiling when she returned to the hall to open the final door into the kitchen.

The room was a dated, higgledy-piggledy mess. Windows overlooking the rear garden were too small to let in much light; it needed French windows to brighten the room. It was small for what she wanted too. With her hands on her hips, she eyed the back wall. If that could come down, and the walls dividing the small useless rooms behind were removed, this would be a fabulous space with light coming from both sides.

She could imagine it. A big fancy kitchen. A huge table for when friends visited. A comfy seating area with a TV. The other space could be converted into two bedrooms, and a huge luxury bathroom. She hugged herself. It was going to be absolutely perfect.

There was a key on the bunch she held to open the back door. Outside, outhouses stretched along one side of a dusty yard. She realised then why the gate had been so hard to open. There was another access here. It wasn't locked and opened easily. Irritation flared. Why hadn't the estate agent directed her to this gate? Then she remembered it was his partner who'd been supposed to show her around; perhaps Chris Baker didn't know about this access gate.

It was annoying. She could have driven right in. Next time. And she knew there'd be one, because despite requiring more work than she'd expected, she was still convinced it was the perfect house for her.

On the other side of the yard, she saw what might have been a kitchen garden at one time. And behind that an orchard, the trees already laden with fruit. She couldn't see the boundary of the land. There was plenty to explore, but not that day.

The agent had said it was a repossession and was being sold by the bank. She'd make a low cash offer citing the leak, and the extensive renovations required as a reason to justify it. It had been on the market for almost two years; the price had been dropped twice in that time. She couldn't see them rejecting her offer.

If it went to plan, she could be the owner in less than a month. Get the work started. Make that damn dream come true.

She'd make it come true if she had to kill someone to do it.

After all, hadn't she done that already?

4

The low offer Cassie made for Hindon House was rejected. She offered the asking price, and sat chewing the nails of one hand, the fingers of the other curled around the phone waiting for it to ring. When it did, she yelped, then took a deep breath to calm herself before answering. She wasn't sure if the estate agent was convinced by her casual air, as if she didn't care, as if this didn't mean absolutely everything to her.

'They've accepted your offer,' Chris Baker said. 'Subject, as you'd insisted, to a structural survey.'

She'd debated not bothering with having one done and saving the cost. It would have been a foolish step to have missed though. The house was in poor repair – she needed to make sure it was structurally sound and wasn't going to fall around her ears.

It took a further week to get the survey done. According to the detailed report she'd commissioned, the house was solid, built on a stone, mortar and compacted clay foundation which would have been typical of the time. This, they suggested, may need to be reinforced with concrete. As she'd discovered herself, the cause of the damp to the walls downstairs was caused by that one stupid dripping pipe. There was no other sign of damp. They did list a catalogue of problems, but all were ones she already knew about, and none made her change her mind about the purchase.

And then it was hers. The first step in getting the future she'd longed for.

Conveyancing seemed to generate a mountain of paperwork. She printed out any emails that came and added them to a growing folder of documentation in her determination to keep everything straight. Her late husband, Richie, had been the organiser, the one who would pore over documents, checking details, dotting every i, crossing every damn t until she was fit to scream. She hadn't though, not till that last day.

And because of that, she was now the one doing the dotting and crossing, the checking and double checking. The dream designed for two, had become a solo option.

As soon as the contracts were signed and exchanged and she was the new owner of Hindon House, Cassie handed in her notice. The same job since she'd left school: all her working life. Twenty years. How mind-bogglingly boring. She could have moved into the private sector as so many others had done. Perhaps she would have done if she hadn't met Richie.

* * *

Ten years, they'd been married. Happy years mostly. She'd expected to have children. When they didn't come, she readjusted without much difficulty. *She* had. Richie hadn't. It was he who'd pushed for the tests, he who'd been devastated when it turned out it was his fault – if any fault was going to be assigned. It never had been by her. He on the other hand bemoaned his low sperm count and the lack of vigour in the few he had, constantly referring to himself as a failure, less than a man, as if the lack of those wriggly little buggers had emasculated him. And nothing she could do or say made a difference. It came down to a simple truth. He was desperate to have children; she wasn't.

But she loved him and went through the multiple rounds of IVF, where they'd taken one of his more determined buggers and inserted it into her accommodating egg and then plopped the resulting mini babe back into her nursery. As it happened, it seemed her nursery wasn't the safest place to put the budding babe, because she lost it each time.

And then, he'd wanted more tests. More invasive procedures. More IVF. But after having had the first three attempts on the National Health Service, now they needed to pay. Using their savings. Money they'd been saving for so many years for the dream they'd had as newlyweds. To allow them to someday give up their civil service jobs and buy a B&B or maybe even a small hotel. To work for themselves.

It was what kept her going when life seemed grim. It was what had mattered when Richie's obsession with having children began to impact on their relationship, damaging it, damaging *them*. Worse, she saw him looking at other women, wondering if they could give him what he wanted.

She hung on, clinging to memories of how it had been, how it still could be.

Because she loved him, and he loved her.

Until he didn't.

5

Cassie put her small apartment on the market the same day she handed in her notice. It had always been her plan to camp out in Hindon House while she was doing the renovations. The sale of her apartment would free up the money she'd need to pay for them.

It sold on the first day. To her relief, the new owner, who was planning to rent it out, was happy to buy all the furniture Cassie was willing to sell.

'Everything,' she'd said bluntly. She was starting anew; she didn't want anything to remind her of the past. As soon as she'd worked her last day, she packed up all her carefully co-ordinated suits and blouses and dropped them all to a local charity shop. Any gold jewellery she'd acquired over the fifteen years she'd been with Richie – the ten years they were married, the five years before – was taken to a jeweller and sold. At the last minute, she slipped her wedding and engagement ring from her finger. With the weight she'd lost in the previous few months, they came away easily and she dropped them onto the counter with the rest.

'You don't think you're taking things to extremes,' her friend

Toni said over a glass of wine in a pub they favoured, not because it was a particularly nice place, but because it was an easy stroll from where both lived.

Cassie swirled the ice around in her G&T and took a long drink before answering. She'd been tempted to buy a bottle of gin after the accident. Several bottles. If she had, she'd have drunk it neat in her desperation to forget. She'd got as far as loading a trolley in her local supermarket, bottles of their cheapest gin clinking together as she pushed it towards the checkout.

There was a long queue. She found herself staring into the trolley and wondering if she could open one of the bottles there and then, guzzle it while she was waiting and start that process of disappearing into alcoholic oblivion. The need was so strong, it frightened her. Leaving the trolley where it was, she headed for the exit.

Since then, she'd kept her drinking for nights like this, when she was with friends who'd make sure she didn't sink too low. It was the downside of moving from the city – she'd miss her friends.

Ignoring Toni's comment, she said, 'You'll have to come down, spend a few days. I really could do with your flair to get the interior design just right.'

It was the perfect thing to say to her uber-stylish friend and soon they were deep in discussion of the best décor to suggest country-house chic.

'When are you planning on moving down?' Toni asked.

'Next week. I packed most of what I was bringing and brought it down last weekend so there's not much left to go. The new owner of the apartment bought all the furniture which made it so much easier.' She'd also bought some of the paintings and knick-knacks Cassie and Richie had collected over the years and what wasn't wanted was donated to a local charity shop. It was brutal but necessary. Telling Toni would start a conversation Cassie didn't want, so she didn't bother. 'There's no point in delaying when there's so much to do. I've organised for the hire of a Portaloo until I can get the plumbing sorted.'

Toni's mouth dropped open. 'You've no plumbing? A Portaloo? Are you kidding me?'

Cassie grinned. 'Afraid not. You still coming?'

'I don't mind roughing it, Cas, but that's taking things to a different level.'

'I'm teasing you; I don't expect you to come down yet. Give me a few weeks to get the basics sorted. I'll need your help when it comes to choosing paint, wallpaper, stuff like that. You've such good taste, and I want it to look right.'

'I'll be down, don't fret. Louise too,' she added, mentioning their mutual friend. 'And when you're ready to take guests, we're planning to be the first.'

Cassie might have made a mess of a lot of things, but she'd chosen her friends well. Reaching over, she planted a loud smack on Toni's cheek. 'You're the best, you know that?'

'We've been friends a long time, Cas, we'll always be there for you when you need us.'

As she had done, for months. And they'd never complained. She'd like to think she'd have the opportunity to return the favour but her two closest friends seemed to lead charmed lives. That, or they were far better at hiding the bad times than she'd ever been. Most of them anyway. When it came to it, when she'd really had to, she'd managed to hide exactly what she'd done.

'I'll miss having you nearby,' she said. And she would. They lived so close to each other, not a week went by that she hadn't seen them at least once. They'd come and visit, of course, but it wouldn't be the same.

Toni, always the more pragmatic of the three, shrugged. 'You'll make more friends there, broaden your horizons. Country people are friendlier than city dwellers, you'll soon have a new network of friends.'

'Yes, of course I will.' Cassie wasn't so sure. The locals might resent her buying up the big house, moving in and making changes. The proprietors of The Lamb Hotel in Hindon might resent the competition. She'd looked at the rooms on their website and had been impressed with the way the twelfth-century inn had been decorated. It was exactly what she'd dreamed of for her B&B. There was room for both, wasn't there? She hadn't intended on doing evening meals, so she could direct her customers to The Lamb. Perhaps even offer a lift there and back. She made a mental note to give that idea more consideration in the future. It could work very well.

She'd tread carefully and not make waves.

Unless she had to. The one thing she'd discovered about herself in the last few months was that she was made of tougher stuff than she'd imagined, more than people, even her friends, gave her credit for.

6

On Cassie's final day in London, the last day of her old life, her closest friends, Louise and Toni, came to see her off. They found her flapping around in a panic. 'I thought everything remaining would fit in the boot of the car.' She nudged the box on the floor beside her with the toe of her shoe. 'This is the rest of the stuff from the kitchen cupboards and I'd thought they were almost empty.'

Toni laughed. 'There's always more than you think. If you can't manage to squeeze it in, I can take it and bring it down when I come.'

Cassie shook her head. Having really no idea what was jammed into the other boxes, she didn't want to leave anything behind. 'I'll make it fit, squash stuff on the back seat, the passenger seat and the footwells.' With her friends helping, every spare inch of space was used to load what remained.

It took a lot of laughter and reorganising to get the car doors to shut, and then they were done.

'Are you sure you can see out the rear?' Louise asked, walking to the back of the car to peer through the window.

Cassie sat into the driver's seat and adjusted the rear-view mirror. 'Yes, it's fine, honestly. I'll take my time, drive slowly.' She saw the sympathetic smile on both her friends' faces. They thought she was so brave: driving again after the accident, getting on with a life without Richie. She liked the version of herself she saw in their eyes. Would it change if they knew the truth? Pushing that thought away, she got out of the car, reached an arm around both women and pulled them into a group hug. 'Right, before you soppy pair start bawling, I'll head off.'

Back in the driver's seat, she shut the car door and opened the window. 'Thanks, girls. You're the best friends I could ask for.' If she wasn't careful, she'd start bawling. Maybe even climb out and say she wasn't going. That this was a crazy idea. She'd seen that thought in their eyes when she'd shown them the photographs she'd taken of Hindon House. What they didn't know was that she'd shown them the best of it, not the worst. When they'd suggested travelling to Wiltshire to see the house in the flesh, she'd put them off. They'd have been horrified at the magnitude of what she was undertaking. They might have made the doubts in her head take form and grow. Might even have made her change her mind.

They might have tried to persuade her that it was grief making her flee from London. They'd never have understood the truth. That it was guilt, not grief, that steered her ship. Worse, it wasn't guilt over what had happened... over what *she* had made happen... no, it was guilt for finally making her dream come true.

Her friends were leaning against the car, peering through the open window. 'Watch out for those ruggedly handsome country men,' Toni said.

Louise laughed and thumped her arm. 'She's going to Wiltshire, not Alaska!'

'Same difference,' said the confirmed city girl. She leaned

through the window and planted a kiss on Cassie's cheek. 'Go carefully. Let us know when you get there and send lots more photos of the house when you can.'

'Yes, and ones of the garden too,' Louise said, pushing Toni aside and reaching through to give Cassie's arm a squeeze.

She hid a smile. If she sent photographs of the jungle that surrounded the house, they'd definitely think she was crazy. 'I'll send so many photos, you'll be sick of them.'

'Never, keep them coming,' Toni said.

The two friends stood back, arms around each other's waist. 'We'll miss you,' they said in perfect unison.

'And I'll miss you both.' With a final wave, Cassie drove from the car park and started her journey.

She left London far later than she'd planned, and typically the traffic on the way out of the city was worse than usual. An hour into the journey, the sky darkened, and the rain started, a deluge that hammered on her windscreen. Even on their highest setting, the windscreen wipers struggled to cope. Since the crash, every time she'd driven, she'd felt a simmering tension. She'd thought it was getting easier with each journey, but now, faced with the rain, it exploded into fear. Straining against the seatbelt, she leaned forward, peering through the rain-washed windscreen to look for somewhere to stop. In desperation, she indicated and pulled into the driveway of a house and turned off the engine.

Resting her head on the steering wheel, she took a deep breath. It didn't help. She needed to get out. A glance towards the house told her someone was home, the lights of a TV flickering in a downstairs room. She should move on, but she couldn't. She felt suddenly hemmed in by the crush of stuff packed around her, by the rain on the windows, by the claustrophobic feeling of being trapped. She flung open the car door, her fingers struggling to undo the seatbelt, and then she was out.

Within seconds, the long-sleeved cotton shirt she wore was soaked through. She shut the car door to turn out the interior light and stood leaning against the car, letting the rain beat down on her, the heavy drops ricocheting off the wet fabric of her shirt. It was several minutes before she felt able to climb back in. The fear hadn't gone away, she wasn't sure it ever would, but she'd manage it. She had to. Had to get a grip. She reached into a bag jammed into the footwell of the passenger seat, pulled out a sweatshirt and used it to wipe the rain from her face and hair. A quick change into a dry T-shirt, and she was back on the road.

The rain didn't let up for the remainder of the journey. By the time she arrived in Hindon, her shoulders ached from stress and her fingers were cramped from gripping the steering wheel so tightly. The one-hundred-mile journey which should have taken two hours, had taken almost four. It wasn't the best start to the rest of her life.

It was almost dark when she turned into the narrow lane that led to the gate at the back of the property. On her first visit as owner, she'd pulled away weeds that prevented it from opening smoothly and now, in the driving rain, it was a moment's work to open the gate wide and drive through. She left it open, drove to the back of the house and parked as close to the door as she could.

All she needed was her handbag and mobile. Everything else could remain in the car. It would mean getting up early in the morning to unpack before her nine o'clock meeting with a local building company, but she couldn't face doing it now. She had to hope that by the morning the rain would have stopped.

'Hopefully,' she muttered, slamming the car door behind her, and pressing the fob to lock it. The clunk was loud in the silence. When the interior light of her car switched out, the sudden and complete darkness startled her. The bunch of house keys she'd taken from her bag fell from her hand. 'Shit!' She bent down to feel for them, pulling her fingers back when they dipped into a puddle. 'Bugger!' She turned to aim the fob at her car, relieved when the interior lit up again. The house keys were there, a few inches in front of her feet. They were wet, and slippery. She grabbed them, found the one for the back door and inserted it in the lock before her car light went out again.

It was such relief to get inside, out of the rain and the cold, that Cassie laughed. She dropped her bag on the floor and did a twirl. This was it. This was the start of the rest of her life.

She flicked the switch to turn on the kitchen light. When nothing happened, her cheery mood faded and she pressed it up and down several times, as if by some miracle it would combust and give her light. It didn't.

The electricity supply had been reconnected. She'd checked the lights were working when she'd been down, only a week before. Frowning, she remembered she'd plugged in a kettle, thinking about having a coffee before she left for the drive back to London. She hadn't bothered in the end, but had plugging it in tripped a fuse? It was a reasonable explanation, or was it? Wouldn't the sockets and lights be on a different fuse? *Richie would have known.* The thought made her groan. He wasn't there, he was never going to be again. She had to learn to cope. Anyway, there was nothing complicated about fuses, you unplugged the last item you'd used, then pressed the fuse switch back up – or down – or whichever way it bloody well went.

It didn't matter – she'd no idea where the fuse box was, and she was damned if she was going to poke around in dark creepy corners in search of it. Using the torch on her phone, she made her way up to the ground floor and tried the light switch there. Nothing. There was a lamp in the bedroom where she'd left her stuff. Maybe it would work? With the torch lighting a circle ahead, she climbed the stairs.

She'd never been in the house at night. Couldn't remember being in any house, anywhere, this dark. In the city, there was always light sneaking in from somewhere. Here, there was nothing. If her phone died... she checked the battery in a panic. She was okay for a few hours. She tried to think where her charging cable was and couldn't remember what bag or box she'd shoved it into that morning. It was in the car, somewhere, which meant going back down. Back out. Searching for it by the light of the car, feeling the darkness circling around, waiting.

She tried a laugh. It didn't work.

The beam from her torch lit the floor in front of her. It left darkness creeping along the walls and across the ceiling. Every few steps, she'd stop and aim the beam upward. Only when she'd convinced herself she was being foolish, that there wasn't anything crawling along the walls waiting to pounce, did she shine the torch back to the floor and move on.

The door of the bedroom she was using was ajar. Hadn't she shut it after her on her last visit? She'd been in a hurry. Perhaps she had left it open. The darkness was stressing her, making her unsure of everything. She swept the beam along the corridor ahead, then back the way she'd come. There were so many dark corners. *Where anything could be hiding.*

With a shiver, she pushed the door wide open and slid the light inside. Everything looked to be as she'd left it, although it was hard to be sure. She'd pulled things from the boxes and bags on her last visit. Would she really know if anyone had rifled through them since? Stupidly, she moved towards the boxes that stood against one wall, remembering the inflatable bed she'd left stretched across the floor only when she stumbled over it. The mobile phone with its precious torch went flying from her hand and skittered across the floor.

Tears of frustration and self-pity welled as the torch went out and the room was plunged into complete darkness. She could lie down on the bed and stay there till morning. Or take her bag, pick up her phone, go back to her car and drive. Go somewhere. Maybe check into The Lamb Hotel for the night. Or keep going. Back to London with her tail between her legs. Louise or Toni would put her up. They'd be sympathetic.

But there was no going back, was there? No going back to the life she'd had, the woman she'd been. The happily married woman, with the adoring husband. The life that had been one big fucking lie. One lie, more lies. No. she couldn't go back there.

She couldn't stand there like an idiot either. Hunkering down, she slid her hand over the dusty floor in front of her, shuffling forward, doing the same, until *eureka*, her fingers closed over her mobile. Pulling it to her, she picked it up and breathed a sigh of relief to find it wasn't damaged. She switched the torch app back on and stood. Self-pity was self-defeating. She brushed away her tears and shone the torch around the room to find the lamp she was pinning her hopes on. Crossing her fingers, she switched it on. Nothing. Her shoulders slumped in despair, her head hanging as tears came yet again. She couldn't stay there. It wouldn't be light for hours. Her mobile would go flat, then she'd be in the dark and alone.

She never used to be scared to be alone, but these days, the silence was always uneasy, her thoughts always churning, and sometimes, if it was very quiet, she would swear she could hear that awful sound of metal scraping against metal, and Richie's last scream. Sometimes, she thought she heard him scream her name.

In desperation, she flicked the switch off and on again, then shone the torch down the flex to where the plug sat in the socket. The socket switch! She'd forgotten about it. Leaning down, she pressed it. 'Woohoo,' she shouted, punching the air in relief as the room was flooded with light. Then she was laughing, and crying, tears of both running down her cheeks.

The sheets and duvet she'd laid over the inflatable mattress had been sent flying when she'd tripped over it. She tidied them, kicked off her shoes then, leaving the lamp on, she slid between the sheets.

She used to be one of those enviable people who could sleep no matter what dramas were going on in her life. She'd read somewhere it was the sign of a true extrovert – that once external stimuli were gone, they could sleep. But Richie's death and the guilt corroding her heart had impacted this ability and since the crash, she'd rarely slept a night through. Cruel dreams woke her, ones in which she believed the last six months had been a nightmare. She'd lie still for a few seconds, relieved to be awake, then reach an arm out to find the bed beside her cold and empty, and she'd cry out. Asleep was a dream, awake was a nightmare.

A couple of times during that night she woke, startled by monsters hiding in the darkness outside her bedroom door. The glow from the lamp didn't reassure her and she reached for her mobile and shone the torch around the room. Only then, did she pull the duvet tighter under her chin, remind herself that monsters didn't exist, and try to get back to sleep.

7

When Cassie woke again it was barely bright, but a glance towards the window told her the rain had stopped. Scrambling up from the mattress, she reached to turn out the lamp, then stood at the window to stare out at the wilderness she could now, officially, call home. The portentous dark clouds of the day before had gone, the sky a cheerful, hopeful blue. Everything was going to be all right. It might be forced optimism, but she'd hold on to it.

She thought about taking a photograph to send to Louise, only then remembering that she hadn't contacted her friends to say she'd arrived safely.

She wasn't surprised to find messages and missed calls from both Louise and Toni. They'd have been worried, would have rung each other and debated what to do. The last thing she either needed or wanted that day was to have them arrive to fuss over her. Plus, if they did, they'd be horrified at the state of the place, and would know she'd lied to them. She hadn't, not really, just hedged the truth a bit. She quickly tapped out a message designed to allay their fears.

Sorry, it was a long journey. Fell asleep on arrival. Just waking now. All good here. Photos to follow later.

She just needed to find something decent to photograph. Some of the plasterwork, maybe one of the fireplaces. She'd work on that later.

But her first plan of the day was to get the lights working. To do that she needed to find the damn fuse box. It took an hour of searching, starting in all the logical places. Finally, when she was almost screaming in frustration, she found it in an almost hidden cupboard built under the main stairway. A modern fuse box, she was glad to see, with everything neatly labelled. The switches for both the upstairs and downstairs lights were down, she flipped them up. Everything else appeared okay. And she'd been correct. The sockets in the kitchen were on a different fuse. Plugging in the kettle hadn't caused the problem.

In the kitchen, she held her breath and pressed the light switch, unable to resist a crow of excitement when it worked as if she'd just invented electricity. Her excitement was short lived. By the time she'd returned to shut the fuse cupboard door, she was frowning. She distinctly remembered switching off the kitchen light before she'd left on her last visit. So what had blown the fuse? She wasn't sure what could. In her experience, fuses were tripped by faulty appliances – she'd done it often enough with a faulty iron or kettle. Once with a lamp. But nothing had ever affected the main lights.

She stared at the row of fuses, as if they were going to offer enlightenment. They didn't and she shut the door with unnecessary force, the bang an echo of her annoyance. Now, despite the certificate she'd received to say the electrics were satisfactory, she'd need to spend money getting them checked.

It had taken her far longer than she'd planned to sort the lights out and she looked at her watch in alarm. Her appointment with the manager of the building company was at nine and it was already twenty to. She was still wearing the scruffy sweatshirt she'd pulled on yesterday. Dashing back upstairs, she flung open a suitcase and rummaged inside for clean underwear. In less than five minutes, she was running through the kitchen door pulling a jacket over a creased cotton shirt and denim trousers.

She locked the door behind her and turned to open the car, only then remembering she hadn't unpacked the night before, and cursing herself for being so stupid. It was too late; she'd have to go with things as they were and hope she'd be able to park somewhere safe. If not, she'd leave the car door open; if anyone wanted to take a bag of dirty laundry, or a box of kitchen utensils or any of the other paraphernalia she'd jammed into the car, they were welcome to it.

It was a minute after nine by the time she drove into a parking space in front of Cody's Building and Renovation Services. It was one of three companies within a ten-mile radius of her new home. From a close perusal of their websites there wasn't much to choose between them. Cassie was starting with this company because it was closest, only a few miles outside Hindon. It was probably sensible to get a quote from all three. It depended on how this meeting went. The work was going to take months – she wanted someone she could connect with.

Directed by a large arrow towards reception, she pushed open the door into a small room and was immediately greeted by a cheery, 'Hello.'

Shutting the door behind her, she approached the desk. 'Hi. I'm Cassie Macreddin, I'm a little late for an appointment with Daniel Cody.' She felt herself being assessed by the older, elegantly dressed woman, and was suddenly conscious of every wrinkle in her shirt and jacket. She'd dragged a comb through her hair before she'd left, but she wasn't sure it had made any difference and wished she'd made time to slick on some lipstick.

'We only worry if people don't turn up at all.' The woman waved towards a seat. 'Sit, Dan isn't actually here yet, I'll give him a shout. There's coffee if you'd fancy one.'

Coffee! Cassie could have hugged her. She pressed a button on the fancy machine and a minute later was inhaling the aroma of what turned out to be very good coffee. She hoped Daniel Cody didn't arrive till she'd managed to get some caffeine into her bloodstream.

It was ten minutes later before the door opened and a man hurried through. With her coffee finished, and feeling more human as a result, Cassie assessed the rugged, rather raggedly dressed man who perched on the side of the desk to speak to the woman behind it. If this was Daniel Cody, Cassie wouldn't feel underdressed. At least her clothes, wrinkled as they were, were clean.

He stood, turned to look at her, then walked across with a hand extended. A very dirty hand. He seemed to realise it and pulled it back with a gruff laugh. 'Probably not a good idea,' he said. 'My apologies, there was a bit of an emergency, and I haven't had a chance to change.' He lifted both his hands and frowned. 'If you're not in a hurry, can you give me ten minutes?'

It would give Cassie the chance to have a second coffee. 'Sure, no problem.' Once he'd gone, she got to her feet and refilled her cup. 'Seems like a hands-on kind of guy,' she said, sitting again. If she hoped her comment would start a dialogue with the woman behind the desk, she was disappointed.

'Yes, he is.' With a smile, she swivelled slightly in her chair, her eyes focused on a computer screen. Soon the tapping of keyboard keys filled the silence.

Only in books or TV series were the main characters able to pump minor ones for information. Cassie sighed, crossed her legs, and settled in to wait.

Slightly more than ten minutes later, the door opened again and a cleaner version of the man she'd seen earlier came through. He grinned at her and lifted both arms out. She thought he was going to do a twirl. If he had, she'd have upped and left. Luckily for their future relationship, he didn't. Instead, he crossed to her with one hand extended as he had earlier. 'It's safe this time,' he said.

His hand was rough. It closed over hers and held it for seconds while he looked at her. 'Cassie Macreddin. The new owner of Hindon House.'

'That's right.'

'Well, let's see what we can do for you.' Taking his hand back, he pointed towards a door in the corner. 'Come through to my office, we can have a chat. See what's what.' He held up a finger to stop her before she'd done more than stand. 'Or, since I've not had breakfast yet, we could go to a café, chat over something to eat. What d'you think?'

She thought it was a bloody marvellous idea. 'It's always easier to make a decision on a full stomach, Mr Cody.'

He laughed. 'Well, we'd like to help you make that decision, but please, call me Daniel, Dan, Danny, or Cody. I answer to all.' He waved a hand towards the exit, then turned to the woman behind the desk who was looking slightly exasperated. 'If anyone's looking for me—'

'I'll tell them you're in an important meeting and can't be disturbed.' Her voice was resigned rather than caustic.

Cody leaned across the desk and planted a kiss on her cheek. 'You always know exactly the right thing to say.'

Outside, he turned to Cassie. 'Just in case you think my behaviour is overly familiar, I should explain that she's my mother.'

'Ah,' Cassie said. There didn't seem to be anything else to say. The familiarity had worried her. It might be the twenty-first century but there were still men who thought that kind of behaviour was welcome. And there were still women who willingly accepted, even encouraged it. She wasn't one of them.

He pointed to a car. 'It's easier if I drive. Your car will be safe here.'

Cassie hesitated. She'd been blasé about her stuff being stolen. Caffeine had made her brain sharper. 'I didn't get a chance to unpack when I arrived last night. There's nothing too valuable but I wouldn't really like to lose it.'

Cody pointed to the roof of the building they'd just left. 'We've CCTV, it's a good deterrent but we've never had any trouble. This isn't London.'

As if crime only happened in the city. She watched the news. It happened everywhere. Especially if people were foolish and put themselves or their property at risk. Like leaving her belongings in her car. He'd climbed into his as if the matter was settled. It irritated her; she didn't like her worries being brushed away so easily.

When she stood hesitating, he wound down his window. 'Seriously, there isn't any need to worry. Ma keeps an eye on any car that pulls in. If there's anything suspicious, she'll be out the door with her cricket bat before you can shout *all out*.'

'Her cricket bat?' It was hard to imagine the elegant woman wielding anything more dangerous than a fork.

'Yep, she keeps it under the desk.'

It was bizarre enough to be true. Cassie opened the passenger door and got in. 'Has she ever had to use it?'

'Only on my brother and me, when we arrived home so drunk we couldn't get the key into the lock and tried to get in through a bedroom window.' He started the engine and pulled the car onto the road. 'She didn't break any bones, but we were pretty bruised.'

'She didn't recognise you?'

'She says not.'

It was hard to picture the elegant woman she'd met behaving with such ferocity. It reminded Cassie never to make snap judgements. 'You don't believe her.'

'My brother, Patrick, was shouting *Ma* over and over.'

'I bet you never got that drunk again.'

He turned and winked at her. 'Let's just say we never came *home* that drunk again.'

This drew a laugh from Cassie. 'It was one way of dealing with it, I suppose. Is your brother in the business with you?'

'No, he went into a different one.'

'In competition with you?' A falling out among the siblings. It wasn't unheard of, but it would be interesting to know why.

'No. Patrick's a thinker, not a doer. He takes after our father, who's a history professor.' Cody lifted a hand from the steering wheel and wagged it. 'Patrick's more interested in people's souls than their homes.'

'He's a vicar?'

'To be exact, he's a priest. A Catholic priest.'

The Codys were proving to be an interesting family. A hands-on business owner, bat-wielding mother, history professor father, and a priest. Cassie wanted to ask if there were more of them. Sisters perhaps. But this wasn't a social meeting. Or, God forbid, a date. Toni's remark about meeting a ruggedly handsome country man popped into her head, almost making her smile. Cassie needed to get her thoughts back to business.

The last thing she needed was any kind of romantic entanglement.

Been there, done that, had the scars to prove it.

8

Cassie stared out the car window, surprised to see they were back in Hindon. More surprised, a few seconds later, when the car turned down a side street she hadn't known existed and pulled into a parking space in front of a café.

'Here we are,' Cody said. 'They do the best breakfast here.'

The café was spacious, and not busy. Cody pointed to a table in the corner. 'Take a seat. This is my treat. What can I get you?'

She was starving. 'I'll have a full English, with all the trimmings. And coffee.' She crossed to the table he'd indicated, resisting the childish temptation to choose a different one. He'd chosen well, there were no seats too close. When they'd eaten, they could talk without fear of being overheard.

She dropped her bag on the spare chair and sat back. Cody had his back to her, allowing her to stare without fear of being caught. He was tall, well built, with the hint of a paunch that suggested he liked his beer. The cricket bat hadn't knocked that out of him. He'd changed into a clean shirt and trousers neither of which had been ironed. She wasn't in a position to criticise, but whereas her clothes, though wrinkled, still managed to look expensive, his looked cheap and were poorly fitting. His hair was short but not styled. In fact, with one side shorter than the other, it looked very much as if he cut it himself. Not a vain man then, Cassie decided. She'd done enough research on the company to know it was a highly successful one. He wasn't a man who felt he had to advertise it by flashy dressing.

He turned suddenly, saw her staring, and smiled. It softened his weather-beaten face. He was, she estimated, about her age. No wedding ring: it didn't mean he wasn't married though. Not that it mattered. Mere curiosity. It was sensible to know as much as possible about a man she might be doing business with. A man to whom she'd be giving a hefty amount of money. She had to remember that. This was business.

'They'll bring the food over when it's ready,' Cody said, placing a mug of coffee in front of her and sitting with another in his hand. He took a mouthful before putting it down. 'I drove out and had a look at the house after you made the appointment to talk to us.'

She wasn't surprised. He already struck her as the action man type. 'You managed to get in through the gate?'

He frowned. 'It wasn't locked.'

'Ah, you came in through the back gate.'

'Sure. I don't think the front one has been opened in years. The two guys who bought it a few years ago didn't use it.'

'Did you know them?' She was curious. The estate agent didn't have much to say about them and she was naturally interested to know why they'd failed. And what they had planned in the first place.

'No, not really. I called around shortly after they moved in. Touting for work.' He shrugged. 'We get lean times, like any other business. But they weren't interested. They said they were in no hurry so planned to do most of the work themselves. I gather that one of them was a plumber.'

She remembered the dripping pipe and shook her head. 'He left a bit of a mess.' She explained about the damp and the leak. 'I stuck a bucket under it.'

'I think they were doing everything on the cheap. It's not always a good idea.'

Their breakfast arrived and for several minutes they dedicated themselves to demolishing the lot. 'You were right,' Cassie said as she polished off the last piece of sausage. 'That was really good.'

'Best place for miles around.' He pushed his plate away and sat back with the remains of his coffee and picked up the conversation. 'They hired an electrician from Warminster. A guy I know, so that work should be okay.'

'I had a problem last night. Something tripped the fuses for the lights. I pushed them back this morning, and everything seems to be okay but...' She didn't want to sound stupid or, God forbid, helpless.

As helpless as she'd felt the day before the crash. That awful day when it seemed as if someone had taken the world from under her feet and left her swaying dangerously. She'd reached for something solid, her fingers only grasping puffs of the reality she thought she'd had. A mirage. It had all been a stupid fucking mirage. She saw Cody frown. Shit, had she said that aloud?

'But?' he said.

Whew! Relief almost made her smile. It didn't, but it did make her lift her chin, and say firmly, 'There's obviously something wrong with the electrics for it to trip in the first place.'

'I can have Tom, our electrician, have a look if you like.'

She wanted to jump up, grab him in a hug and say, *yes, please, take care of everything for me.* But her days of depending on a man, any man, were done. What was that old adage – *fool me once, shame on you, fool me twice, shame on me.* 'I think it's best if I explain what I want, then you can tell me if your company can meet my needs. I don't have time to waste.' It came out sharper than she'd intended and she saw his expression harden. Good, she didn't want to be seen as a pushover.

Reaching for her bag, she pulled out the plans of the house. Quickly, and concisely, she went through it, room by room, using the plan to show where she wanted walls removed, others added. 'So in the end, all the bedrooms will be en suite. There'll be no need for a separate bathroom.' She pulled out the plans of the lower ground floor. 'This is where I'll be living, so I'll need a bathroom put in here. And this area,' she ran a finger over the wall between the kitchen and the corridor behind, 'I'd like these walls knocked down, have this a huge open-plan area with light coming from the back and front.'

Cody pored over the plans silently. She watched him, and waited for his comments, curious for his reaction.

'What's your timescale?'

Cassie had given this question a lot of thought. She hoped she was being realistic and watched his expression carefully when she said, 'I need to be ready to take paying customers as soon as possible. Realistically, I'd like to be ready to go within six months.'

'Six months,' he echoed.

He wasn't giving anything away. 'That's doable, yes?' He made no comment, merely continued his perusal of the plans. Maybe he was looking for a polite way to say he wasn't interested. There were other companies she could go with. It was no big deal. It was stupid to feel disappointed. 'I'm going to be living there while the work is going on. I'll be helping. There's a lot of junk to be cleared out. I can hire skips, get rid of it all.'

'There's a skip hire company we use. They give us good rates.

It will save you money if you do some of the donkey work. It can be very time consuming, getting the crap of years removed.'

'You are interested in doing it?' She tried to keep the hint of desperation from her voice. There were other companies, but she suddenly wanted this one.

He looked surprised. 'Of course. It's not going to be cheap though.' He collected the plans together, neatly, lining up the edges with his blunt fingers. 'I've seen the outside of the house, so I have a fair idea what needs to be done there, but I'd need to see the interior. I can come around this afternoon if that suits. I'll bring Tom, see if he can find out what caused the lights fuses to trip.' He smiled. 'No charge for that, in case you're worrying.'

She wasn't. It was his *not going to be cheap* comment that bothered her. Perhaps she should get quotations from the other companies too. It was time consuming, but probably safer. 'When can you let me have a quotation?' She reached for the plans, folded them carefully and slipped them back into her bag. 'I'll be getting other quotes, of course.'

'I'd assume you would. It's always sensible.'

He didn't look the slightest bit perturbed by the idea, as if he knew his quotation would be the best. Cassie couldn't decide if his confidence was annoying or reassuring.

'Once I've seen the house, I can do you up a quote in a couple of days. It'll be for the basic work: the building of the en suite bathrooms, replacing the windows, knocking the walls down, etcetera. It'll all be explained in the quote. The cost of fixtures and fittings will come later. That depends on what you want. I can recommend some companies but it's up to you how expensive you want to go.' He pushed up the cuff of his shirt and checked the time. 'Right, if you're done, I'll drop you back to your car. Is about three okay for you?'

Cassie didn't want to admit she'd nothing else planned. 'That's fine. I have a few other appointments, but I should be back by then.'

Her car was as she'd left it. Nobody had attempted to steal any of her precious cargo. She left Cody with a casual wave and climbed in. He was gone, tearing up the road, before she'd started her engine.

It was a feeling she was being watched that made her look towards the office. Mrs Cody was at the window. Staring out. Cassie raised a hand in greeting, and mouthed a thanks she knew the woman couldn't possibly see.

Perhaps she hadn't seen the wave either. Because she didn't respond. Instead, she reached up and shut the blinds.

It was an unexpectedly unfriendly response that instantly put Cassie on edge. She'd barely spoken to the woman; how could she possibly have offended her?

Maybe she thought Cassie had designs on her son? Maybe she was, that very moment, reaching under the desk for the cricket bat and would come out, waving it at Cassie, warning her off.

She huffed a laugh. If Cody's mother knew about her, what she'd done, what she was, she'd have reason to be so protective. Maybe with mother instincts, she could see it in Cassie's eyes... that she was a wrong 'un. *Toxic*. The word still made her want to cry.

When no bat-wielding mother appeared to chase her away, Cassie climbed into her car and seconds later was speeding from the car park.

9

It didn't take Cassie long to unpack the car when she got back to Hindon House. 'Home,' she said, testing the word. It didn't seem to fit. But then it wasn't supposed to be like this; it should have been the two of them, excitedly enthusiastic about this renovation. Richie's voice, his bellowing laughter, should be echoing around the rooms. There shouldn't be this strangely unsettling silence.

The unpacking didn't take long, simply because there was no point in putting anything away. All the kitchen paraphernalia, she left sitting on a counter in the kitchen. The rest she took upstairs to the bedroom she'd use until the lower ground floor was sorted. Months away.

There was so much to do, it was impossible to know where to start. She supposed she could start bringing all the rubbish from the other bedrooms down to the hallway. As soon as the skips arrived, she could clear it out. Instead, she crossed to the bedroom window. It was a pretty morning, blue skies, the odd puff of cloud. In the glare of the sun, the extent of the work ahead of her was clear. She couldn't see the drive, or the gate, all was covered in greenery. Had she taken on too much? She could have bought a going concern in some seaside town, jumped straight in to being a landlady.

Her fingernail scratched at the window frame. Paint flaked away. Underneath, the wood was rotten. Her eye followed it to the top. It might be repairable rather than needing to be replaced. Or was that false economy? She'd have to see what Cody thought.

She turned, rested her bottom against the windowsill and stared around the room. It was spacious, with high ceilings, ornate coving, and an elaborate ceiling rose. All looked tired and worn.

A bit like how she felt.

Self-pity. It was corrosive. Determined to do something, she went with her plan to start clearing out the bedrooms. Stupidly, she'd moved the junk she'd found in the room she was using to the one next door, and would now need to move it again. Making work for herself, as if there wasn't enough.

She stood in the doorway and sighed. Perhaps it would be easier to simply chuck everything out the window when the skip arrived. If they could bring it in through the main gates, they could place it right outside.

The change of plan injected her with energy. She'd seen gardening tools in a shed outside the kitchen. Rummaging among the selection of mostly broken and rusty implements, she found a pair of secateurs. It mightn't have been any good for pruning precious plants, but she thought it would be just the thing for hacking the brambles and ivy that prevented the main gates from opening. She took a shovel with her too and walked the perimeter of the house to the front, then the quarter mile along the weed-strewn avenue to the gate. It was only mid-morning, but the sun was already hot. It would have made sense to have worn a hat, even more to have worn gardening gloves.

Not possessing the latter, she started to work, cutting along the line of bramble and ivy that had crept back around the gate since she'd first pushed through weeks before. It took brute force and persistence rather than finesse and it was satisfying to see her progress. The bramble didn't give in easily, springing back and jabbing her with thorns. Luckily, the secateurs were sharp enough for the job.

She needed to be able to open both sides of the gate wide enough to allow the skip delivery. It took almost an hour to get one side free – an hour of chopping, wrenching, digging, swearing, and sweating. Cassie leaned on the handle of the spade and calculated it would take her at least another hour to do the other side. Her hands were scratched, bleeding and dirty. She looked down at her blood-streaked filthy clothes and shook her head. The rest could wait till the following day. She had time to make herself look a little more respectable before Cody and the electrician turned up.

She shut the gate over, relocked it and rested the spade against it.

There was no running water in the house. Something she'd have to get resolved as soon as possible. Until she did, she'd have to make do with the piddling supply of cold water in the Portaloo. She grabbed soap, a flannel and towel and did the best she could. Clean clothes made her look almost presentable.

There was a supply of bottled water in the kitchen. She emptied enough into the kettle to make a mug of coffee, then sat to await the arrival of Cody.

The kitchen was her least favourite room in the house. It made her feel uncomfortable and put her on edge. Toni, with her passion for interior design, would probably say there was something wrong with its energy and suggest moving everything around to create balance with the natural world. Cassie wasn't sure how much she believed in feng shui but if it improved the feeling in the room she'd be all for it.

They couldn't do much about the ceiling being lower than in the rest of the house but they could change the dismal décor. And when the far wall was knocked down, and the small rooms behind were all incorporated into one big space, it would all feel so much better. First thing she'd do was to get those damn bars removed from those windows.

But that was some time in the future. She found herself sweeping a hand over her arms to dislodge any creepy crawlies, twisting and turning to check for cobwebs, unable to rid herself of the irritating sensation that something was brushing gently over her skin.

Refusing to give space in her head to the idea she was being chased from the kitchen, she took her mug and headed outside. There was so much of the garden she'd yet to explore. She meandered slowly along as she drank, trying to distinguish the weeds that needed removing from plants that needed to stay. This part of the garden probably would have been planted with vegetables at some stage. There were certainly apple and pear trees. Unfortunately, brambles had wound their way around these too.

After a few minutes, she came upon an old brick wall and walked along it to find an opening. She didn't need to move far to find a gateway, the brickwork on either side crumbling away, the wrought-iron gate that had once hung there now lying flat on the ground, weeds growing through the bars.

She stepped through, curious to see what lay beyond the wall, but she should have been careful and watched where she put her feet. If she had, she wouldn't have tripped over a rock and stumbled, the mug flying from her hands as she sought to save herself from hitting the ground. The sycamore sapling she grabbed was of little help, slowing rather than preventing her fall. More rocks on the ground. Her head whacked into one. She lay in the shade of the wall, her face half buried in moss and grass, an earthy smell oozing from the soil underneath.

She didn't move.

10

Dazed, Cassie wondered if she'd died, how long would it be before she was found? Cody would arrive, get no answer and leave, assuming she'd changed her mind, or got held up with those other appointments she'd conjured up to make herself seem important. Her friends would worry. Eventually they might come down, see her car, and find the unlocked back door. They'd go inside and shake their heads to see the state of the place – far worse than she'd admitted. They'd see the deception. And they'd assume it had all been too much for Cassie. They'd wait, and when she didn't return, they'd leave a note and go back to London.

Her body would begin to decompose. Then winter would come, and rain and frost would break down her flesh until there'd be little left except tatters of material on a skeleton.

She wasn't normally so morbidly dramatic. When had she changed? If she had to pinpoint one moment, it wouldn't have been the crash, not even the moment when she'd climbed from the car and seen Richie's crushed body, his eyes wide and lifeless. No, it would be the moment – frozen in time – when he'd told her he was leaving her. Didn't love her any more. Didn't want to be with her. That heart-stopping moment had changed her.

Before that day, she'd been a glass half full kind of person. Nowadays, that glass seemed empty. The negative effect the house was having on her wasn't helping. Or not the house, as such, that damn kitchen and those small rooms with their barred windows.

She might have stayed lying on the ground, wallowing in self-pity, if she hadn't opened her eyes and seen a quabble of woodlice heading straight for her nose. The thoughts of the little grey horrors marching into her nostrils had her jerk upright, the sudden movement making her dizzy. She lifted a hand to her head, her fingers moving gently over the graze and the already swelling bump. There was a trace of blood on her fingers, not much, she wasn't going to bleed to death, but she was going to look a sight.

And ache all over. She shuffled on her bottom, grimacing when she felt yet another rock underneath. Standing, she shook off the bugs and leaves that clung to her legs. Not rocks, she realised, looking around with growing dismay. It was a graveyard. There was a damn graveyard at the bottom of her garden.

There had been nothing in the sales details. *Nothing*. She wouldn't have bought it had she known. She didn't want this memorial to death in her garden. It was macabre. She'd left London... had fled it, if she were being honest... to get away from all the memories, to try to put Richie's death, and her part in it, behind her. How could she, if death was in her damn garden?

They were unusually small gravestones, some almost obscured by moss and weeds. Her mug had hit one of the taller ones and lay beside it in two pieces. She bent to pick them up, reading the deeply carved inscription on the stone as she did so.

Here Lies My Best Friend, Topsy.

Enlightenment almost made Cassie smile. Topsy was a good name for a rabbit, or perhaps a cat. It was a *pet* cemetery. She investigated a few more of the stones, hobbling from one to the other. Previous owners had obviously been pet lovers, there must have been twenty or more stones. Most of the inscriptions, worn away by weather and time, were indecipherable. Of the ones she could read, only two mentioned the type of pet that was buried. Sam, a beloved beagle, and Sunshine, a canary.

A pet cemetery, not a graveyard. Many historic houses had something similar in their grounds – it was part of their history. There was nothing at all macabre about it. But if she'd known it might have made her reconsider buying. She stood looking around at the monuments to death and shook her head. There was no *might* about it. Graveyard or pet cemetery, she didn't want it in her garden.

She crossed to an entrance on the far side. Two gateways for such a small area seemed excessive. This one, however, was in a better state of repair, the gate still hanging. She went through and closed it over – it immediately swung back against the wall. She left it there and turned to look back over the cemetery.

It made sense to have this gate fixed and the other crumbling entrance bricked up. She'd lock the gate, allow brambles and weeds to take over. Over time, the stone markers would be further eroded and she could pretend the cemetery never existed.

Death and pretence, who knew they could go so well together?

With the two halves of the broken mug in her hand, she headed back to the house. She was almost there when she heard an engine, and seconds later Cody's car pulled through the rear gate.

'Hi,' she said when he climbed out.

His response wasn't the standard 'Hi' in return. He stared at her in concern. 'What the hell happened to you?'

She lifted a hand to her forehead. It hurt. 'Do I look a state? I fell over one of the gravestones in the pet cemetery.' She made it sound as if it were perfectly normal to have a burial ground in her garden, as if she'd known about it all the time. Maybe he did because he didn't look surprised.

'You need to be more careful.'

The implied criticism irked. As if she'd been dancing around the wilderness like a hapless fool rather than tripping over a gravestone she hadn't realised was there. Ignoring him, she turned to the passenger who'd climbed out and was standing silently by the car.

'You must be the electrician,' she said. 'Tom, isn't it?'

'That's it.'

There was an awkward silence as if the two men were waiting for Cassie to say or do something. Be hospitable perhaps. 'Can I get you both a coffee or tea? Or there's mineral water.'

Cody's eyes settled on the broken pieces she held. 'If you have another mug, I wouldn't say no to a coffee. And Tom never refuses food or drink.'

The electrician held his hands up. 'Guilty as charged, but it's only because he doesn't pay me enough so I have to eat on the job.'

Cassie gave this the laugh they appeared to expect, then led the way into the kitchen. 'Since I saw the leak from the bathroom, I've been afraid to turn the mains water on, so I'm using mineral water,' she said, picking up the bottle and filling the kettle.

'There should be no problem,' Cody said. 'Turn it on while we're here and I'll check to make sure it's all okay.'

Cassie wanted to say no, that she'd prefer to wait till she'd decided who to give the business to, that she didn't really like the idea of his muscling in with his offer of electrician and now plumbing. She really wanted to, but the thought of having unlimited water was too good an offer to refuse. 'Thank you, that would be great.'

As soon as everyone had their drink of choice, she decided it was time to get into business mode. 'I'll show you where the fuse box is,' she said to Tom. 'It was the main lights that fused.'

'I know the company who did the electrical work a couple of years ago. They're good,' he said with an emphatic nod. 'I'm sure it's all kosher, but I'll run a quick test to make sure.'

Leaving him with it, she led Cody through the reception rooms, where he spent several minutes checking the mould-streaked walls. 'Nothing that can't be fixed,' he said.

It seemed to be his attitude to any problem. She hoped it showed his experience rather than an indication that he made little of every problem.

In the first bedroom, she sighed at the mess of rubbish and old furniture. 'As soon as I get a skip, I'll be able to start clearing all this stuff out.'

Cody bent to lift a small broken table. He looked at it briefly before shaking his head and dropping it. 'Doesn't look as if there's anything worth keeping.' Ignoring the rubbish, he shoved his hands in his trouser pockets and looked around. 'It's a lovely spacious room though. Even taking a chunk out to make an en suite, it'll still have generous proportions.'

'Yes, that's what I thought, and all the rooms are of similar size.'

The final room to show him was the attic space. A narrow stairway led to it. Cassie had opened the door to look inside on her last visit, but that was as far as she'd gone. Too narrow to walk up side by side, once more she led the way, stupidly conscious of the silent man walking behind.

'I'm hoping to put another bedroom up here,' she said, pushing the door open. There was a light switch on the wall inside – she slid her hand down the wall and pressed it. 'It's jammed to the rafters with all sorts of stuff. I'll have to go through it all, see if there's anything worth keeping or if it's all just junk.'

Cody came through the door behind her, forcing her to take a step forward. She'd half turned to speak to him when she felt the floor give beneath her feet.

11

Cassie's first thought was that it wasn't her day. Her second that accidents came in threes, so she'd better watch out. And her final one was to wonder how much this was going to cost to fix.

'Bloody hell,' Cody said. 'Don't move.'

Even if she could have done, she wouldn't – the floor below had high ceilings. If the fall didn't kill her, it would certainly break something, possibly several somethings. Her right leg had gone all the way through the floorboards, and she was wedged at an awkward angle. 'I'm not sure I can anyway.'

Cody used his foot to test some of the surrounding boards until he was on the other side of the damaged floor. 'Okay,' he said. 'Cross your arms, I'm going to pull you out.'

She had no option but to trust that he knew what he was doing, but when the simple movement of her arms made the floor creak ominously, she couldn't help it, she squealed. Before she had a chance to speak, to ask if he was sure this was going to work, she felt his hands slip under her arms and grab her wrists. Suddenly she was free. The temptation to turn in his arms and hug him was too much to withstand. 'Thank you. Oh my God, thank you.' If she'd been there on her own… it was the second time within the space of a few hours that she'd had the same thought. She'd been alone since Richie's death. In London, with her friends dropping in, and neighbours within shouting distance, it was easier. Here, she wasn't so sure she could cope. Had it been sheer obstinacy that had made her follow the dream she and Richie had had, a determination to have the life he'd tried to deny her? She no longer knew her motivation.

'Let's get out of here,' Cody said. He held her away from him. 'Step where I step, okay?'

She couldn't trust herself to do more than nod. Then they were back out on the stairway. 'Probably best not to go back in there until you've had the place assessed,' Cody said. He pointed to the ceiling. 'There's a damp spot there. I'm guessing water is getting through the roof. It might only be in one place, but it's better not to risk it.'

Cassie didn't need to be told twice. 'I suppose I'm lucky that the weight of the stuff stored there didn't bring the whole lot down.'

'The rot would have spread, and that'd have happened eventually. You've been lucky.'

Lucky? The house and the damn garden had attacked her. The broken floorboard had torn her jeans and scratched her leg. It stung. So did the graze to her forehead. And every part of her ached. She'd have liked to have rested her head against the wall and wailed.

Perhaps her expression gave her away because Cody shut the attic door. 'No point in worrying about that just yet.'

They went back to the kitchen where Tom was sitting staring at his mobile. 'The electrics all look okay to me,' he said as Cassie came through the door.

'Good, that's good.' She didn't care. Didn't care if the whole damn place went up in a puff of smoke.

'I'll make you a cup of tea,' Cody said.

As if that was going to help. Cassie bit back the retort. He was being nice. It wasn't his fault that she'd bought this nightmare. And there it was... that one word. It was a nightmare. What had she been thinking? She sat at the table and buried her face in her hands. She could hear the two men talking in hushed tones behind her. If Cody brought her over a cup of tea laced with sugar, she'd have hysterics. She was so near to it; it would just take that one last push to get her over.

Like the one last push Richie had given her. *I'm leaving you.*

'Here you go.'

She spun back from the memory of that day, an eight on the Richter scale of awfulness, to the current terrible one which might have hit a nine or even a ten if she'd fallen through. The tea Cody handed her was milky, but not sweet. Then she laughed hysterically anyway. He couldn't have put sugar in it, she didn't have any. She wondered if he'd looked. The thought made her laughter grow and take on that hysterical slant she'd been so afraid of. She stopped abruptly. 'Sorry, there's nothing funny about anything.'

'You've had a shock,' Cody said taking a seat opposite.

'Yes.' She sipped the tea. 'I'll be okay now though.'

He didn't look convinced. 'I'll have a look at your mains water, see if I can get that working for you.'

She nodded. It was all she could do. She didn't have the energy or inclination to argue. Having water would be good. What she'd have liked was a long soak in a bath, but she didn't have a bath. It almost made her giggle again. Instead, she lifted her mug and sipped the tea.

The two men messed around under the kitchen sink for a

while, then vanished into the hallway and it was several minutes before they returned. 'Right,' Cody said, a self-satisfied smile brightening his face. 'You have mains water now. I checked that pipe in the bathroom, it's not going to cause any further problems.'

Mains water to the one working sink in the house, and that one in the kitchen. She had to struggle to sound grateful. 'You've been great, thank you.' And then, because she really was grateful, and because he'd possibly saved her life, she made a snap decision. She couldn't change the past, she needed to get her future sorted. 'I'd like your company to do the work, assuming,' she added hurriedly, 'that your quotation isn't crazy.'

'Are you sure?' He sat opposite her again. 'You really should get a few quotes to compare.'

'Are you going to rip me off?'

'No.'

'Then that's settled. When can you start?'

12

Cassie discovered that Cody wasn't a man to delay when a decision had been made. He returned the following afternoon with a quotation, and a contract that was, he insisted, designed to protect them both. He'd do the work; she'd pay the agreed cost.

She'd dragged the kitchen table and chairs outside that morning to make the most of the weather. As good a reason as any, certainly a better explanation to give Cody when he arrived rather than telling him the truth that there was something *wrong* with the kitchen, that being in it for any length of time made her skin crawl. It was impossible to explain the inexplicable.

Cody, as it happened, made no comment. Almost as if the furniture had always been there. He sat down, rested an ankle on his knee, and waited for her to finish poring over the paperwork he'd given her.

'If we discover problems along the way,' he explained, 'if, for instance, there is a major problem with the roof, I'll discuss it with you before we proceed.'

The damn roof. 'You think there might be?' She had a contingency fund set aside, but it was small. The roof on the other hand, was huge. She'd been assured it was intact. That it had been repaired a couple of years before.

'It might simply be a slipped tile. We had some bad storms over the winter. I think if it was anything more serious, you'd have seen more evidence inside. It's the first thing we'll check, that and the floor in the attic.'

'Good.' She picked up the pen he'd left on the table and scribbled her name on the contract. 'There you go.'

'I'll have a copy made for you.' He stretched his arms up, then rested his cupped hands behind his head and looked up at the house. 'If you're looking to start taking customers in as soon as you can, it makes sense to start with the bedrooms.'

He was right, of course. She'd told him it was the priority. As soon as the bedrooms and common areas were ready, she could start letting them out. There was no reason she couldn't cook breakfast in the kitchen as it was now. There was no logical explanation for asking Cody to start the renovation there. That getting rid of those small rooms and gutting the kitchen needed to be a priority. No reason. She needed to think with her business head and not let stupid irrational emotions take over.

She'd take down the blinds from the kitchen windows, get rid of the excess furniture, replace the light fitting for something more effective. And she'd shut the doors into those small rooms. And stop being such an idiot.

'Yes,' she said, bringing her attention back to Cody. 'That does make sense. So when can you start?'

'We're finishing off a barn conversion in Devizes. If everything goes to plan, we should be able to start here on Monday. Meanwhile, I can have a skip delivered tomorrow and you can start clearing those rooms out.'

Cassie rubbed the pad of her thumb over the scratches on her other hand. It looked like she'd have more by the end of the day if she was going to get that front gate open. 'Okay, have them deliver it through the front gate, I'll leave it open for them.' She got to her feet. 'I'll go and transfer that advance you've requested.'

He got the hint and stood. 'Right. I'll send you a message later to let you know what time the skip will be arriving.' And with a wave, he was gone, and Cassie was alone.

She'd lived alone before. The years before she met Richie, the months since he'd died. But she'd never felt quite as alone as she did when she turned to walk into the house. The sun that warmed the patio didn't reach inside and the kitchen was chilly, making her shiver. There was probably damp behind the awful floor-to-ceiling tiles that covered each wall. Ugly, cold and damp. She didn't linger, heading up to her bedroom to use her laptop to transfer the money to Cody's company.

Rather than eating in the kitchen, she'd taken to bringing food to her room. Despite the peeling wallpaper and the moth-eaten carpet, it was more peaceful there. It was easier to stay positive, to make plans, to imagine she had a future. That everything was going to work out. There was none of the creeping sense of unease that smothered her almost as soon as she walked into the kitchen.

Perhaps there was a rational explanation for the way the room affected her. Early in the previous century, a house this size would have had servants. The lower ground floor would have been their domain... maybe they'd been mistreated, beaten or in some way exploited. She had read some of the history of the house in the sales details, but there wasn't much. All she could remember was that prior to the two men who'd bought it last, a family had owned it for a short time, and before them it had been owned by another family for a couple of years. Before that? No idea.

The house seemed to have changed hands a lot.

It was a bit late to be wondering if there was a very good reason.

13

Cody sent a message to say the skip would be delivered the following afternoon. Cassie thought of all the ivy and bramble she needed to pull away to release the front gate and groaned. Maybe by the morning, some of her aches and pains would have eased. Maybe it would be just as easy to have the skip delivered around the back of the house. She dismissed that thought. It wouldn't. There were two bedrooms to the front of the house chock-a-block with rubbish. It made sense to have the skip directly outside so she could toss it all from the window.

Exhausted from the drama of the day, she didn't bother with getting something to eat. She had a bottle of water in her bedroom to sip if she was thirsty. A pile of books sat on the floor beside her blow-up bed. She reached for the top one and sat back to read. Usually, she'd have put her earbuds in and listened to music at the same time, but she was strangely loath to cut out the sounds of the house. Or perhaps, it was more honest to say that she was afraid someone would sneak up on her unheard.

What she'd do if she did hear someone, she wasn't precisely sure; it simply seemed better to know if there was someone creeping about. And if there was someone? For the first time, in a worrying downward slant to her general unease, she jammed the back of the chair against the handle of the door. Nobody could surprise her now.

The added security didn't completely allay her fears. Reaching for the bottle of water, she popped a couple of paracetamol into her mouth and took a slurp to wash them down. Hopefully, they'd take the edge off her aches and allow her to sleep.

Rather than undressing, she lay on the air mattress fully clothed, her eyes wide, straining to listen for any sound. When the only thing she heard was an owl, a sad lonely *toowhoo* that seemed to drift through the darkness, she shut her eyes.

The painkillers took the edge off her aches, exhaustion shut her eyes, and finally she slept.

She slept long enough for the pain relief to have worn off, and her first thought on waking was that she was going to die. Every part of her seemed to be hurting. Even raising her arm to look at her watch seemed to be an effort. Finding it was early, she crawled on her hands and knees to where she'd left the water and packet of pills and took two, then crept back to bed to hope they'd work quickly.

She gave them half an hour, then struggled to her feet. Not perfect, but better. It was probably as good as it was going to get. Using a small make-up mirror, she checked her face. Her forehead was a lovely shade of purple, but the abrasion was dry. The cuts and scrapes to her hands were too. She slipped off her jeans and T-shirt and checked the rest of her injuries. Some artistic splashes of colour on her arms looked interesting. She brushed a hand over them; although tender to touch the bruises weren't painful. The scratch along her thigh, sustained when she'd fallen through the attic floor, stung like hell but didn't appear serious. There was nothing to stop her tackling the rest of the ivy and bramble that prevented the main gate from opening. The very thought of the work involved made her groan.

It had to be done. *She* had to do it. Her friends hadn't said, but she knew they thought she was crazy. That this whole idea was daft. *And they hadn't seen the house.* Louise had wanted her to wait, spouting something she'd read about not making any big decision within a year of a major life change. Poor Louise, she'd no idea just how big that life change had been. Thinking about her friends made Cassie straighten her shoulders. They were right, of course they were. This whole stupid idea was ridiculous, but she was doing it. Her marriage had failed, she had to make her future work. But if she was going to tackle that damn gate, she couldn't do it solely on paracetamol. The breakfast she'd eaten – when was it? Two days before? That had been her last proper meal. It seemed like a good idea to fuel up before starting any work.

She wasn't going to eat in that nice café dressed the way she was. As the new owner of Hindon House, it seemed vital to look the part. To ooze confidence, professionalism, to fool everyone into thinking she knew exactly what she'd taken on and wasn't afraid of any of it. The bruise to her forehead, the scratches and scrapes – damn it, she'd wear them all with pride. Proof that she was willing to get stuck in to make her endeavour a success.

She took fresh clothes down to the kitchen and did brief ablutions. Later, she'd figure out how to get hot water. The heating system had been installed by the last owners; it was probably easy to use.

The thought of a good breakfast rushed her out the door and into her car, and then she was on the road to Hindon. She parked outside the café and headed inside. It was already surprisingly busy with solo diners who sat with their eyes glued to folded newspapers or the screens of iPads or mobile phones, forks moving with regular motions to their mouths. Passing through, or locals for whom the café was a regular haunt, like her they were probably fuelling up for a day's work.

There was a queue at the counter. Neither of the two people in it turned to look at Cassie as she joined. Maybe it was too early in the morning for friendly banter. She glanced around the room. Nobody looked up from what they were doing to pay her any attention. She liked the idea of being a local, of getting to know people, becoming part of the community. Her thoughts drifted to a time when she'd walk in and be greeted with a smile, or a wave. It would be good to feel less alone. No harm in fantasising and painting her future in rosy colours. It was easy to do that here in the warm bright café. She wished she could hang on to that feeling, to bring it back with her, perhaps to paint the kitchen in Hindon House with it.

The queue moved quickly, and it was Cassie's turn to give her order to the smiling, pleasant-faced woman who was serving. 'I'll have the big breakfast, please. And coffee.'

'Brown or white?'

Cassie blinked, confused. Brown or white coffee? 'Black, please.'

It was the server's turn to be confused. 'Black toast? Like you want it really burnt?'

Brown or white toast! Cassie felt colour rising in her cheeks and was conscious of the queue of people behind her. 'Sorry, no. Black coffee, white toast.'

'Okey dokey,' the woman said, ringing up the till. 'That'll be £12.'

Cassie tapped her credit card against the card reader oddly

relieved when it beeped the way it was supposed to. Every little thing going her way was a boost these days.

'Take a seat, we'll bring it over as soon as it's all ready.'

'Great, thanks.' Avoiding the curious glances from the queue behind her, she crossed the café to the table she'd already earmarked and sank gratefully onto a seat. Black toast! How embarrassing. Keeping her eyes down, she pulled out her mobile and whiled away time sending messages to her two friends, telling them how well everything was going.

'Here you go.' It was a different, younger woman, who balanced a laden tray on the edge of the table as she unloaded a plate spilling with Cassie's breakfast. 'Toast... not burnt.' The woman winked at her.

'It was crossed wires,' Cassie said, feeling her cheeks burn again.

'Debbie speaks in shorthand. It takes a bit of getting used to.' She stood there, the tray dangling from one hand, until curiosity got the better of her and she blurted out, 'You were here the other day with Danny, weren't you?'

The aroma from the breakfast was tantalising and made Cassie's mouth water. She wanted to chat, but more than anything she wanted to eat. 'Dan Cody? Yes, he's doing some work on a house I've just bought.'

'Ooh, how exciting for you. In the village?'

She didn't seem in a hurry to rush away and was standing that bit too close so that Cassie had to twist her neck awkwardly to look up at her. 'Just outside. Hindon House.' She expected the woman to look impressed, to smile perhaps, and say how great that was. What she didn't expect was for her to look horrified, lift her tray, and hold it across her chest like a shield. A call from behind made her turn, and when she turned back, she'd regained her composure. 'I'd best get on. Enjoy your breakfast.'

Cassie watched her scuttle away. Not back to the kitchen, though, where the call had come from. Instead, she stopped beside Debbie and whispered in her ear. They tried to be discreet but Cassie didn't miss the glances both threw in her direction.

She picked up her cutlery and started on her breakfast. But the hunger that had hurried her to the café decided to abandon her, and she picked at it, eating a little of each item before giving up with a sigh. Pushing the plate away, she nibbled on a piece of toast, drank her coffee, and tried to put a positive spin on the woman's reaction. Perhaps it hadn't been horror she'd seen, merely surprise that Cassie had bought Hindon House. A big run-down old house sitting in the middle of a jungle, one that had languished empty for the last two years. Perhaps the locals were surprised that anyone would want to buy it.

Lost in her thoughts, it was a few seconds before she registered that the softly spoken *excuse me* was addressed to her. 'Sorry,' she said. 'I was miles away.'

'I hate to interrupt, but there's no free table and I wondered if I could sit here.' As if to make her request clearer, the woman placed a hand on the back of the spare chair.

Cassie hadn't even noticed the café filling up and glanced around now in surprise. Many of the tables were occupied by lone diners, all men. It was possible the elderly woman standing patiently waiting preferred to interrupt another woman. There wasn't much choice but to say yes. 'Of course. I'm almost finished anyway.' She picked up the last piece of toast and smiled.

The woman echoed the smile and sat. Although it was already warm, she was dressed for a cooler day. Slowly, she unbuttoned her navy raincoat, slipped her arms out and dropped it on the chair behind her. Underneath, she was dressed in a navy blouse buttoned to the neck, and navy trousers. Grey hair, clipped boyishly short, suited her slightly elfin face. Prim was the word that leapt into Cassie's head. Prim, neatly turned out, and at least eighty.

'Please don't feel you have to rush away.'

Her voice was soft, gentle. Every word carefully enunciated. A retired teacher perhaps. 'I really need to get on with the day,' Cassie said.

'It does fly past. Especially at my age.'

There was a distraction as the waitress arrived with coffee and a plate of toast. 'Here you go, Mrs Morgan, enjoy.' An eyebrow was raised at Cassie's half-eaten breakfast. 'Was there something wrong?'

'No, it was fine, it was just a case of my eyes being bigger than my stomach, you know the way.' Cassie smiled, expecting a reciprocal response but the waitress merely nodded, picked the plate up and left.

'I can never manage more than toast in the morning.'

The comment drew Cassie's attention back to the woman sitting opposite. 'I usually just have cereal and toast; the fry-up was supposed to set me up for the day.' She regretted the comment as soon as it was out, seeing curiosity immediately light the older woman's face. It wasn't a surprise when the question came.

'A busy day planned, have you?' And then without allowing time for a reply, followed with, 'You're not from around here, are you?'

Cassie dropped the end of her toast on the plate and lifted the remnant of her coffee. 'I've recently moved here.'

'How lovely! It's nice to have new blood in the village. It's a friendly place to live. I hope you'll like it here.'

'Thank you.' Cassie glanced towards the counter. Neither of the two women there were paying her any attention. Perhaps she'd imagined their reaction. 'I've bought Hindon House,' she said. Her fingers clenched on the mug she was holding as she waited for a response.

'Hindon House?' Mrs Morgan tilted her head. 'You're going to live in it?'

With her elfin face and short hair, Mrs Morgan resembled an inquisitive robin. Cassie felt an instant liking. 'Yes,' she replied, relieved to see surprise and curiosity. Nothing negative. It loosened her tongue. 'I'm going to open it as a B&B.'

'A B&B! Well, fancy that! You and your partner, is it? She indicated Cassie's left hand with the slightest tilt of her head. 'I don't see a ring.'

Cassie glanced at her hand. The slight indent that years of wearing a ring had made was almost gone. She was glad. 'No, it's just me,' she said. 'No husband, partner or children.'

'It isn't a house for children.'

The words were sharply spoken, taking Cassie by surprise. She was going to ask what the woman meant when Mrs Morgan spoke again. 'I understood the house was derelict.'

And a derelict house wouldn't be suitable for children. Of course, it was simple concern. Nothing more. Cassie had to stop putting hidden meanings into words where they didn't exist.

Mrs Morgan spread butter on her toast, then cut each slice into quarters before finally picking up one piece and taking a bite with her small slightly yellowing teeth. 'Have I been misinformed?'

Cassie smiled. 'I think someone may have exaggerated its shortcomings perhaps. It's structurally intact, but needs a lot of redecorating, and modernising.'

'A lot of money and hard work, eh?'

'Yes, to both.' Cassie shook her head. 'Which I should be starting.' She drained the last of the coffee and put the mug down. 'My name is Cassie Macreddin, by the way. We'll no doubt meet again.' She glanced around the café. 'I can see this becoming a regular.' As long as she wasn't subjected to more odd looks by the staff.

'Good to meet you, Cassie. My name is Elsie Morgan. I've lived in Hindon most of my life.'

Most of her life – suddenly Cassie didn't want to leave. 'You must have known the previous owners of the house. I'd love to know more about them.'

Mrs Morgan nodded slowly. 'The house is so close to the village, it's impossible not to get to know whoever lives there.'

Cassie wanted to bombard her with questions and probably would have done if she hadn't seen the tremor in Mrs Morgan's hand. Had it been there when she'd arrived, or had mention of Hindon House caused it? 'I'd love to hear all about it. Would you like to come around and have a look before the work gets done, then you can see it afterwards and judge whether I've done a good job.'

Elsie Morgan stopped with another piece of toast halfway to her mouth. She lowered it and smiled sweetly. 'That would be so lovely. The last time I was inside was many years ago. It would be interesting to see what time has done to it.'

And interesting to hear the tales she had to tell. Cassie would prise the information out of her. 'The work is starting on Monday, so come before that. We'll have tea, and chat.'

Agreeing on a day and time, Cassie headed away but not before she noticed the two waitresses stare and whisper. Maybe she wouldn't make the café a regular haunt after all.

14

Back in Hindon House, Cassie changed back into her rags, grabbed the secateurs and spade, and headed down to the front gate. She had a few hours before the skip was to be delivered. She might need every minute. Although it had only been a couple of days since she'd been there, it was frustrating to see that the ivy had already succeeded in joining the two gates together again. She took a ridiculous amount of pleasure in chopping it away. Pulling open one side of the gate, she started on the other. Chopping, hacking, pulling, trying to duck the bramble when it sprung out, lashing at her, scratching her, determined to cause harm. Every now and then she'd stop, wipe the handle of the secateurs on the bottom of her T-shirt, and dry her hands on the leg of her jeans.

She thought she had it all free and dropped the spade she'd been wielding onto the ground to pull the gate back. It didn't budge. She kicked it in frustration, then took the spade and chopped at the soil that had piled up at the base of the gate. Loosening it, she shovelled it up and tossed it to the side. Her yell of satisfaction when the gate opened startled birds from the hedgerow on either side. They flew into the air, then settled back twittering complaints.

She used clods of soil to secure the gates open and trudged back to the house with the spade dragging noisily on the ground behind her. She still hadn't checked out the heating system but at least she had water in the kitchen to wash the blood and dirt from her hands and arms.

The skip arrived only ten minutes after it had been promised, the delivery truck rolling through the open gates and trundling down the driveway.

Cassie waved at the driver and pointed to where she wanted the skip dropped, then hurried back out of the way. 'Perfect,' she said, when it was dropped in just the right spot.

'Cody says you want it swapped out tomorrow afternoon, that still the case?'

Tomorrow afternoon! Maybe she'd given Cody the wrong impression of her abilities. She wasn't bloody superwoman. No, she was a bloody idiot. 'Yes, that's fine. Same time?'

'Same time.' He gave a wave, reversed and rolled back down the drive.

Cassie wondered about leaving the gate open, then reconsidered. Better to have some level of security. The lock and chain were where she'd dropped them. With the gate secured, she went slowly back to the house. Clearing the rooms was going to be exhausting work. It seemed a good idea to have coffee before starting. And something else to eat since breakfast had been a failure. She'd brought food down with her and a mishmash of items were piled willy-nilly into the too-small fridge. Mushroom soup tempted her. A few minutes later, feeling like a slob, she was sitting at the table in the back yard eating it from the carton.

She lingered over it, putting off the work that needed doing, but too long without moving had the inevitable effect. Every overworked muscle in her body had seized up. There was probably a part of her that didn't hurt, she just wasn't sure where that was. A few stretches loosened the tightness and she popped two more paracetamol to ease the aches and pains.

Determined to get started, she opened the door of the first bedroom she planned to tackle. Already crammed with old furniture and all sorts of rubbish, it hadn't helped that she'd moved stuff from the bedroom she was using and shoved it on top. Making her way through the piles to the sash window, she hauled the lower window up as far as it would go, leaned out and grinned. The skip was almost directly below.

Throwing everything from the window worked well. There was something therapeutic about sending things flying and hearing them crash as they landed in the skip or smashing on the ground when she missed. Heavier items, two old chests of drawers, she took apart first. It wasn't difficult, most were rotten or already broken. A few well-aimed kicks were all it took, then she sent them sailing piecemeal through the window.

Once she'd worked her way through a large portion of it, she headed down to the skip. Most of her shots had hit the target; some items lay in pieces in a circle around it. Bending, picking, dumping – she got into a rhythm and hummed as she worked. She kept going until the light started to fade, and every muscle in her body was screaming for her to stop. One room almost done. So much still to do. She'd been way too optimistic. The skip was half full. If she got up at first light, she could finish the first bedroom, start on the next. There were two days before Cody and his team arrived. She had to make the most of it.

She'd no energy left to eat. Instead, she opened a bottle of chilled white wine, poured a glass, and took it outside to sit and watch the sun set. The busy hours had prevented her thinking about the café, and the waitress's strange reaction to Cassie buying Hindon House. In the quiet of the evening it came thumping back with heavy steel-capped toes to give her a headache as she tried to make sense of it. She'd like to think she'd misinterpreted it, but she was sure she hadn't. It hadn't been simply the young waitress's reaction, it had been the whispering between the two women, and the looks they kept darting in her direction.

Elsie Morgan... when she came the following day, perhaps she'd be able to offer an explanation. She'd said she'd known the people who'd lived here. Perhaps some had caused trouble and had left a bad taste in the mouths of the villagers and made them wary of any new incumbent.

Mrs Morgan struck Cassie as a level-headed, no-nonsense kind of woman. It would have been nice to have asked her if there was anything in the house's history to account for the bad vibes in the kitchen. It would have been nice – but Cassie didn't want to appear a bit flaky talking about bad vibes and negative atmosphere. But she'd ask about the previous owners, see if she could learn something that might account for it.

And if Mrs Morgan told her that all previous owners had been saintly generous kind people, if there was nothing in the house's history to account for the increasing unsettling feeling that Cassie experienced, what then? Did it mean she'd brought it with her? That last ghastly night with Richie had taken place in the kitchen – was that it? Nothing to do with Hindon House – all to do with her and the cloud of guilt she carried.

On that depressing thought, she tossed back the last of the wine in her glass and got to her feet.

She'd left the kitchen light on, with the door shut to stop the enormous moths she'd seen fluttering around from getting inside. It was only a few feet to the door from where she'd been sitting in the glow of light that came through the dirty window. A few steps would take her back to the door.

But then, the light went out.

15

Cassie froze. In the darkness, she felt disconnected from reality. Between her and the house lay a black hole she might fall into and never be found. Mrs Morgan would call the following day and leave assuming she'd got the day wrong. Cody would call on Monday and leave in a temper to find nobody home. And no one would look down to see her in the hole under their feet, her fingers worn to bloody stumps as she'd tried to crawl free.

She could have jumped into her car and driven away. Gone back to London, admitted it had been a crazy idea, learned to ignore the *I told you so* stares from her friends. She could have if she'd not been city-girl careful and locked the car when she'd come home earlier, her keys resting peacefully in her handbag. In her room. Up the damn stairs.

The complete darkness was scary, but what was seriously terrifying was what was lurking unseen. That nice electrician had checked the system. There wasn't anything wrong with it. So, someone had to have turned the light out.

There was a torch app on her phone. She'd left it on the kitchen table. All she had to do was open the door, dart in and grab it. Then she'd have light, and the means to communicate if she needed to call for help. It was a good plan. It needed her to move though, and she couldn't. Not one step.

It was one of those huge moths that eventually forced her to move when it fluttered against her face, making her squeal and bat her two hands backwards and forwards to chase it away. If it was a toss-up between the moths and facing whatever might lie within, she'd choose the latter.

Before she had time to change her mind, she started towards the house, moving slowly, arms stretched out, hands seeking. Her sense of direction was off, and it was the wall of the house she felt. Swearing softly, she moved sideways till she felt wood under her fingers. Then she was inside.

In her hurry to get to her phone, she walked into a chair, the seat of it catching her knee. It was one more pain to add to her collection. Ignoring it, she ran a hand over the surface of the table, sure she'd left her mobile there. Panic sent her heart racing, both hands now sliding over the unseen table. It was there. It had to be.

And then she had it, relief making her eyes fill. The torch was good and provided a strong beam she could shine around the room. Into the corners. Even under the damn table.

Reassured the room was empty, she went to the door and turned the key in the lock. Was she locking someone in, or something out? Fear made her hesitate with her fingers on the key. The door had been unlocked for all the hours she was busy freeing the gate that morning and all afternoon while she'd cleared the bedroom. Anyone could have gained access, kept themselves hidden to wait for the opportune moment.

She tried the light switch, on and off, on and off, the clicks loud in the silence. It had to be the fuse board again. Aiming the beam towards the door to the hall, she followed it out. She shone it resolutely ahead, refusing to look right or left, hurrying past the entrance to the corridor. Fear escalated; it sent her running up the narrow stairway to the hall, breathless, almost crying. Too afraid to stop to check the fuse board, she ran up the stairs to the first floor, taking the steps two at a time, shining the torch on the space ahead to frighten whatever might be lingering in the shadows.

In the bedroom, she hurriedly shut the door, grabbed the chair, and wedged it underneath the handle. Trembling, she leaned an arm against the wall and rested her forehead in the crook of her elbow. Only then did she realise she hadn't checked she was alone in the room. Anyone could be hiding in the darkness behind her. Was that a breath she heard? Was someone creeping towards her? When she was sure she felt a touch on her arm, she squealed, and turned to shine the beam of light on her tormentor.

There was nobody there. Nothing hiding in the shadows. Carefully, she shone the beam behind the suitcases and carefully stacked boxes, and into the further corners of the room. She was alone.

Trembling in a post-adrenaline slump, she dragged herself over to the inflatable mattress and lay down.

In the silence, all she could hear was her breath hitching.

As she lay there, afraid to even take off her shoes, she had one further regret. That glass of wine. Because suddenly, she desperately needed to wee. The Portaloo, outside, was totally inaccessible. She wasn't leaving the safety of this room until daylight. If that meant lying there with her legs crossed, so be it.

And that's what she did.

Lay there, wondering what the hell was going on.

By the time the first glimmer of daylight appeared through the branches of the overgrown trees that surrounded Hindon House, she was crying from a mixture of frustration, desperation and cold anger.

It made sense to harness the anger, at least till she'd visited the Portaloo. That was her first stop, the second was the cupboard housing the fuse box. The row of switches, all neatly facing the same way, apart from one. Clearly labelled *kitchen lights*, the switch was down. She shut her eyes, mentally kicking herself as she realised she'd never tried the main lights upstairs. She'd made a stupid assumption that they wouldn't work.

Reaching for the fuse switch, she flicked it, then went to check the lights were working. They were. She stood underneath the fixture, wondering if the electrician had been wrong, and there was a fault. A fault, or human intervention? Someone playing tricks on her? She checked the front and back doors – both were securely locked. She knew she was being silly – paranoid even – but she went to each of the downstairs windows and checked them. The wooden frames were rotten in places; it wouldn't have taken much to have forced them open, but none had been. So nobody had got in. And since she didn't believe in ghosts, it had to be a fault in the electrics. On Monday, she'd ask Cody to have the system checked again. Maybe, she'd also have a lock put on the fuse box, just to be sure. She refused to entertain the idea that a lock wouldn't stop a ghost. Hindon House was *not* haunted.

Back in her bedroom, she debated trying to get a few hours' sleep before starting work, but when she lay down, too many worries were scampering around her brain. The growing feeling that she'd made a mistake in buying the house, the strange reaction of the waitresses in the café, the increasingly unsettling sensation that there was something wrong just out of reach. The unreliable electrics were just one more weight to add.

She clambered up from the mattress. There was no point in lying there wallowing in worries when there was so much to do.

Perhaps buying the damn house mightn't have been the smartest move, but it was done – she had no choice but to make the most of it. She'd have something to eat, then get on with emptying the rubbish from the rooms. Luckily, it was mindless work, she'd have no problem doing it half asleep.

16

It was mindless work, but exhausting. Tiredness slowed Cassie down, making every item seem heavier, every distance she had to walk appear longer. Further from the skip, everything landed on the ground, needing to be picked up and hefted over the side when she went down.

Late morning, hot, sticky and utterly weary, she remembered Mrs Morgan was calling around that afternoon. Stupidly optimistic, Cassie had expected to be much further ahead with the work. With no way to contact the woman to cancel, she had no option but to work till she arrived and hope she had the skip filled by the time it was due to be collected at 4 p.m.

She'd deserve a break for something to eat then. An hour chatting – and maybe getting the answers to some of her questions – then she'd get back to it and start filling the next skip. Cody had thrown down a challenge by organising it to be picked up within twenty-four hours – she was determined to prove herself.

It was hot, sweaty, exhausting work. Monotonous too, leaving far too much space in her head to be filled with conflicting, crashing thoughts, convinced she was imagining things one minute, that someone was intent on causing her mischief the next. She stopped, a broken lamp in her hands, and wondered if that was it – if someone was trying to drive her from the house. Someone who wanted the house for themselves. It might be worth asking the estate agent if there had been anyone else interested in buying it. Perhaps someone Cassie had outbid.

The property market was a notoriously cut-throat one.

Or perhaps, it was a local who didn't like the idea of opening the house as a B&B? The owners of a rival business? She'd have to ask Mrs Morgan about the owners of The Lamb. Maybe they were terrified of competition denting their profits. That idea made her laugh – if they saw the state of Hindon House they'd realise they'd nothing to worry about. It would take a lot more money than Cassie possessed to be able to bring it up to the level of the twelfth-century inn. The most she could aim for was to be their poor relation.

With a heavy sigh at the amount of work that needed to be done before she could even reach this level, she threw the lamp out the window and heard it crash to the ground below.

By early afternoon, the skip was full. She swept up the remains of the glass and breakages and emptied them in, then stepped back with a satisfied grin. She deserved a break.

She'd advised Mrs Morgan to come by the rear gate. After a quick wash, she set the table outside, covering the surface with pretty cloths she'd found in a drawer. In some dim future, she planned to buy old cups and saucers and offer her customers afternoon tea. For the moment, it'd have to be china mugs. She left them ready to use, upside down to prevent bugs investigating the interior. Then searched for the packet of biscuits she knew she had somewhere, finally locating it in a box she'd yet to unpack.

Just in time. The sound of a car engine made her cock her head and move to the window in time to see a shiny Mini pull up beside her dustier battered car. She quickly tore open the packet she was holding and emptied the contents onto a plate. Leaving it on the counter, she hurried outside.

'Hello, welcome,' she said as her visitor climbed slowly from the car.

Mrs Morgan raised a hand in greeting before opening the rear door and reaching inside. When she stood up, she had a cardboard box in her hands. 'I made you a cake.'

Cassie was touched. After a wretched night and the hard work of the morning, the simple kindness brought quick tears to her eyes. 'That was so kind of you.' She nodded to one of the chairs around the table. 'Have a seat, I'll go put this on a plate and we can have some with a cuppa. Tea? Or would you prefer coffee?'

'Tea would be perfect.' Mrs Morgan eyed the seating arrangement, then looked up apologetically. 'Would you mind if we moved a little into the shade. I burn very easily, and that sun is strong.'

'Oh yes, of course.' Embarrassed that she hadn't considered this, tiredness making her more flustered than usual, Cassie put the box down on the table. 'I can move it over.'

'We can do it together.'

It wasn't difficult to move it a few feet into the shade. Cassie fussed about moving the chairs, straightening the cloths that had ruffled up. 'Right, have a seat, I'll have tea made in a sec.'

It took more than a sec to organise everything and it was almost five minutes later before she rejoined her guest. 'Thank you so much for the cake,' Cassie said, putting the tray down on the table. 'Chocolate cake is one of my favourites.' It wasn't but it seemed the right thing to say, and she saw Mrs Morgan's face light with pleasure, a smile creasing her face and rippling the thick foundation she used. Cassie re-evaluated her age upward. Nearer to ninety than eighty. A very sprightly ninety. She wore the same subdued, reserved clothes she'd worn in the café. Grey rather than navy this time. Cassie pictured a wardrobe of identical garments in various dull shades.

With tea poured, milk added, cake cut into slices – large for her, a sliver on request for Mrs Morgan – the conversation went from the usual discussions about the weather, to how Cassie was settling in and on to a discussion of the work involved in turning Hindon House to a successful B&B.

'It'll be nice for Chris to have some competition in the town,' Mrs Morgan said.

Chris? 'Chris Baker, the estate agent?'

'The very man. He has notions, wants to be seen as this big businessman. I think he was interested in buying this place at one stage, but nothing came of it.'

'Really!' Cassie was taken aback. He'd never mentioned having had an interest in the house. She wondered if that was why he'd not been the easiest person to deal with. He'd wanted the house for himself. The bastard!

'It's going to be hard work, getting it all done,' Mrs Morgan said unaware she'd put a great big furry cat among the pigeons.

Putting thoughts of Baker's perfidy to one side, Cassie concentrated on her guest. 'I have Daniel Cody's company starting on Monday. I'm trying to get all the rubbish cleared from the rooms before that.' She shook her head and smiled. 'So much stuff has been dumped over the years.' It was the perfect opportunity to bring the conversation around to the previous occupants. 'The two men who bought it a couple of years ago, did they actually live here?'

Mrs Morgan sipped her tea, then dabbed at her lips with a tissue she'd taken from her pocket. 'They did for a couple of months, but they arrived mid-November and it was particularly cold. When they discovered the heating system was shot, they moved into The Lamb. I think they stayed there for a couple of weeks while a new boiler and radiators were installed.'

'A couple of weeks in The Lamb would have made a dent in their finances.'

'No doubt.' She reached for her mug and sipped her tea.

Cassie had wolfed down her slice of cake, suddenly ravenous. She eyed the rest of it, wondering if it would show a level of piggishness to cut herself a second slice when her visitor hadn't started to eat her first.

Instead, Mrs Morgan was drinking her tea, dabbing her lips after every sip. 'They moved back here, but within a few months, they were gone,' she said. 'Everyone assumed they'd run out of money.' She looked towards the house and sighed. 'I suppose they didn't realise what a big endeavour they'd taken on.'

Cassie heard the underlying criticism. Was this elderly woman and everyone in Hindon waiting for her to fail too? 'Foolish to buy something this old and run-down without having thought things through.' Foolish too to only think of the finances, to give no thought to the enormity of the task, to the sheer *loneliness* of following a dream made for two. Steering the conversation away from her shortcomings and finances, she asked, 'Tell me about the people who lived here before them.'

There wasn't the hint of a tremble in her hand as Mrs Morgan used her fork to break a piece off her thin slice of cake and lift it slowly to her mouth. It wasn't until she'd swallowed the miniscule piece that she answered the question. 'I didn't know them at all well, you understand. If I remember correctly, they were called Willard. A couple, and their two teenage daughters. There was a newsagents in the village then, so I'd see them in it the odd time. They kept themselves to themselves.'

Meaning, Cassie guessed, that they hadn't stopped for a chat, or to exchange gossip. 'How long did they live here?'

'Not long. Maybe a year.'

A year! A couple and two teenagers. Maybe there was some tragedy in the family that would account for the negative atmosphere in the kitchen. Maybe the family had gathered there, and there had been discontent, arguments, perhaps even violence. The Willards may have been strict disciplinarians who locked their girls in those little cell-like rooms with their barred windows as a punishment. 'Do you know why they left?'

'No.' Mrs Morgan looked slightly offended. As if Cassie was accusing her of being a tittle-tattle who knew everything about other people's affairs and was happy to gossip and pass on what she knew. 'They simply moved out.' She relented a little to add, 'Back to London where they'd come from, I believe.'

'It's fascinating to know about the people who lived here before me.' Mrs Morgan wasn't being as forthcoming as she'd hoped. She risked trying one more question. 'Who lived here before the Willards?'

Mrs Morgan pushed her barely touched cake away and sat back with her mug of tea. 'Before them? Goodness, I don't know. There was an older couple here for a couple of years, I think. As far as I can recollect, it was empty for many years before that. During the war, and for a few years after, it was used as a rehabilitation unit for injured servicemen with five or six beds in every bedroom. Many of us from the village helped to look after them.

Now that was interesting. Injured servicemen. Pain and suffering. Maybe that's what she felt. Perhaps their misery had seeped into the walls of the house. Maybe the worst of them, the ones suffering from mental debilitation because of what they'd suffered and seen, were housed near the kitchen. In those cells. Perhaps the windows had been barred for their protection. 'Did some sleep in those small rooms in the corridor behind the kitchen?'

Mrs Morgan looked puzzled. 'Goodness no, I think they were only ever used for storage. The servicemen – and it was only men, things were stricter in those days – needed space and fresh air. They sat outside during the day when they could, benefitting from the country air.' She looked towards the house again as if remembering a different time. 'The grounds back then were pretty, the house itself was showing signs of wear and tear but it was still very grand.' She put her mug down, looking suddenly tired, and even older. 'I should go soon. I get tired easily these days. Thank you for the tea.'

'Thank you for coming, and for the cake.' There was one other thing Cassie needed to ask. 'The café in Hindon have a very tempting selection of pastries, no doubt I'll work my way through them. When I was there the other day, I mentioned I'd bought this place' – she laughed, hoping it didn't sound as forced as it was – 'I don't want to sound paranoid, but they looked at me very oddly.'

Mrs Morgan smiled, shook her head then lifted a hand and with her index finger drew a circle in the air in front of Cassie's face. 'Perhaps it had something to do with that horrendous bruise. I didn't like to mention it, but it looks as if you've been in a particularly nasty fight.'

Instinctively, Cassie put a hand to her forehead, fingers gently palpating. 'I fell and banged my head on a rock.' A gravestone to be exact, but it seemed a bit overdramatic to elaborate.

Mrs Morgan's finger was still moving. Now it waved up and down Cassie's bare arms. 'Between the bruise and the scratches, you do present a startling sight.'

She lifted her arms. Some of the scratches looked raw. It was no wonder the waitresses had looked at her so strangely, almost fearfully. Did they too think Cassie had been in a fight? That she was a bit of rough. A criminal type from London. She looked at the bruises and scratches on her arm. What a sight! No wonder they'd looked wary. 'I've been cutting back brambles, they don't take kindly to it.'

'Thorns are a nasty but effective defence mechanism. The plant is struggling to survive, you're determined to chop it down, it's bound to be difficult.'

It was a strange way to look at it and Cassie wasn't sure what to say.

Mrs Morgan obviously didn't expect a reply. Pushing back her chair, she got to her feet with an ominous creaking of old bones. 'Before I go, you promised to show me around.'

'Of course.' Cassie pushed back her chair and stood. 'You'll need to watch your step though, there are floorboards up and a lot of stuff lying around.' She moved slowly, matching the pace of her elderly visitor.

'It's still a beautiful house,' Mrs Morgan said as they returned to the kitchen following a tour of the ground floor. She'd shaken her head when offered a glimpse of the bedrooms. 'That stairway looks a little too exhausting for me, my dear.'

Cassie was alarmed at how frail her visitor suddenly looked. 'I hope you haven't overdone things.'

'Age is a terrible thing.' Mrs Morgan smiled. 'I enjoyed the tour and I'll look forward to seeing it when it's all done. Where are you planning to start the work?'

'I need to get the bedrooms, the front hall and sitting rooms done, so I can open for business.' Cassie waved a hand around the kitchen. 'This, unfortunately, will have to wait a while.' She pointed to the back wall. 'I'm thinking of having that knocked through, incorporating the space behind, getting rid of those old storage rooms. It would mean there'd be light from both sides.'

She was imagining the space. It would be so much better when it was done. She didn't realise how lost she was in her plans till she felt a hand on her arm and looked down in surprise.

'It sounds like you have exciting plans. Thank you for showing me around. But now, I really must be going.'

Cassie walked the older woman to her car feeling suddenly guilty for having bombarded her with questions earlier. The poor thing had probably hoped for a pleasant afternoon. Sometimes, Cassie worried that she'd become self-centred rather than focused. She sighed and lifted a hand in farewell as Mrs Morgan drove out through the gate.

Checking the time, Cassie saw it was almost four. The skip would be picked up soon. There was one more room to the front of the house she could empty directly through a window. The two remaining rooms were at the back. Perhaps she could get the following skip set down on this side of the house. She looked around for the best place for it and as she was doing so she heard the rumble of the truck on the front drive.

This time, she went through the house, carefully locking the back door behind her. By the time she got to the front, the new skip had been deposited, and they were in the process of lifting the filled one. She waited till they were finished before approaching the cab. 'Hi,' she said. 'When you bring the next skip back, can you deliver it around the back?'

'Sure.'

She told the driver how to access the road. 'Around the same time tomorrow then.'

When he was gone, she leaned against the empty skip. It was Saturday afternoon. If she was in London, she'd probably be shopping in the city, maybe having a late lunch or a glass of wine in her favourite wine bar. When Richie had been alive, they'd sometimes go to an early show, to a gallery, or for a walk on Hampstead Heath. A different life.

There was no time for dwelling on the past – neither the one filled with good memories, nor the one filled with bad. Both were history. This place, despite the problems, was her future. She'd make damn sure it was.

It was that determination that kept her going despite the exhaustion that weighed her down more heavily by the hour. It kept her going till the third bedroom was empty, and everything that had smashed to the ground around the skip was picked up and dumped inside. It kept her going until night fell, when she came down the stairs after changing out of her filthy clothes into a pair of pyjamas to find the ground floor in darkness.

The last thing she'd done before going upstairs had been to switch on the lights. Her feet slowed to a halt on the stairs as she looked down into the pit of darkness below, then slowly, slowly she stepped backwards to the landing where she turned and walked... no ran... to her bedroom where she slammed the door and wedged the chair into position.

17

This time Cassie wasn't so stupid and she tried the main bedroom light. It didn't work. Neither did the lamp. There had to be a problem with the electrics. Simple as that. She'd been verging on paranoia and stupidly making mountains where there were only little molehills – the waitresses in the café had been understandably disturbed by her bruised and battered appearance, and there was a problem with the electrics. If Richie had been here, he'd have laughed her out of her fears before they grew to be terrors. But he wasn't. She had to deal with the molehills herself.

There was only one more day before Cody and his team arrived. She'd manage till then. She just wished she'd had something more nutritious and filling to eat that afternoon than chocolate cake. Very good cake, as it happened. Stupid to think of it, because now, with her mouth watering, it was all she could think about.

An electrical fault was tripping the fuses, nothing else. A mere molehill that would be sorted. There was no reason why she couldn't use her phone as a torch and go down to the kitchen to get something to eat. Get a piece of that cake too. There was no reason at all.

What was she afraid of, after all? Ghosts – or rather, one ghost. Did she really believe Richie was going to reassemble himself from the dust she'd scattered on Hampstead Heath and come back to haunt her? It would be impossible. She'd stood on Parliament Hill and watched as he'd blown away in the early morning breeze, swirling once before vanishing into the view they'd loved.

Richie was gone, but in a way, she'd brought him with her. The memories at least – the grim tense relationship they'd had at the end when they tiptoed around one another, until she hadn't been able to hold the words in and they'd burst out in a long shrill tirade full of pain, betrayal and soul-crunching hurt.

The darkness that had troubled her after Richie's death hadn't gone away, instead it lay hidden, waiting for its opportunity. And now it was back, like a disease.

It all suddenly made sense and having something concrete to blame for her fear washed it away. This she could handle. She gave Richie too much power when he was alive, she was damned if he was having any now that he was dead. Grabbing her mobile, she switched on the torch app and opened the bedroom door. The circle of light didn't look too inviting. She followed it anyway, stepping carefully and descending the stairs one slow step at a time. When she opened the fuse box door, she was unsurprised to see the same switches down. Snapping them up, she smiled when all the lights came on. A fault. She'd have a sharp word with Cody on Monday about his electrician.

Humming under her breath, she switched off her torch and headed down the narrower stairway to the kitchen. The cake box was on the table where she'd left it. She was still humming as she opened it, the sound cut off suddenly as she pulled the flaps back and stared into... nothing. For one long gut-churning terrifying moment, she was afraid to look up from it, afraid of what she might see. A cake-eating ghost? The stupidity of the thought was enough to calm her scrambled mind and she thumped the heel of her hand against her forehead, wincing as it hit the bruise. She'd put the damn cake into the fridge, hadn't she?

Hadn't she?

She glanced across the kitchen to where the appliance in question sat humming softly. Looking all innocent. 'Cake-eating ghosts,' she muttered, walking slowly over to the fridge. 'Scaring myself stupid with such bloody nonsense.' Her hand rested on the handle for a few seconds before she pressed her lips together and pulled it open with such vigour that the carton of eggs balanced precariously on the edge of a shelf tumbled to the floor.

The ominous crashing sound of cracking shells would have upset her if she hadn't been so relieved to see the chocolate cake sitting on the shelf where she'd put it. She didn't remember the action; it was one of those things done with little thought.

Taking the cake from the fridge, she stepped over the mess on the floor, and put the plate on the counter. It was silly to make a drama out of things that were happening. Incredibly stupid to turn things into a ghost story. Now that the mystery was solved, she was able to smile at the cake-eating ghost notion.

Still, she didn't fancy sitting in the kitchen where a skin-prickling damp lingered despite the warmth of the weather. In any case, there was no knowing when the light would go out again. It was better to take whatever she wanted upstairs with her.

Unable to stir up any enthusiasm for something more nutritious, she cut a slice of the chocolate cake, then shrugged and cut a second. Cake and a mug of tea were the perfect combination. Working as hard as she was, she'd soon work off the extra calories. She picked up the plate and mug. With both hands full, she'd no option but to leave all the lights blazing after her. It was nothing at all to do with being afraid of the dark.

The bedroom door was ajar. She pushed it open with a tap of her hip. Inside, she placed the plate and mug on a small table then, because she felt better for doing it, she wedged the chair back into place.

Being refrigerated had changed the texture of the cake, it was drier than earlier and needed a mouthful of tea after every bite to wash it down. All that could be said in its favour was, it had filled a gap.

She'd no concerns about finishing the tea. Earlier, when she was clearing out the other bedroom, she'd found an ugly orange flowerpot. It was destined for the skip, and almost went flying out the window before she stopped and looked at it more closely. It was chipped, and well worn, but not cracked. It was just what she needed. Now, it sat on the floor in the corner of the room waiting to be useful once more. No more desperately waiting till morning if she needed a wee. It was surprising how you adjusted when you needed to.

Adjusted, and accepted what was necessary.

It's what she'd done when Richie died.

What she'd done *before* he died.

She'd bought this house to make her dream come true – eventually she'd learn to accept that it was blood money that had paid for it.

Blood money.

She needed to stop thinking of it that way – as Richie's wife, she'd been entitled to the life insurance money.

It didn't matter that he'd asked her for a divorce the day before he died.

18

The lights in the kitchen were still blazing when she came down early the following morning and she left them on, relieved to find them still shining every time she popped back at regular intervals for a caffeine fix. There had to be an intermittent fault somewhere. Often the hardest things to repair. When things were completely broken, smashed to pieces, lying at your feet crushed, that was far easier. That's when you knew you had to throw out the old and replace it. It was how Richie had seen their marriage. He'd judged her as faulty, *toxic*, and decided to replace her with something in better working order.

Annoyed with how easily her thoughts drifted back to him, Cassie worked even harder, hoping the exhausting backbreaking work would leave little time for reminiscing. If it didn't completely stop her mind from drifting into the past, it did get the last of the front bedrooms emptied before she heard the faint rumble as the new skip was delivered to the rear of the house. She hurried down to gather up the last of the rubbish she'd tossed from the window, finishing just as the truck came to pick up the filled skip.

She waited till it was loaded before approaching the driver. 'Same time tomorrow?'

'Yes.' He looked behind her to the house. 'How many more d'you think it's going to take?'

Cassie had no idea. There was all the old junk in the remaining two bedrooms, then the contents of the attic whenever she could get access to it. Plus the ground and lower ground floors with their moth-eaten carpets, curtains and dated furniture, most of which would need to go, and the contents of all those horrible little cells behind the kitchen. There'd also be the rubble that the building work would create. 'Quite a few,' she said finally.

She stood watching as the truck drove away, then turned and looked at the house. What she'd have loved to do was have a long soak in a hot bath. What she was going to do was to make a start on the last two bedrooms. Cody and his team would arrive in the morning. She wanted them... him... to be impressed with how hard she'd worked, to see how serious she was about this project, how committed she was to making it a success.

The final two bedrooms were even more chock-filled with rubbish. Cassie sighed, and peered at the mound of old, worn and broken furniture, assorted boxes, and bags. Ragged moth-eaten curtains hung at the window from bowed window poles. One pull would have the lot down. They'd be the first to go.

The curtains came down over her head as soon as she laid a hand on them. She grimaced and pulled the dusty shredded material away. She'd have liked to throw it straight out the window, but one glance told her that wasn't going to happen. Someone, sometime in the past had painted them shut. Even knowing it was a waste of time, she hauled on the lower sash, willing it to move upward. The wood was rotten; if she had a knife or something she could probably prise it free.

Never one to put off things, she headed downstairs to find

something suitable. The lights were still on. Something was going her way. She unlocked the back door and headed to the shed for something she could use to lever the window open. Spiders scurried out of the way as she searched through the rusted tools, settling finally on a flathead screwdriver and a hammer.

Back at the window, she jammed the tip of the screwdriver between the sash and the window frame. A tap of the hammer and it sank into the wood. It took longer to pull it out, then she moved it along, and hit it again. Maybe she was getting tired, maybe she was basically an idiot, but for whatever reason she didn't pay enough attention to where she placed the tip of the screwdriver and when she hit it, it slipped from the window and hit the glass. Her reflexes were quick, but not fast enough to miss the rain of broken glass that fell on her. She stumbled back, fell over a heavy box on the floor behind, and crashed onto a wooden chair that shattered under her weight.

She lay, winded and shocked, afraid to move, terrified to lift her head to see blood pumping from her body. From the recesses of her mind came some alarming bits of information. If she'd sliced a small blood vessel, it could take hours for her to bleed to death. A major vessel... she'd be dead in less than five minutes. How many minutes had it been? How ridiculous if her last thoughts on this earth were worrying about numbers.

Everything hurt. Was that a sign she wasn't going to die? Not that day at least. Maybe it was relief, or pain, or the feeling of being a total idiot that made the tears come. She didn't consider herself to be a particularly clumsy person, yet all she seemed to do recently was fall over. Exaggeration wasn't usually one of her traits – she'd fallen over twice, this being the second time. It wasn't her fault she'd fallen through the damn attic floor. She needed to stop berating herself. Taking over from where Richie left off.

It was irritation that her thoughts had once more circled to her late husband that forced Cassie to sit up, instantly relieved to see no blood pumping or oozing from her at any great speed. Trickling, definitely. There was a long, and painful slice down her right arm and a piece of glass embedded in her left hand that made her eyes widen in horror. Shards of glass stuck porcupine-like from her T-shirt, some of them piercing the skin of her breasts, small pinpoints of blood showing through the grubby material.

Using the edge of a chest of drawers to give her support, she struggled to her feet, testing each limb, reassured that all were in working order. It didn't appear she'd broken anything. But she'd certainly added to her bruise collection.

It was only the glass from the lower sash that she'd broken, the top was still intact. She tried to look on the bright side – at least she'd have no need to open the window, she could simply throw stuff through.

Not with a large piece of glass sticking from her palm though. She stared at it. It hurt like hell and had to come out. There was a small amount of blood pooling around its base, not enough to signify major damage. It would be okay to pull it out, wouldn't it? Wouldn't it? Or would she bleed to death?

Tears came again. She could ring someone. One of her friends. They'd come down, she knew they would. And they'd look after her, sympathise, be there for her. *Pity her.*

Annoyance with the stupidity of her predicament made her act without further thought. She grasped the piece of glass, shut her eyes, and pulled it out.

Too late, she realised it would have been more sensible to have gone back to her room and taken out a clean towel to wrap around her hand. All she could see to use was the tatty curtain she'd pulled down what seemed like hours before.

Her legs were unsteady as she climbed over the obstacles to leave the room. So much for getting the room cleared; she wasn't sure when she'd be fit to do any more clearing out. And if she had to get one of Cody's team to do it, it would slow things down and cost more.

Guessing tears weren't going to be of much use, she snuffled, and headed into her room to grab some clean clothes and towels.

Down in the kitchen, where she sighed in relief to see the lights still working, she filled a basin with water, stripped off her dirty clothes and used a flannel to wash away the blood and dirt from her skin. Her hand was bleeding, as was her arm, but neither to any great extent. Small cuts on her breast were oozing slightly. Only when she wiped a damp flannel over her face did she realise she'd some cuts there too. Luckily, she wasn't vain, but it might be best to stay out of the café for a while. The thought of what those waitresses might say if they saw her even more battered and bruised made her giggle, the sound loud and with a trace of mania at the edges.

Of course, she didn't possess a first aid box. Nor did she have even a simple sticking plaster. When she was up to it, she'd drive to the nearest big town, find a pharmacy and stock up. For the moment, she'd have to improvise with clean towels.

She was crying again by the time she'd managed to tie a makeshift dressing around both her arm and her hand. The clean T-shirt was baggy enough to slip easily over her head, catching the tears and snot and bubbles of blood as she dragged it on. That was as much as she was going to wear.

Weary beyond reason, she forced herself to take something out of the fridge to eat. When the microwave pinged, she took it out, put the hot container on a tray and brought it upstairs to her room.

She sat on a chair in the barely habitable room, every part of her either aching or stinging, cut to pieces, battered and bruised, and as she chewed her way through some barely edible chicken pasta, she finally admitted that she couldn't do this. She'd made a mistake. A great big fucking unbelievable mistake.

Life had defeated her once again: she couldn't carry a child to full term, she couldn't make her dream come true. She was a great big fucking waste of space – worse, a *toxic* fucking waste of space. She called herself every name she could conjure up, castigating herself for everything that had gone wrong for her, for the country, for the damn world. Tossing the fork on top of her half-finished meal, she screamed in frustration. Loud yells that echoed around the room and bounced off the glass in the windows. It didn't matter; she could scream all she liked because she was alone. Nobody was going to care.

Defeated, and pathetic? This wasn't who she used to be. Tears were running down her cheeks. Was she going to give up now after all she'd been through? Using the back of her hand, she swiped away the tears. Hadn't she already learned that when life and circumstance pushed you down, when it held you squirming in the dust, you did what you could to drag yourself back onto your feet, dust off all the crap and get on with living.

She'd done it before; she'd do it again.

She might be a little pathetic, but she was not defeated.

19

Although she didn't have any dressings in stock, Cassie did have a supply of painkillers. Taking a combination allowed her to get a few hours' sleep, waking early morning when the effect had worn off. She lay for a moment with every part of her body hurting. She'd promised herself she wasn't going to waste any more tears, but they came anyway as she struggled from the air mattress. The only way she could manage was to roll onto the floor on her belly and push up from there, every action making her wince.

Once on her feet, she examined her injuries. Blood had seeped through the makeshift dressings on her hand and arm. She peeled them off one at a time, gritting her teeth against the pain. Both were still oozing a little and she used clean towels to wrap them up again.

As soon as Cody and his team arrived, she'd go in search of a pharmacy. The nearest town was only a twenty-minute drive away – she was sure to find one there. It mightn't be any harm to stock up on some disinfectant as well as dressings. The earlier scratch, courtesy of that blasted bramble, was looking very angry.

Feeling as if she'd aged fifty years, she dressed in the loosest clothes she could find, and went downstairs where not even the lights still burning in the kitchen managed to cheer her up. Nor did the bowl of cereal she forced herself to eat prior to swallowing more painkillers, or the mug of coffee she took outside where the empty skip seemed to taunt her.

Twenty minutes later, with the edge of the pain softened by pills, she went upstairs to the back bedroom. She had one undamaged hand; she might as well put it to some use. Unfortunately, the hand was attached to her shredded arm and after throwing a few small items through the window, she faced the unwelcome reality. Until the wounds healed, or at least till she bought some proper dressings, she was stuck.

Refusing to be seen as a pathetic failure, she went back to her bedroom. With the help of a make-up mirror, she applied some concealer to the bruises and scratches on her face. Since her hair was a few days past needing a wash, she'd have liked to have tied it up in a bun. Impossible with one hand, she resorted to a tight ponytail with the end doubled over. She found a long-sleeved shirt loose enough to cover the towel wrapped around her arm. Everything was a struggle and took far longer than it should. She was just ready when she heard the beep of a car horn.

It would have been nice to have run down the stairs and greet them at the back door with a cheery *hello*. That wasn't going to happen. She hobbled down, her good hand gripping the banisters, every foot placed with understandable caution.

Two vans and a car had pulled up and a group of men had gathered. At a quick count there were six of them including Cody.

'Hi,' she called drawing their attention. They moved towards her en masse. She felt their eyes sweeping over her, no doubt taking in her bruise collection.

'Morning,' Daniel Cody said. He looked as if he wanted to ask what had happened to her. Instead, he nodded towards the skip. 'I spoke to the hire company. You've done well. They said the first two pick-ups were full. Once we get going, this one will soon be too.'

'I've cleared the front bedrooms. I'm using one but I can move as needed. I have the back bedrooms yet to clear.' It was time to come clean. She lifted her right hand. 'Unfortunately, I had a bit of an accident yesterday.' She looked up to the window. 'As you can see, the glass broke. It slowed me down I'm afraid.' It had dragged her to a full stop and sent her into a spiral of self-loathing, but he didn't need to know that. 'I'm going to drive into Gillingham to get some supplies, so I'll leave you to it, okay?'

He was looking at her hand and frowning. 'You sure you're okay to drive?'

She had no idea until she tried. 'Yes, it's just a nick, I'll be fine.' He didn't seem convinced and looked as if he was about to argue. To forestall him, she turned to look at the house. 'If you could get on with checking the roof, and start the work for the en suites, that'd be great.' She turned back to him. 'Your electrician isn't here? Is he coming later?'

'No, we won't need him for a while.' Cassie's disappointment must have been obvious because he quickly added, 'I can have him call around if necessary. Has something happened?'

'The fuse for the lights keeps tripping.'

He smiled slightly. 'I did wonder why the lights were on, on such a bright sunny morning. You afraid to turn them off?'

Cassie wasn't happy being a source of amusement. 'It was dark when I came down this morning, I simply forgot about them.' She shoved her good hand into her jeans pocket. 'Right, I'll let you get on with it. I'll be back in a couple of hours, and we can chat then. If you could get the electrician to come back, that'd be good.' She turned to walk into the house, then turned back once more. 'There's plenty of tea and coffee, help yourselves.'

Five minutes later, she was on the road to Gillingham.

* * *

It turned out to be a small but well supplied town. She parked in the car park and walked... very slowly... back to the High Street. A café caught her eye. Decent coffee would be a good start. She bought a large cappuccino and a slice of lemon drizzle cake. Her diet had certainly taken a turn for the worse recently, but she needed something to sweeten her day.

She'd liked to have lingered, to have remained there by the window watching the world go by, to forget she'd ever taken the notion into her head that renovating an old house to convert to a B&B was a good idea. She might have stayed longer if she hadn't caught strange looks from the other customers. Perhaps she'd been fooling herself that the concealer she'd used on the cuts and bruises had worked.

Heading out, she noted the Lidl further down the road, and what looked like an interesting delicatessen opposite. They were shops to visit on another day. That day, visiting the pharmacy was as much as she was able for.

It was a large store. She found the aisle for painkillers and picked up a couple of packets. Further along she saw boxes of plasters – too small for her current needs, but they'd be good to have. She picked up the largest box and headed to the counter. 'I'll take these,' she said when it was her turn to be served. 'Do you have any larger dressings?'

The assistant was an older woman, smartly dressed, her grey hair shot through with pink, make-up applied with skill that Cassie found enviable. She was also extremely pleasant and helpful. 'We have a huge selection out the back, what size would you like?'

Cassie lifted her arm and used a finger of her bandaged hand to trace a line along it. 'About that long, I was cutting back some bramble, it got its revenge.' She turned the hand wrapped in the torn strips of towel. 'And a smaller, square one for here too. I've none at home and had to improvise.'

'Goodness, you have been in the wars. Bramble can be so vicious.'

'Yes. Plus, I've a lot more to do. I've recently bought an old house.' Cassie shrugged. 'It looks as though I'd better stock up.'

'Leave it with me, I'll put together a selection.' She must have seen the weariness in Cassie's face. 'Why don't you have a seat. I'll collect some things, bring them out to you, you can decide what you want.'

Grateful for the woman's kindness, Cassie crossed to a chair and sank onto it. All the pains were returning; as soon as she got back to the car, she'd open one of those packets of pills.

'Okay, here you go.' The assistant sat in the chair next to Cassie. 'A few long dressings, several smaller ones. A tube of antiseptic gel. A bottle of disinfectant. That should keep you going.'

It was exactly what Cassie had wanted. 'That's perfect, thank you.'

She left minutes later with a plastic shopping bag dangling from one hand. Retracing her steps, she was conscious that she was slowing as she approached the car. It had been a nice couple of hours. No drama, no disquiet. *No fear.*

All were coming barrelling back now.

She had nobody to blame for yesterday's accident apart from her own stupidity and maybe there was a fault with the electrics that was making the lights go out, but she couldn't get what Mrs Morgan had said about Chris Baker out of her head. He'd wanted Hindon House for himself.

Maybe he still did.

20

Cassie found Cody standing in the kitchen drinking coffee when she returned. She dropped the bag she was carrying on the counter, careful to bend the top over to hide the contents. She didn't want his sympathy. 'Were you waiting to speak to me?'

If he was, she hoped it was good news. Perhaps, that he'd miscalculated, and it was going to cost less, or it wasn't going to be as difficult as he'd expected and they'd be finished far sooner. Her forced optimism passed in seconds. His wasn't the face of a man bearing good news. In fact, his handsome features looked decidedly grim. Annoyingly, he was also proving to be a man who didn't rush to speak. Or maybe what he was about to say was so awful, he didn't know how to tell her.

'What is it?' Fear made her voice harsh.

He indicated a chair with a wave of his mug. 'Why don't you sit?'

She wanted to tell him to get on with it. That she could take whatever he was going to throw at her. That she was tougher than she looked, with steel in her spine and platinum in her veins. Unfortunately, she also appeared to have marshmallow in her legs. It seemed a better option to sit rather than collapse in a heap at his feet. 'Right,' she said, trying hard not to wince as she sat. 'Now would you please tell me what's going on?'

Instead of replying, Cody crossed to the kettle and flicked the switch. 'You look like you could do with a coffee.'

There was an open bottle of wine in the fridge beside the milk. He'd have seen it, yet he wasn't suggesting she might need a drink. She took some solace from that. Maybe, whatever was wrong – and she knew from his expression there had to be something – it wasn't that bad.

'Coffee would be good,' she said. There was no need to explain that she wanted to wash away the taste of the tablets she'd dry-swallowed in the car in Gillingham. The first instinctive reaction of fear faded as she watched Cody rinse out two mugs, shake them dry in lieu of using a towel, and ladle a heaped spoonful of coffee into each. The distinct echo of banging coming from upstairs was also a relief. Work was proceeding regardless.

The kettle hissed as Cody poured water into both mugs. He stirred and looked at her. 'Milk and sugar?'

'Just milk.' She swallowed the *I'm sweet enough* that was on the tip of her tongue, colour washing over her face in embarrassment that she'd even thought about uttering such a cringe-worthy comment. Luckily Cody was too busy taking the milk from the fridge to notice.

'Here you go.' He handed her the mug, then took a seat opposite.

She took a sip. It was far stronger than she liked. Her heart would be racing all afternoon. More than it was as she waited for him to speak. 'You'd better tell me what's going on.'

He put his mug on the floor beside him, then leaned forward, his elbows resting on his thighs. The movement brought his face closer. She could see where he'd carelessly missed a spot when he'd shaved that morning, the finer lines that fanned from the corner of his eyes, the creases that said he was quick to smile. Not now though, he was frowning, obviously weighing up his words. Perhaps she should be grateful he was being so considerate. She wished he'd just get on with it.

And then he did.

'I checked the roof,' he said slowly. 'There were a few loose tiles that needed to be slotted back into place, but overall, it's in good nick.'

Cassie was confused. 'That's good news, isn't it?'

'Yes.' He laced his fingers, tapping his thumbs together. 'I paid particular attention to the area of the roof over that water stain I saw on the attic ceiling. If there was a problem, it'd been fixed.'

'Right.' It was Cassie's turn to frown. 'So that damp patch we saw is a historic one, yes?'

'Yes.' He heaved a sigh. 'There's no problem with the roof at all. Where there is a problem, is with the floor, the one you almost fell through. The one you would have fallen through had I not grabbed you.'

The floor. She pictured the rot spreading through the floors, maybe even through the rafters, the house crumbling all around her. Pound signs flickered before her eyes. If she spent all her money on stopping the rot, there'd be nothing left to do the rest. It was better to know the worst. 'How much is it going to cost?'

He looked puzzled. 'What?'

Maybe he was a bit dim. She knew she was. Only a dim, idiotic moron would have bought a house that was about to collapse around her ears. She wondered if she could sue the surveyor. He'd never mentioned rot. 'How much is it going to cost to make it all right? The rot,' she added when Cody continued to look confused.

He shoved his hand through his hair with such force that Cassie wasn't surprised it was getting a little thin on top. She didn't understand why he was getting so upset, he wasn't the one who was going to be coughing up the bucks. Or maybe that was it, maybe he was afraid she didn't have it and he'd be out of a job.

'There isn't any rot,' he said.

Cassie would have liked to press a reset button, to start this conversation over, because it wasn't making any sense. 'You said the problem was with the floor, didn't you?'

He laughed, startling her. 'Yes, I suppose I did, but I didn't mean it was rotten. That's the problem. The floorboards are perfect, or at least' – he shrugged – 'they were until someone sawed through them.'

21

Cassie must have misheard. 'What did you say?'

'The floorboards aren't rotten. I assumed they must have been because you went right through them.' He got to his feet so abruptly, she was startled and only just managed to stop the cry of alarm. 'Hang on,' he said. 'It'll be easier to show you.'

He was gone for a few minutes and when he returned, he was carrying several sections of floorboard. They were dropped onto the chair he'd vacated. He picked up one and held it out. 'See,' he said, pointing to the cut edge. 'That was made by a circular saw.' He tossed it onto the floor and picked up the next. 'This one too.' It landed with a clatter on top of the other, and he picked up the next. 'And this.'

She held up her hand. 'Enough, I get the picture. Or at least, I think I do.' She looked at the wood on the floor and swallowed the lump in her throat with difficulty. 'Someone deliberately cut them so that the next person who walked on them would fall through.'

'It wouldn't be hard to do with the correct tool.' He bent to pick up yet another piece of wood. 'This bit... you can see where it was sawed all the way through. I'm guessing this was the first, then they eased up a bit. They didn't want to cut all the way through, just enough so that when weight was put on it... and by that, I mean a person... it'd give way.'

'It was a deliberate trap.'

'Looks like it.'

Cassie put her mug down on the floor, reached for one of the pieces of wood and ran a finger over the sawed edge. 'An insurance thing perhaps. Those two guys who owned it last, I know they went broke, maybe one of them planned it.' It was a reasonable explanation. Obviously, they hadn't gone through with it, and had stupidly left the trap for some other unsuspecting person to fall into. How high were the ceilings... possibly ten feet. A fall would more than likely result in severe injury, if not death. She shivered.

'No, I don't think that's it.' Cody said. 'The police would have investigated, they're not stupid, they'd have seen exactly what I did.'

'Maybe that's why they didn't go ahead with it?'

He reached for one of the pieces of wood on the chair. This time, instead of the cut edge, he ran his hand over the flat side. 'I don't think they were responsible.'

Cassie could feel her heart thumping. It was so fast, so loud, she was surprised Cody couldn't hear it. Her dream, it was already worn thin, spider-like crackling spreading over parts of it, one more push... one more disaster... might send it splitting into tiny little stabbing shards of pain. 'Maybe the people before them?' Desperation was making her look for even the remotest and most unlikely of explanations. When she saw sympathy in his eyes, she wanted to scream, wanted to take one of the pieces of wood and hit him with it, keep on hitting him till he bled.

She was horrified at the violence of her thoughts. This wasn't who she was. At least it hadn't been. Could she blame Ritchie for this? Why not? He was to blame for everything else, even... and the thought almost made her laugh... for her being there. His healthy life insurance policy that had given her the freedom. She drew in a long calming breath and let it out slowly. 'Tell me,' she said, seeing that Cody had more he wanted to say.

'I checked the attic carefully.' He smoothed his hand over the wood he was still holding. 'The area around the damaged floorboards is clean.'

'Someone swept away the sawdust.' That made sense. She was trying to think rationally, logically, it was a struggle.

'Yes, but outside of the damaged area, where the floor is visible, there's a layer of dust.'

A layer of dust – but not around the damaged floor. Cassie wasn't stupid. Someone had used a circular saw to cut the floorboards, then had cleaned up after themselves, sweeping up evidence of their work, and taking the dust with it. 'This was done recently.'

'That'd be my guess.'

But why? Cassie had no enemies that she knew of, certainly nobody who'd want to harm her physically. To kill her. She might as well face it – someone had laid a trap directly inside the attic door, and if Cody hadn't been with her, she'd have fallen through. If she'd been injured, she'd have lain there waiting for someone to come and rescue her. How many days would she have waited? Or had whoever was responsible for the trap intended to return and make sure they had the outcome they wanted? The same person who'd been playing with her lights perhaps – she'd wanted to believe there was a fault with them, but maybe there wasn't.

It would have been good to ask Cody what he thought; what she should do. But she wouldn't. This was her problem.

She got to her feet. 'How soon can you fix it?' She was impressed at the calm tone of her voice. She sounded professional, not at all like a woman who was falling apart and was annoyed to see that Cody looked unconvinced. In fact, he looked like a man who was going to argue, and she really couldn't handle that. 'As soon as it's done, could you assign someone to clear the attic out.'

He tossed the piece of wood he was holding on top of the rest. 'Sure, but what about—'

She held a hand up to stop him. 'I'll take care of it. Now, on to more important things, is the electrician coming back today?' She was relieved to hear he was. One problem would hopefully be sorted. 'Right, well I'll get on with emptying the bedrooms.'

'Like that?' He nodded to her bandaged hand.

Cassie lifted her other one. 'I have two. I might be a bit slower, but I'll get there. If there's anything too big for me to lift, I can leave it for one of your lads to do.' She didn't wait for an answer. She didn't need one. If she could save a few quid by doing some of the work herself, that's what she'd do. It wasn't like she had much of a choice. Cody hadn't said, but the repair of the floor would cost and eat into her already small contingency fund.

She waited till he had left before picking up the bag of supplies she'd bought in the pharmacy. It took several minutes, lots of wincing and muttered curses, even a few tears, before she had the makeshift dressings off. More grimacing when she washed her wounds, relieved to see they didn't look too bad. Even the bramble scratch along her arm appeared to be healing. A smaller, neater dressing on her hand allowed her to wriggle her fingers. Not perfect, but it would help.

She was forcing herself to stay positive, to concentrate on what needed doing. The sound of the workmen whistling and calling to one another, the rhythmic sound of someone hammering, the occasional whine of a drill, they were the music that would allow the dream she was still desperately clinging to to come true.

That other sound, the insistent beat inside her skull that told her something was terribly wrong – until her aches and pains faded enough and she could stop popping painkillers like a desperate junkie – she'd ignore it. It didn't make any sense – there was nobody who'd want to kill her, nobody who'd want to see her hurt.

Not any more.

22

Cassie concentrated on clearing a passage from the bedroom door to the window and when that was done, worked methodically, using her one good hand to lift, the fingers of her injured hand to balance. As with the previous rooms, most of the contents were junk. Occasionally, she found something that might be useful, a small table, an unbroken lamp or unchipped vase. They were put to one side; she'd put them to good use when she started the decorating and furnishing.

The shock of Cody's revelation faded as she worked, and as it did, she was able to consider the situation calmly. She couldn't believe someone would deliberately try to kill her, but maybe frighten her away? That idea simmered as she worked. When she went down in the early afternoon for something to eat, she found Tom, the electrician in the kitchen, some kind of monitor in his hand, a deep frown between his eyes. He merely nodded at her, then moved out into the corridor. She assumed he was going to look at the fuse board again. Hopefully, he'd be able to pinpoint whatever was wrong.

She took a sandwich and mug of tea into the garden and

lowered herself gently onto a seat. It might be wishful thinking, but the pain was a little easier. No more painkillers, they made her head a little muggy, and she needed to be able to think straight.

Her sandwich was finished, and she was sipping her tea, when Tom came out obviously looking for her. She'd made no headway in thinking of a solution to the problem she already had, and she could see by his tight expression that he was going to land another on her.

'Hi,' she said.

He pulled the chair opposite out with the toe of his boot and sat. 'I'm not interrupting, am I?' he said, with the air of someone who didn't really care if he was or not. 'I've done a thorough detailed electrical survey.' He enunciated each word carefully, as if by doing so it would make everything clearer. 'The system is working perfectly. There is no fault with the lights. I checked the fittings, the bulbs, the switches. Everything is as it should be.'

'So why does the fuse keep being tripped?'

She saw it then... the quickly hidden flicker of disbelief. He didn't believe her. Or perhaps it was more a case that he was so sure he was right, so certain that there was no problem with the electrics, that she had to be lying. She knew she wasn't. That left only one logical reasonable explanation – the lights weren't tripping the fuse; somebody was manually switching them.

The electrician was waiting for a comment. What did he expect? That she'd confess she'd been wasting his time. Maybe he thought she was looking for attention. An older woman, living on her own. The thought that he might be regarding her in such a way brought Cassie to her feet so abruptly she had to swallow a cry of pain as her mistreated muscles made clear their dislike of such treatment. She felt old, decrepit, useless as she pressed her hands on the table trying to regain her composure.

'Are you okay?'

The genuine sympathy in his eyes made Cassie feel immediately guilty for thinking badly of him. 'I'm fine, thank you. Just a few aches from unaccustomed physical work.' She rustled up a smile. 'Thank you for checking the electrics again, I do appreciate it. Perhaps I just imagined it all.' Making herself out to be an idiot.

'Not the kind of thing you can imagine, really.' He shrugged. 'All I know is, I can't see anything wrong.' He stood and picked up the bag he'd dropped at his feet. 'I'll be back in a couple of days to do the electrics for the en suites, but if you need me before that, just give a shout.'

Cassie watched him go, then turned to head back inside. There was a clatter of dirty mugs by the sink, she added hers to it wondering if they were going to be left for her to clean up later. Then she sighed. What else had she to do?

Outside the kitchen, she hesitated at the entrance to the narrow dark corridor with its eerie little rooms. The dirty windows filtered the light that came through the bars. Strange striped shadows on the walls flickered as weeds growing outside swayed in the summer breeze.

Cassie shivered. It did make sense to get what would be the money-earning part of the house renovated first, but she'd really like to get these rooms done. They were damp. She could smell it, feel it. When they were all knocked together, and the wall dividing them from the kitchen was gone, light would come from both sides and it would be a much happier space.

Happier? It was a strange thought to have. Buildings weren't happy or sad, that was down to the people who lived in them, wasn't it? But as she stood there, with the cold and damp creeping over her skin, she knew her first thought had been right. It would be a happier space when the work was done, but for now it was a sad, dismal, blood-chilling place.

She trudged up the stairs to the ground floor and crossed to the fuse board. It all looked as it should be. There was no reason to doubt the electrician, but unlike him, she knew she hadn't imagined it: someone had, somehow, got into the house and switched the fuses off. Twice.

If it was to frighten her, they'd succeeded. If it was to mess with her head, they'd succeeded there too. But if they'd hoped to chase her away with this, or with that booby-trapped attic, they didn't know a thing about her. If they did, they'd know that when she was knocked to the ground, she always came up fighting.

23

Cody came to find Cassie before his team finished for the day. She was still working on the bedroom and, although it was slow work, she'd made progress. Most of the small stuff was gone, another hour would see her finished.

'You've done well,' he said, looking around the room.

She wiped perspiration from her forehead with the back of her hand. It had been sweaty dirty work. She guessed she looked a state, but so did he. His brown hair was thick with dust and there were dark smears of questionable origin across his cheeks. There was an expression her mother used when Cassie would complain about having to study instead of joining her friends in the pub – you can't make an omelette without breaking eggs. Her mother was right, of course, Cassie would never have got the grades without putting the effort in. It was the same here – even if it meant getting battered, bruised and filthy in the process.

She felt Cody's eyes on her. 'I'll get all I can moved out of here by this evening.' She pointed to some of the furniture too big to lift. 'If someone could throw those out, that'd be good.'

He picked up a small but heavy table and tossed it from the

window straight into the skip. 'Lucky shot,' he said, turning with a grin. 'I'll have the rest removed tomorrow.'

'Good, and I'll make a start on the last bedroom.'

Perhaps she sounded weary. Or maybe she looked worse than she felt because he shook his head. 'There's no rush, you know, we're not going to get to it until next week sometime.' He nodded towards the remaining furniture. 'This lot will fill up the skip. I'll have it picked up tomorrow and ask for the next one to be dropped outside the other window. You'll be able to start emptying the room on Wednesday.'

She didn't know whether to be pleased or annoyed that he appeared to be giving her permission to take a day off. It didn't matter, she was grateful for it. Burying herself in work hadn't prevented her mind trying to grapple with the who and why someone would have booby-trapped the attic, and whether the same person was responsible for interfering with the electrics.

If she was going to strike back, she needed to know who to aim for. 'Before I forget, Tom is finished. He can't find anything wrong with the electrics but I'd be happier if there was a lock put on the fuse box door, can you organise that, please?'

'Can do.' Cody seemed reluctant to leave. He leaned a shoulder against the wall and gave her a rundown on how far they'd progressed that day in a level of detail Cassie struggled to find interesting. She truly didn't care what kind of wood he'd used to repair the attic floor and didn't need to hear a treatise on the merits of treated studwork timber for the bathroom walls. A bit like when she had a nice meal out – she didn't need to know every ingredient or how it was cooked, she simply wanted to enjoy the taste.

'I trust you to use what is best,' she said when there was a break in his report. The only thing she really needed to know was how much more the attic work had cost her.

'Negligible,' he said. 'It was pretty straightforward.' He pushed away from the wall. 'You look done in; why don't you tidy up a bit and come into Hindon with me for something to eat?'

She looked down at her clothes, brushing dust from her jeans, hiding the flush of colour that had flared across her cheeks. 'A bit?' She laughed and looked at him. 'I think you're being kind.'

He held his hands up. 'We'd be a matching pair. Do come, the food in The Lamb is excellent. We can eat in their pub where they won't raise as much as an eyebrow at two scruffy hard workers going for a bite to eat.'

She should have said no. Of course she should. Their relationship was professional; it was better to keep it that way. But it had been a long time since she'd spent time with a man who wasn't her husband. Since his death, there'd been nobody, nor any inclination to fill the space he'd left. It was too filled with pain. Cody seemed like one of the good guys, but she'd thought that of Richie too, and look how that had ended. *Richie!* Was she going to let him ruin her life forever?

'Okay,' she said. 'Give me ten minutes to make some attempt at restoring order. At least I have water.'

'Hot water too, he said with a smile. 'I had a look at the boiler and got it working.'

Hot water! 'Right, well, that'll make a difference. I might be able to make myself respectable.' She filled a basin with gloriously hot water, took it upstairs with her and did the best she could with what she had. It was impossible to wash her hair. Instead, she untied it, brushed the dust from it, and tied it back. Unfortunately, the style highlighted the bruises. Swearing softly, she applied a little more make-up than usual and thanked whatever genius had invented concealer. Chinos, and the least creased shirt she could find, and she was ready.

Almost twenty minutes had passed before she rejoined Cody

in the kitchen. He'd obviously made the most of what facilities were available. His clothes were still grubby but his face and hands were clean, his hair dampened and smoothed back.

He didn't appear irritated at the long wait, getting to his feet when she opened the door, and giving an appreciative smile. 'You've scrubbed up well.'

She felt colour flare in her cheeks again. Annoyed with herself for being so damn susceptible, she grabbed her keys and opened the back door. 'I'll drive myself, meet you there.' It was better, he wouldn't need to drive her home, she wouldn't be tempted... What was she thinking! He was merely being kind. She was behaving like a stupid teenager. Ignoring his surprised expression, she crossed to her car, climbed in, and took off without another glance in his direction.

He'd think she was a moody cow, but better that than he thinking she had the hots for him. *The hots?* God, how pathetic! By the time she pulled into The Lamb's small car park, she'd regained both her equilibrium and her sense of humour.

Cody pulled into the space beside her, and they walked in together.

The pub with its flagstone floors, inglenook fireplaces and wooden beams instantly made Cassie feel relaxed. 'This was a good idea, thank you,' she said. 'I'm suddenly starving.'

The pub was busy, with several customers at the bar and a few tables already occupied. Cody pointed to a vacant one overlooking the High Street. 'How about there?'

It was perfect. They sat and a comfortable silence settled between them as they perused the menu.

It didn't take Cassie long to decide. 'I think I'll have the beer-battered fish and chips.'

'And a burger and chips for me,' Cody said. He picked up both menus and stood. 'What'll you have to drink?'

'A small white wine, please.'

With a nod, he headed to the bar to order.

He was obviously well known and stopped to have a word with several people. He had a comfortable way with him, shaking hands with the men, kissing the cheeks of the women, all done with obvious charm. When Cassie found herself staring at him, she dragged her eyes away and looked through the window to the street outside. There was nothing to keep her attention, but she kept her eyes resolutely fixed there until she saw Cody's reflection in the window.

'Sorry, to be so long,' he said, putting a glass of wine down. 'I hope Chardonnay is okay.'

He sat with a pint of beer in one hand and raised it in a salute. 'To Hindon House.'

She laughed, raised her glass, and tipped it against his. 'To Hindon House.'

Their food arrived soon after, and they made polite small talk as they ate. Only when they were finished, did Cody sit back, and with a more serious expression ask, 'Have you reported the attic sabotage? To the police, I mean.'

The police! It hadn't entered her head. It did now, making her shake her head emphatically. 'There's nothing to report. Someone was playing a silly trick.' She held her hand up when she saw he was going to argue. 'I'd prefer to leave it at that, if you don't mind.' Maybe she'd been too sharp. Too *I'm the boss, what I say goes*. She saw a shutter come down over Cody's face. As if he was thinking the same.

He shrugged, drained his glass, and put it down. 'I don't mind. It's your house, and your neck.'

Cassie probably should have been grateful he was concerned. It wasn't that she was reluctant to involve the police. They had, after all, been extremely kind to her following the crash, and patient with her as she'd stumbled through her account of what had happened. She just didn't want to tempt fate by bringing herself back into their orbit unnecessarily. Stupidly eager for Cody not to see her in a bad light, she was about to trot out some excuse about not wanting to waste police time when she saw him smile.

She blinked in surprise, then realised he was looking over her shoulder at someone who'd come through the door behind. A woman? Cassie waited to see what vision of loveliness was going to appear, taken aback when she turned her head, to see a dark-suited man approach.

Cody got to his feet and reached out to envelop the man in a bear hug. Pushing him away, he kept an arm around his shoulder, and introduced him to Cassie. 'Meet my brother, Father Patrick Cody. Patrick, this is Cassie Macreddin who's bought Hindon House.'

Patrick Cody shared his sibling's good looks, but they were a softer, gentler version, his eyes warmer. And when he spoke, his voice was almost peaceful. 'How nice to meet you,' he said.

'And you,' she replied.

Cody grabbed a chair from the free table behind. 'Here you go, sit and join us for a while. D'you want something to eat?'

Father Cody sat. 'No, thank you, I can't stay. I only popped in to have a word with someone.'

He didn't say who, and Cassie noticed Cody didn't ask. Some parish business, no doubt. She was fascinated by the difference in these two men, so alike, yet so different. Cody sitting slouched in his seat, hands shoved into the pockets of his cargo pants, the priest sitting upright, his hands resting on the table in front of him, one atop the other, palms up, as if he was begging for alms. One man so restless, the other so peaceful.

'I assume you have big plans for the house,' the priest asked.

'It's going to be a country-house B&B.' She smiled and added, 'Eventually.'

'Good things take time, and it doesn't do to rush.'

'Next he'll be telling you that when God made time, he made plenty of it,' Cody said.

Cassie thought this was quite funny and was about to laugh until she saw the priest's face. His expression had sharpened, hardened. He didn't, it appeared, share his brother's sense of humour.

'I'm hoping to have the bulk of the work done within six months,' she said, bringing his attention back to her. 'There's a lot to be done, but your brother has assured me it can be done within that time frame.'

'Promises easily made are as easily broken. It is better to trust in the Lord.'

'I know when Patrick starts to get all religious, that it's time to leave,' Cody said. He jerked a thumb towards the bar. 'I'll go and settle up.' He held up a hand. 'And before you decide to argue, this is my treat, call it a working dinner.'

And with that, he was gone, leaving Cassie with his brother.

'Daniel is a good man.' The priest got to his feet. 'But when it comes to business, he is like all the others. So be careful.'

He walked away before Cassie found her tongue to ask what he meant. She was still frowning when Cody returned a minute later. He didn't seem surprised to see his brother had left without saying goodbye. Perhaps they had an odd relationship.

But the priest's words had unsettled Cassie. Worse, they'd dented the confidence she had in Cody. She'd quickly classified him as one of the good guys, but truly what did she know about him?

It was probably for the best to keep him at a safe distance. Keep her on her toes.

Keep her from doing something stupid, like becoming romantically involved with a man working for her.

But she was still frowning as she returned to the house, and only seeing the lights blazing from every window managed to shift her low mood a little. She was being silly. It was probably a version of fraternal rivalry. The businessman versus the priest – religion versus capitalism.

She had enough on her plate without getting involved.

24

The following morning, with a huge amount of difficulty and a lot of swearing, Cassie managed to wash her hair at the kitchen sink. It felt so good to have it washed that when she blow dried it, she left it loose. The bruise to her forehead was a nice shade of pale green. She had eyeshadow a similar shade; it was almost tempting to use it. She was going to the café in Hindon – it would give the staff something to stare at. Resisting the temptation, she applied foundation she hadn't used for a long time. A final touch of concealer blended the discolouration away and helped disguise the many nicks her skin had sustained from the broken glass. She brushed a finger over one cut close to her eye: a lucky miss.

A white T-shirt, and pale blue chinos made her feel summery and brightened a mood that couldn't make up its mind to be glum or glad.

Still undecided, she stood at the back door drinking a mug of coffee until Cody and his team arrived.

'Morning,' she said. 'I've some business to look after so I'll be gone for a few hours.' She was annoyed at herself for explaining, but she didn't want him to think she'd taken his advice and was skiving off for the day. 'If there's any problems that can't wait until I'm back, you can get me on my mobile.'

'Good,' Cody said, then with a nod, he vanished into the house.

Good? That she was going to be available if needed, or that she was away for a few hours. She played the one word in her head over and over, checking the tone. Was it a tad patronising? As if he knew what was good for her. Or worse, as if he was the big strong builder man putting everything to rights, whereas she was the idiot who'd bought the house and was set to pour every penny into doing the renovation in the hope of making her dream come true.

Or was she overthinking things. It was a throwaway word. He could as easily have said *okay*. It was her own doubts that were colouring her thoughts.

Grabbing keys and bag, she went outside, climbed into her car, and without a backwards glance drove through the gate and took the road for Hindon. She felt a sense of release to be free of the house again for a few hours. It was understandable. With all the cuts and bruises she'd sustained in the last week, it was hard to rid herself of the nonsensical idea that this grand new home of hers had it in for her. During one of her many periods of wakefulness that night, she'd remembered that Stephen King book, *The Shining*. She'd read it many years before – the scariest book she'd ever read, it had given her the chills. It hadn't helped that it had been a clear night, the full moon a bright hole pressed into the sky. Bizarrely, its light seemed to be shining on her bedroom door, and she'd lifted her head from the pillow and stared at it. What had she expected to see? A hatchet blade breaking through the wood? A disembodied voice crying *here's Johnny*?

She'd crept from the bed and wedged the chair under the handle as she'd done before, almost laughing at her stupidity. If there was a hatchet-wielding maniac prowling outside, it wasn't going to prevent him from entering.

In the daylight, driving through the pretty countryside, she was able to laugh at herself, even count her blessings – her aches and pains were easing, and she was able to move the fingers of her right hand without wincing much. Nor was she immune to the charms of the dappled sunshine as she negotiated the narrow tree-lined road. She used to be a positive person, she needed to grab some of that back.

It was difficult. There'd been no problem with the lights the previous day or night but instead of being reassured, it made Cassie more unsettled. More convinced by the day that it was somebody who wanted her out of the house, someone who wanted it for themselves, she knew they wouldn't have given up so easily. Perhaps they were playing a long game, taking a breather to lull her into a false sense of security, then they'd come back and hit her with some other nightmare.

Chris Baker. The estate agent's name was rattling around in her head but it would be foolish to allow herself to be blinded by it. There may have been other under-bidders, other people who might have been glad to see her fail. Her plan for that morning was to have a decent breakfast in the café, then go and pester the estate agent for information on who else had made a bid for the house.

Parking in a space directly outside the café, she checked her face in the rear-view mirror. She looked okay. There was nothing to draw attention to her, nothing to make the staff look at her askance. She fluffed her hair with her fingers, bringing her fringe a little more over her forehead. She wasn't sure if it made things better or made it look as if she was hiding something.

Overthinking again. With a shake of her head, she grabbed her bag, and stepped from the car. The café was busy but there was a table free near the rear wall. Cassie sat, and picked up the menu that was propped against a salt and pepper duo. Someday she'd try the pancakes, but that morning she had a craving for a big breakfast with all the trimmings. Leaving her bag on the table, she crossed to the till where a woman she didn't recognise was busy scrolling through messages on her mobile, her thumb moving rapidly.

'Good morning,' Cassie said.

The woman was probably her age, maybe a few years older, a little more worn around the edges, a little heavier around the middle. Heavily made-up eyes flicked up, then back to the screen. One more swipe of her thumb and she put the mobile down. 'My cousin in America. She was married at the weekend and has sent me what seems like a million photos.'

'And expects you to ooh and ahh and comment on each one, eh?'

The woman laughed. 'If she does, she's living in cloud-cuckoo land.' She tilted her head. 'You must be Cassie Macreddin.'

Perhaps Cassie hadn't done such a good job in hiding her battered face after all. Her fingers went up to fiddle with her hair, drawing her fringe self-consciously further across the fading bruise. 'Yes, that's me.'

'I'm Milly Baker, Chris's sister. He told me a London woman had bought Hindon House.' She grinned conspiratorially. 'He described you so well, I think he might have a penchant for you.'

Penchant? Not a word she'd heard used outside a novel, but Cassie laughed as if flattered, pleased to be recognised for something other than her battered face. There was no reason to mention that all she could remember of the estate agent was that she'd wanted to strangle him with the shiny blue tie he'd worn. 'I think his penchant was for the sale and the commission he'd be getting.' She'd said the wrong thing, she could see it in the sudden tightening of Milly's expression.

'It's not easy keeping a business afloat these days, and with his partner, Joe, on long-term sick leave, it's even tougher for him. So you can hardly blame him being pleased to get the sale, can you?'

'Not in the slightest,' Cassie said. 'And he made it all so easy for me too. I really appreciated his help.' The lie came easily but the words nearly choked her. Chris had been an absolute nightmare to deal with, not answering emails promptly, or returning phone calls until days later. Of course, thanks to Mrs Morgan, Cassie thought she knew why. It must have been so galling for him to sell the house he'd wanted to someone else.

Praise for her brother didn't help to smooth Milly's ruffled feathers. It seemed she wasn't an easy woman to placate and her voice was decidedly chilly as she asked, 'What can we do for you this morning?'

'I enjoyed the big breakfast so much the other day, I'm going to have it again. With coffee please and white toast.'

Milly scribbled the order down. 'Big breakfast. Coffee. White toast. That's £12 please. Take a seat, I'll bring it over when it's ready.'

Cassie tapped her credit card against the card reader to pay, then returned to the table, annoyed with herself for putting a foot so badly wrong. She hoped Milly wouldn't have a word with her brother before she'd had a chance to speak to him – it might get his back up and make him less willing to answer her questions.

As on her previous visit, the rest of the customers were either buried in newspapers or on their mobile phones.

Milly arrived with her drink a couple of minutes later.

'Thanks,' Cassie said. 'You make great coffee here.'

Although praising the brother hadn't worked, it seemed Milly was willing to defrost at approval of the coffee. 'I only use organic,' she said. 'It's a little more expensive but I think it makes a huge difference.'

'This is your café?'

'Yes, I thought you knew. Didn't Chris send you here?'

Chris hadn't even mentioned the place, or his sister. Cassie had learned her lesson though. 'He told me there was a fabulous café around the corner, but I didn't have a chance to come in that day. I was rushing back to London. It was Daniel Cody who took me here when we were discussing the renovations.'

Milly's eyes lit up at the mention of Cody's name. 'Danny is one of our best customers.' She looked as if she was going to say more, maybe even confess to having a *penchant* for the man, but luckily for Cassie, the door opened and a couple of customers came through. 'Enjoy your coffee,' Milly said, and bustled away.

Cassie hadn't been lying, it was very good coffee. Service that morning was slow, and she'd finished it before her breakfast arrived. It was the waitress who'd served her the previous visit, but she gave no indication she recognised her as she placed a brimming plate on the table. 'I'll be back with your toast in a sec.' She pointed to the empty mug. 'More coffee?'

'Please, that'd be great.' Once the coffee and toast arrived, she was left in peace to eat.

She'd almost finished when she looked up to see Mrs Morgan approaching her table.

'May I join you?'

Cassie was still feeling guilty for her quizzing of the elderly woman when she'd visited and greeted her with a friendly smile. 'Of course.'

'Thank you.'

Although the day was already warm, Mrs Morgan was wearing a wool coat buttoned to the collar. She sat without undoing even the top button, the fabric pressing at her neck.

Cassie felt herself staring, wondering that the woman didn't feel she was being choked. She was elderly, and skeletally thin, perhaps she felt the cold. Dragging her eyes away from the concertinaed skin just above the collar of Mrs Morgan's coat, Cassie tapped the edge of her empty plate. 'I'm glad you didn't arrive in time to see all I ate; I've been a bit of a pig.'

'There's nothing wrong with a healthy appetite.' The arrival of her coffee had Mrs Morgan turn to smile at the waitress. 'Thanks, dear.' She turned back to Cassie. 'This is my morning treat.'

Cassie wondered if it was all the woman could afford. Coffee, not breakfast or even a piece of cake. She'd liked to have offered to buy her something but was afraid to offend. 'It's good coffee.'

'It is.'

Cassie wondered if the woman had chosen to sit with her for a reason, or just for the company. If it was the latter, she was doing a poor job at providing scintillating conversation.

'You're looking a little better than the last time I saw you,' Mrs Morgan said.

Considering Cassie had looked like she'd been in a car crash, the *little better* wasn't hugely complimentary. 'Thank you. The bruises are almost gone.'

'I see the brambles are still out for blood.'

It took a few seconds to understand. Then, she lifted her hand. The dressing, fresh on yesterday evening, was startlingly white. The one on her arm was older and beginning to show its age, the corners rolled up, a few brown spots she guessed were coffee spatters. 'Yes,' she said. It was easier than going into the whole window-smashing explanation. 'But I'm getting there.'

'So it's going okay for you?'

Cassie wanted to laugh, or cry, wanted to describe in detail about the attic floor, the dodgy electrics, the window, the graveyard. Wanted to lay it all out, so that this woman, this virtual stranger, could reassure her and tell her it was all going to be all right. Poor Mrs Morgan, to be quizzed on her visit to Hindon House, and dumped on now. If Cassie wasn't careful, she'd find herself with no friends in the village. 'It's going fine,' she said, hoping she sounded confident. 'It's slow, of course, but I expected that. When it's done,' – she waved a hand around the café – 'I'm hoping it'll be as big a success as this place is.'

Mrs Morgan gave a tight smile, then sniffed, a disparaging sound that told Cassie clearly what the older woman thought of the café owner.

'It was easy for Milly,' Mrs Morgan said. 'She bought a going concern. There'd been a café here for years, run by a very nice couple who retired to Spain about two years ago. I think they hoped to get more for it to give them a good start, but when there were no offers for a few months, they accepted a much lower bid. Everyone was surprised, including them, when the bidder turned out to be Milly.'

All this was said in a low, almost conspiratorial voice, as if she was afraid of being overheard. She glanced nervously towards the till where Milly was ringing up a customer's bill. 'I shouldn't be gossiping,' Mrs Morgan said, shaking her head as if ashamed of herself.

Cassie reached a hand across and rested it gently on the woman's arm. 'You were being kind to me, not gossiping.' She was relieved to see a lightening of the woman's worried expression. Cassie had been right with her first assessment. Mrs Morgan was the quintessential older woman, stoic, old-fashioned, reserved. A stalwart of the community. She also knew a lot about what was going on in the village. 'Can I assume Milly's brother was the sales agent?'

'Yes. So now the Bakers have the estate agent's, the café, and they also own the petrol station. That's a lot in a small town like Hindon.'

'Like a cartel,' Cassie said with a laugh. It was supposed to be a joke, so she was surprised to see Mrs Morgan nod earnestly.

'I told you Chris has notions about being seen as a successful businessman. I heard,' – she leaned closer – 'that he's made the owner of The Lamb an offer several times and says he won't give up until they agree to sell.' She sat back, looking almost satisfied to have painted the estate agent in a rapacious light.

She wasn't, obviously, a woman to get on the wrong side of, and Cassie wondered what the Bakers, sister and brother, had done to annoy her. She had a small cottage in the town, in prime position on the High Street, perhaps they'd been trying to acquire that too.

Mrs Morgan's eyes flicked to where Milly was standing at the till, but as she was deep in conversation with a customer, she relaxed and turned her focus back to Cassie. 'I can't be sure, but I think there were some questions asked about the sale of this place. I think the Sandersons might have written to the ombudsman to complain.'

Assuming the Sandersons were the couple who'd previously owned the café, Cassie nodded. She wasn't convinced though. There was something in the almost cat-like satisfaction on Mrs Morgan's face that said it was she who'd made the complaint. Perhaps the Bakers' ambiguous business tactics went against her stricter moral code. Small town intrigue, Cassie would prefer to avoid it, she had enough on her plate.

Mrs Morgan's gossip had, however, given her food for thought. If a complaint had been made to the ombudsman about the estate agent, Baker might have had a warning and was treading very carefully. Perhaps that's why he hadn't made a bid for Hindon House.

Mrs Morgan was chatting about her garden. Cassie was able to tune out and consider what she'd heard. Was the estate agent playing a clever game? Hindon House had been sold by the bank who'd foreclosed on a loan the previous owners had taken out. They hadn't been in a hurry to sell. Perhaps too, they hadn't been interested in dropping the price?

Cassie had been so terrified of losing out that when her first low offer had been rejected, she'd offered the full asking price. But if she were to sell it now? If she were chased from the house by things that went bump in the night, if she was desperate to sell, wouldn't she take the best offer that was made? Selling it with work half done, she'd be forced to drop the price and someone would grab it and make a killing.

Chris Baker. Getting his hands on the house he'd wanted, at a bargain price. Perhaps. Or maybe even Cody. What was it his brother had said – *when it comes to business, he is like all the others*. Cody could finish the work he'd started and sell on at a huge profit.

She didn't like being sucked into a conspiracy theory, but someone was out to get her. Someone who thought she was a pushover; she'd have to prove them wrong.

25

Cassie left Mrs Morgan with her coffee after promising to meet her another morning. She left her car where it was and headed back to the High Street and the office of Baker and Partner Estate Agents. Her plan had been to ask Chris if there had been any other offers on Hindon House in the hopes of finding out who the under-bidder was, to run them to ground and... well, she wasn't sure what she'd have done then, but she'd have done something. However, armed with the new information gleaned from Mrs Morgan, she decided to change tack. If Chris was hoping to frighten her away and get the house for a knockdown price, it was time to show him what a tough opponent she was.

The unanswered emails and ignored phone calls. They made sense now. He'd apologised, every time, but in a tone of voice that said clearly, he wasn't the slightest bit sorry. She wondered at the time, how he could run a business with such poor customer service. He probably hoped she'd back out, and eventually the bank would weaken and drop the price.

When she hadn't, maybe the slimy rat had come up with a different plan to get what he wanted. She had to be careful not to jump to conclusions though. There were still the underbidders to consider. She needed to gather all the information before she decided what to do.

The estate agent's office had bay windows on either side of the door. One window given over to sales, the other displaying premises to let. Pretending to be viewing the information, she looked through to the office beyond. It didn't suit her budding plan to have onlookers – Chris would speak more freely if they were alone. She was in luck, and apart from the man himself, the office was empty.

Pasting a smile on her face, she pushed open the door and walked in, swinging her bag as if she hadn't a care in the world. 'Hello, Chris, I was passing and thought I'd pop in to say hello.' She looked around the office as if expecting to see customers. 'I've got you in a quiet moment, that's lucky for me.' She took the empty seat, dropped her bag to the floor, and relaxed back, folding her arms. Just as if she'd popped in for a long and pleasant chat. 'I've wanted to call in since I arrived to thank you for all your hard work in making everything run so smoothly over the purchase of Hindon House. Honestly, it was such a relief.'

A smile wavered on Chris's face as if he wasn't sure how to react, his eyes flickering to the door in the hope of rescue by a customer. The door stayed resolutely shut. He clapped his hands on the desktop. 'We aim to please, Ms Macreddin.'

She hoped he'd keep on aiming to please and give her the information she wanted. 'I was curious about the underbidders. You'd said there were a couple. Are they local?' Almost immediately his face tightened, and she knew she was out of luck. He was consistent, at least, he'd been unhelpful during the purchase of Hindon House, he was going to remain that way.

'I'm sorry, I'm not free to give out that information, I'm afraid.'

He sniffed. 'We take client confidentiality seriously as I'm sure you can understand, Ms Macreddin.'

She understood all right. He was a pompous prick. But it was better to keep on friendly terms. 'Of course, I understand completely. And, please, call me Cassie, we'll no doubt see a lot of each other now that I'm fixed in Hindon. Business owners should support one another, don't you agree?' She was pleased to see him relax a little, a tentative smile appearing on his full, rather wet lips.

'I do indeed,' he said. He indicated the door behind, and for one shocking moment Cassie thought he had his own version of support and was inviting her to go back with him for some morning fun. The thought made her skin crawl. 'We have a posh coffee machine; can I tempt you?'

Coffee, he was offering her coffee. Nothing more. Cassie blamed his sister for putting ridiculous ideas in her head. Then she wondered if Milly had had an ulterior motive for having done so. What that would be, Cassie had no idea. Chris was still waiting for an answer. She didn't want any more coffee, but it made sense to say yes. Far easier to chat over a convivial cuppa. 'Coffee would be nice.' Then, in case he exchanged notes with his sister later, she added, 'I can never have enough.'

'Espresso, cappuccino, latte?'

'A latte would be perfect, thank you.' She watched him through the open door. He made a big fuss out of making the drinks. He was, she guessed, the kind of man who loved a barbeque, all the stupid fuss about plonking a burger or piece of chicken on hot embers, using super-long tongs to turn it over, making a fuss about that, as if he was a Michelin star chef cooking an epicurean meal.

The coffee when it came was mediocre at best. Milly would be relieved to know it wasn't a patch on hers. Perhaps it wasn't organic. The thought made Cassie gurgle, drawing a raised eyebrow from Chris. 'It's so good,' she said, taking another sip, hoping she wasn't going to have hysterics. Feeling another giggle building, she took a large mouthful of coffee hoping to wash it down. It was the thought of this man trying to frighten her from Hindon House that brought her thoughts back to a more serious plane.

'Daniel Cody and his team are doing a great job; I might be ready to open ahead of schedule.' It was not quite a lie, not really the truth.

'Good news.' He sat back, linked his fingers together and rested them on the curve of his belly. 'Mind you, with that kind of development, you never know when you're going to encounter problems, do you?'

He was right, of course, but was he talking about problems that might naturally occur, or ones he had caused, or was planning to cause? Were his words a generalisation, or a threat?

'Cody seems like the kind of man who could cope with almost anything. Anyway,' she said, meeting his eyes, 'I'm made of tough stuff, I'll cope with whatever is thrown at me.' His eyes didn't waver, nor did he look the slightest bit guilty. But then, he was in business, he'd probably honed that poker face.

She hadn't managed to learn the identity of the underbidders, but there was more she wanted to know. 'I don't plan on following the same route as…' She frowned as if trying to recall the names, hoping he'd fill in the gaps. He'd already struck her as a man who liked to show off his knowledge.

'Ben Donnelly and Mark Rogers?'

She smiled. 'Thank you, yes, them. I gather they overextended themselves.' With the line cast, she held the smile in place waiting for the fish to bite.

Baker tapped his thumbs together. 'They got the house at a

good price, it should have worked, but they tried to do everything themselves, and that didn't.'

'No, I think it's important to know your limitations, that's why I hired Cody. My strength lies in managing the money, and in being persistent and determined.' Could she spell it out any clearer? She wasn't going anywhere. 'What happened to them, do you know?' She kept her voice casual.

Baker screwed up his mouth as if he'd suddenly bitten into a lemon. 'Things turned nasty towards the end. They were desperate to hold on to the house, and tried to convince the bank they could turn it around, but once it got out that they were in trouble, it was like dominoes. Businesses and trades started to refuse to supply them unless they paid upfront. Worse, they demanded payment for goods already received.' He nodded towards the window. 'There was even an argy-bargy out on the street between Ben Donnelly and the then manager of the garage about an unpaid bill.'

'It must have been tough.'

'It was, there was a lot of ill-feeling in the town towards them. People lost money when they were declared bankrupt.'

Tough on the townspeople, tough on the two men who'd lost everything. Cassie knew what it was like to be obsessed with a dream. Maybe they still were. Maybe it wasn't underbidders who were her problem at all. Her list of suspects was growing. 'Do you know what happened to them?'

It must have come out sharper than she'd planned, Baker stopped tapping his thumbs and regarded her in surprise. 'I've no idea, but men like them, whose only interest is in making a quick buck, usually land on their feet. I doubt if they've gone far. They're probably involved in some other shady deal.'

There was a sneer on his lips, a dismissive tone to his words. Cassie realised suddenly that she didn't like the estate agent. He was the kind of man who'd always think the worst of people, who wouldn't understand the power of a dream, the obsessive need to follow it, no matter what. She'd never met Donnelly or Rogers, so she couldn't comment, but it seemed to her that it was Baker whose interest was in making a quick buck. But being a smarmy git didn't necessarily make him responsible for what was happening at Hindon House. Maybe Donnelly and Rogers really, *really* wanted the house back.

'It seems Hindon House was unlucky for them. And I gather the family who lived there before them didn't stay long either.'

'City folk.' He lifted a hand and held it palm out. 'No disrespect intended, but they had expectations that living in a small town couldn't possibly have met.'

Cassie wanted to ask what he meant, but the door behind opened, and she saw his face light up in anticipation of a customer. There was no time for finesse. 'What was their name? That family?' Mrs Morgan had given her Willard, she needed first names if she'd any hope of tracing them. She was going to spin a yarn about writing a history of previous owners, but it seemed Baker was already in sales mode as he spilled out the information without hesitation in the interest of getting rid of her. 'Alan and Jenny Willard.'

Cassie grabbed her bag and got to her feet. 'Thanks for the coffee and the chat.'

'Always a pleasure to meet a satisfied customer,' he said, his voice pitched to carry to the couple who'd come in.

It was so tempting, so very, very tempting to reply with a seductive, *you always satisfy me, Chris*, before sashaying from the office. But cutting off her nose to spite her face was never a good idea. If things worked out as she hoped, she was going to be living in Hindon for a long time. There was no point in making enemies.

While she was in the town, she took the opportunity to do a

little food shopping. Hindon Village Store, a community shop on the High Street, looked interesting. Inside she found it stocked a huge range of products for such a small premises. Shelves stretched to the ceiling were packed with everything she could possibly want. Even better, it had a small, but well stocked delicatessen counter.

Minutes later, a heavy bag hanging from her hand, she was passing by the estate agent's again. She didn't turn her head to look through the window, but a quick flick of her eyes caught Chris's dazzling red tie. He was standing on the other side of the glass, looking out. Staring at her. It was hard to resist the almost overwhelming need to speed up as she felt his eyes following her. Watching her. Maybe planning his next step in the campaign to scare her away. The two windows seemed to stretch for miles, the bag she was carrying growing heavier by the step. In response to the desire to drop it and run, her fingers tightened on the handles, and she forced herself to keep going, one step at a time.

Even when she'd passed the office, she could feel him staring after her, the heat of his gaze like laser points on her back. She was being silly, fanciful, it didn't stop her speeding up as soon as she turned the corner and almost running to her car. Rather than putting the bag in the boot, she clambered into the driver's seat, pushing it before her, bruising the fruit, squashing the raspberries.

Only when she'd locked the car door, did she feel able to draw a breath, one that came rasping, vibrating with fear. Stupid to allow the man to have such an effect. Stupid to be so upset. It would have been nice to have laid her head against the steering wheel for a few minutes to allow her time to recover, but she was conscious she was parked outside the café. She didn't want to give the locals a reason to talk. They might, horror of horrors, think she was struggling in the same way Donnelly and Rogers had been.

Instead, she rummaged in her handbag for a pen, and a scrap of paper, and scribbled down the names Chris had given her. *Ben Donnelly, Mark Rogers and Alan and Jenny Willard.* There'd be no harm in looking them up. Maybe giving them a call. Baker had made her suspicious of Donnelly and Rogers. Had that been deliberate? Throwing red herrings around.

As if she was an idiot.

Baker would soon learn she wasn't a woman to be messed with. The same way Richie had. She would get to the bottom of the strange goings-on in Hindon House and get back to the future she'd planned for herself.

If Chris Baker was responsible, she'd make him regret it.

26

Cassie wondered if she'd tempted fate by telling Baker that everything was going so well, because when she got out of her car Cody was waiting for her. He had a mug cradled between his big hands. She wondered if he did anything else apart from drink her tea and coffee. Immediately she felt guilty for the thought. The man was entitled to a break. It was the frown creasing his forehead that worried her.

'Problem?'

'Not for me.'

Just what she needed. Someone else speaking in riddles. Maybe it was a Wiltshire thing. 'Why don't you tell me, and I'll see if it's a problem for me.'

'Best if I show you,' he said, lifting the mug to his mouth and gulping down the contents.

'Glad you're not letting it go to waste anyway.' If she thought the sarcasm would hit him, she soon realised he was more than a match for her.

'I like to get value for your money,' he said with a wink, then turned and headed through the kitchen.

Left with no choice, she dropped her shopping bag on the kitchen counter and followed him up the stairs to the hall, then up again to the first floor. She was pleased, and relieved, to hear the loud rhythmic clip-clop of a nail gun, the buzz of a saw, the shouting and laughter coming from the men as they worked.

Cody stopped outside the third bedroom to the front and pushed open the door. 'We were about to start building the en suite.'

'Right.' Cassie looked around. There didn't seem to be any problem.

'You wanted it in that corner.' He pointed, then turned and pointed to the far corner on the other side. 'I suggest you put it there. It'll be easier to run pipes from the en suite next door.'

'Easier, meaning cheaper.'

He nodded, then crossed the room to where he had suggested. 'We'll have to change the configuration slightly, and there'll be room for a shower, not a bath, but I think it'll look good and it won't impact on where you put the bed and wardrobe.'

He was right. It made sense. 'Okay, I'm happy with that. What about the back bedrooms, do we need to make a similar change?' She tried to remember what she'd planned for them.

'No, they'll be fine. The plumbing for them is going to come off the bathroom sitting between them.'

Of course, she should have known that. It was hard having to rely on someone else, but she supposed that was what she was paying him for. 'Is that it?' As if she had a host of work she needed to get through.

'That's it. Everything else is going to plan. I have Toby clearing stuff from the attic. I told him to leave anything that looked anyway decent in the lounge downstairs, and you can decide whether it should be dumped, kept or given to charity.'

'Good.' She'd no idea what was up there. The house had been

sold to include all contents, including the years of *stuff* left behind by previous owners who had probably planned to go through it all one day, in a distant future that had never come.

Cassie had been rigorous when she'd moved from London. She'd gone through the contents of the apartment and everything that wasn't either useful or pretty was dumped, sold or given to charity. It included all of Richie's belongings. She'd wanted nothing to remind her of her late husband.

'I'd better get on,' Cody said.

And so had she. She wasn't entirely confident that the younger Toby would know the difference between trash and treasure. She had a quick peek at the work that was going on in the bedrooms, nodding knowingly when she caught one of the workmen's eyes, then leaving before she was asked for a comment that might show her absolute ignorance. She needed to stop being so hard on herself, she really didn't need to know how the work was done, just that it was.

She hadn't been in the attic since the day of her accident. Despite Cody's assurances that the floor had been repaired, she stopped in the doorway before she slid a tentative foot forward, prepared to retreat at the slightest squeak.

'Hiya.'

The voice came from the far side of the large attic space. Cassie raised her eyes from the floor and saw Toby peering at her from between a mound of boxes. 'Hello,' she said, 'I've come to give a hand.' Forgetting her worry about the floor, she crossed to his side. 'Did you find anything interesting?'

A tall, skinny lad with long straggly hair tied back in a wispy ponytail and a trail of tattoos on both arms, Toby shook his head, then tapped the side of the box he was working on. 'It looks like it holds nothing but old cooking pans, but Dan told me to make sure to look to the bottom every time in case there was something better underneath. He told me to keep anything that looked anyway decent.' He shrugged and gave a toothy grin. 'Your idea of decent and mine might be completely different. Most of the stuff is rubbish, but I erred on the side of caution and piled anything I wasn't sure about into the back room downstairs.'

She looked around. 'Right, well it makes more sense if I can make that decision here. I'll put everything that needs to be skipped to one side, then you can take it down and chuck it out the bedroom window. Okay?' It meant he'd be running up and down the stairs, but he was young, he'd cope.

He was also pleasantly agreeable. 'Sounds like a plan.' He tapped the box again. 'There's nothing more exciting in this than a mummified mouse. Most of the pans are rusty, I'd have said it was for the skip, right?'

Cassie peered into the box, picked up a cake tin, looked at it briefly and dropped it. It rattled noisily, then settled back among the other rusty relics. 'Definitely.'

He stooped, picked the box up and took it away.

Alone, Cassie rested her hands on her hips and looked at the number of boxes, old suitcases, battered and worn furniture. No point in delaying.

By the time Toby returned, she had several items waiting to be taken for disposal. 'It's not as bad as I'd first thought,' she said to him.

'When I came up first,' he said, leaning against the doorframe, 'I thought I'd be here forever looking through stuff, but it's mostly just rubbish that people were too lazy to get rid of. I guess it's the problem with these big old houses, too much space to fill.'

He didn't seem to be in a hurry to get moving. 'Have you worked with Cody for long?'

'Almost a year.'

'And you enjoy it?'

'Sure. There's always something different. I'm training to be a carpenter, but I like to throw my hand in where it's needed. Dan likes us to be flexible. It suits me. I never get bored.'

Cassie looked at the pile of stuff that needed to be brought down and dumped. It wasn't exactly an exciting job. Perhaps Toby was simply being polite.

'It's been mostly extensions since I started with them,' he said, crossing his arms, as if settling in for a long chat. 'Working somewhere like this is better.'

'Because you never know what's going to turn up?' Cassie smiled.

'Yea. Plus seeing a worn-out, run-down place given a new life is good. It's different too cos you're going to be running a B&B. I think Dan's plan was to keep it as a private home.'

Dan's plan? She bent to fiddle with the handle of a locker she'd left for throwing out to hide her expression. 'I might keep this after all,' she said. 'The handles are too good to waste.' Having regained her composure, she turned back to Toby. 'I didn't know Dan had been interested in buying the house.'

Colour flooded the young man's face. 'I don't think it's a secret that he made an offer,' he muttered. He pushed away from the doorframe and bent to pick up the locker. 'So this is to go into the lounge with the other stuff you're keeping, yes?'

'Please.' Cassie frowned. She'd have liked to have asked him how he'd known about Dan's plans, but seeing the guilt on his face she guessed he'd either seen or overheard something. There was no reason to believe he was lying. Dan Cody, the man who owned the company doing the renovations, had been an underbidder for the house.

She sat on one of the tables destined for the skip. It creaked ominously, forcing her to stand again. Surely it was an unethical business move on Cody's part. At the very least, shouldn't he have admitted he'd had an interest in acquiring the house?

Certainly unethical, even immoral, if she was footing the bill for renovations, while he was trying to scare her away. Who better to know how to cause an issue with the electrics? Or maybe the electrician was in on it... he was in Cody's pay after all. And it was Cody who'd told her the floorboards had been deliberately cut. Perhaps that was a lie, designed to make her believe that some unnamed person was trying to frighten her.

The nice friendly Daniel Cody had a hidden agenda. She should have known. His brother had tried to warn her. And it had worked, she'd been made wary, just not enough. Now she was very wary, and angry. With Cody, but mostly with herself. When was she ever going to learn not to trust anyone?

Toby, who seemed to realise he'd put his foot in it, worked quietly for the remainder of the day. Less chat meant they got most of the attic cleared. 'We should get it done tomorrow,' Cassie said with a satisfied glance around the almost empty space. 'Thanks for your help, you did great.'

'I can stay to get it done tonight, if you like?' He was almost too eager to please.

Cassie shook her head. He might not be exhausted, but she was. Physically and mentally. 'No, but thank you. Tomorrow will be fine.'

He lingered by the attic door, his cheeks flushing again. She wondered if he was going to mention what he'd said, maybe even ask her not to say anything about it. Instead, he gave a nod, a wave, and headed away.

Perhaps it would be worth tackling Cody, asking him if it was true that he'd been an underbidder. But he'd be under no obligation to tell her the truth. And after spending the afternoon with

Toby, he'd guess where she'd heard it from. She didn't want to get the poor lad into trouble. Perhaps even lose him his job. She'd liked to think Cody wasn't that vindictive, but she was beginning to wonder if she knew anything about him. He was a handsome, reliable-looking man – but she'd been fooled by appearances before.

There were other ways to find out the truth.

She needed to talk to Ben Donnelly and Mark Rogers, and to Alan and Jenny Willard. Because if Cody was playing games to get his hands on Hindon House, it might not be his first time.

27

It was odd, but having a focus for her anger, sharpened it, made her less scared, more determined. Or perhaps it was just that she wasn't willing to sit back and wait to see what happened. It never had been her way. She was always a dive in regardless, worry about the consequences later kind of person. And look where that had landed her. She brushed away thoughts of Richie to concentrate on her current predicament.

Cody came to see her before he left, as seemed to be his habit. A last catch-up of the day's events before he headed off. Or perhaps he wanted to see how his evil plan was working, to see if there was any sign of her falling apart. Neither the booby-trapped attic floor, nor the problem with the electrics had scared her away, so perhaps he was going to come up with something else. Something more dramatic. Or perhaps he'd wait till more of the work was done. Get her to pay for it, then when he'd managed to scare her off, when she was desperate to sell, he'd swoop in with a low offer she'd be relieved to accept. The bastard!

She put her game face on when she heard the heavy footsteps on the attic stairway. 'Hi,' she said, getting in first. 'Toby played a blinder today. He was up and down those stairs all afternoon, never complained. We're almost finished.'

'It's a great space,' Cody said, walking to the far wall. 'It'll make a nice suite.' He looked up into the rafters. 'I'm assuming you're going to want dormer windows, yes?'

'Yes, natural light would be essential.'

'It won't be a problem.' He pointed upward. 'One there.' He took several steps towards her. 'One there, and one there.' He frowned and walked to the other corner. 'I'm not sure we'll manage to get one in the bathroom, you might need to settle for a vent.'

It was what she'd expected. 'That'd be fine. As long as there's sufficient light in the rest of the space.'

'Good dormer windows will do that. Leave it with me.' He shoved his hands into his pockets. 'The work is going well; I'm planning to get the plumber to start in another day or so. He'll do the plumbing for in here at the same time.'

She dredged up a smile. 'That's good news.' He didn't seem in a hurry to leave but the temptation to confront him with what she'd learned from Toby was beginning to overpower her. She had to stay quiet; it was far better to have more information, more proof before she confronted him. 'I was just about to head down,' she said. She didn't wait for his reply.

She could hear him behind her. Too close. She moved faster, reached the landing, and crossed to the stairway down to the ground floor. Reaching it, she stepped to one side and waited for him to pass. 'See you tomorrow,' she said, her fingers gripping the banister.

He lingered. 'Are you okay?' When she didn't answer, he added, 'You seem a bit stressed.'

She looked up from her contemplation of the smooth oak under her hand. 'Just tired, it's been a long day.'

'Right.' He didn't sound convinced, his eyes sweeping over her and lingering on the fading bruises on her face. 'You should get some rest. I'll see you tomorrow.'

And then he was gone. Cassie waited till the sound of his footsteps receded, till there was total silence, before releasing her grip and wiping her hand over her face. *Stressed?* He had no idea.

After checking the work the men had done that day, pleased with how quickly the en suites were taking shape, she went down to the kitchen, unaccountably annoyed to see the sink filled with dirty mugs and plates. As if it was her job... a woman's role... to sort out the kitchen. It was tempting to make a point and leave them there. She was still grumbling as she filled the sink with hot water. In a temper, she added too large a squirt of washing-up liquid, the resultant foam forcing her to wash, then rinse everything. One-handed, it took her a while and by the time she'd finished, she was banging the clean dry mugs on the countertop, imagining Cody's face under each.

Her temper was always easy come, quickly go, and by the time she'd put the clean crockery away, she was back to simply worrying.

Oddly, she missed the noise of the workmen: the sounds of their various tools, their raucous laughter, loudly shouted orders and demands. She'd been on her own since Richie died, so she was used to her own company but the silence of her apartment back in London was never this quiet. There was always the low rumble of the city in the background, pierced occasionally by the sound of a siren, or a yell from someone passing by on the street outside.

If she went outside here, she'd hear birds twittering, even the sound of the leaves on the trees if there was a breeze. Once night fell though, the silence was profound, broken only by the sound of those who were comfortable in the dark: the hoot of the owl, the sharp bark of a fox.

And other hunters – the human kind. Cassie pictured Cody slithering around in the darkness intent on causing her harm.

But it wasn't dark yet. Unwilling to linger in the kitchen, she slid one of the quiches she'd bought earlier onto a plate and bunged it into the microwave. When it was ready, she grabbed cutlery and took it outside. Although the table was now in the shade, it was still pleasantly warm. She brushed some investigating ants from the table with the back of her hand and sat to eat. The quiche smelled and looked appetising. She should have been hungry but after forcing herself to eat a few mouthfuls, she dropped her cutlery on the plate.

Some people ate more when they were worried, she wasn't one of them. In fact, since Richie's death, she'd lost almost a stone. No wonder she looked so wretched, bruised so easily, and fell over when the wind whispered. The thought made her pick up the fork, but it couldn't make her eat.

She sat for a moment, admiring the trunk of a tall cypress tree as it glowed golden in the light of the setting sun. It looked so peaceful. What a shame she felt totally on edge. Returning to the kitchen didn't help.

The ceiling was lower than in the upper floors. The room was an odd uneven shape too. It made it impossible for cupboards to lay flush against the walls and created dark inaccessible gaps behind which anything could hide. Even when the sun shone through the windows, the room remained chilly. Twilight dropped the temperature and made black holes in the furthest corners.

The one central overhead light didn't make a huge difference. In fact, it made the room even more unsettling... creepier. Cassie dropped her plate into the sink, flushed it with water, then filling a glass, she took it and left the room.

She'd got into the habit of looking the other way as she passed the corridor leading to the small rooms with their barred windows and she climbed the stairs to the ground floor without looking back.

The lights were all working; she switched them on as she passed, leaving them on behind her. It looked as if Cody, or whoever was to blame... she tried to keep her mind even part-way open... had grown tired of that trick. The worry was, what he... or they... were going to come up with next. It was a thought that weighed her down as she climbed the stairs. She was resilient, always had been. Always managed to bounce back from whatever hit her, or duck the crap that life threw at her. It had got harder though. Richie had done that to her. Dented her self-belief. Changed her.

In her bedroom, she hesitated before shaking her head and wedging the chair under the handle. It gave her peace of mind, and she'd take that where she could get it.

She'd tidied all her belongings to the far corner of the room and covered them all with a sheet while they were making the walls for the en suite. It took her a few minutes to uncover everything, then fix her makeshift bed.

It would be such a relief when it was all done. When she could have a shower in the evening to wash the dust away instead of using baby wipes to do a very perfunctory job. In clean pyjamas, she sat on the mattress, her back resting against the wall, and powered up her laptop, grateful for the remarkably good Wi-Fi, one of the few things the previous owners had organised.

Thanks to their bankruptcy, it took only minutes to find details for Donnelly and Rogers. Cassie was in luck. Rogers, an Australian citizen, had returned home, but Ben Donnelly was still living in the UK. He was working for a builder's merchants. Not too far away either. Less than an hour's drive. She used her phone to take a screenshot of the address.

One down, one to go. She hoped to be equally successful in finding the Willards. An internet search didn't throw up anything useful. It made it harder not knowing what either Alan or Jenny Willard did for a living. Finally, she turned to Facebook and breathed a sigh of satisfaction. There were three Willards, but only one called Jenny.

It had to be her. Cassie wrote a message, read it, deleted, wrote another, deleted that. Finally, she settled on a simple short explanation.

I've recently bought Hindon House. I'd love to talk about your experience. Happy to drive to meet.

No mention of spooky goings-on that might put the woman off. No mention of Cody.

It might be a long time before she got a reply – if ever. There was no point in staring at it, hoping to see that little bubble with the three dots to say one was coming. It was highly unlikely Jenny Willard would respond so quickly.

Shutting her laptop down, Cassie closed it and slipped it under the end of the mattress. There were books she could read. One she'd started recently. She picked it up, opened it at the bookmark, and found where she'd left off. A few words, and her concentration waned. She couldn't remember what the story was about, she'd a vague idea it wasn't very good. It certainly wasn't good enough to hold her attention. Slipping the bookmark back between the pages she tossed it to one side, then rested her head back and shut her eyes.

She was drifting off to sleep when her phone alerted her to a new message. Anticipation made her fumble and drop it. Shaking the sleep from her head, she picked it up, the excitement fading when she saw it wasn't, as she'd hoped, from Jenny Willard, but from Mrs Morgan.

Would you like to call here for coffee in the morning?

Would she? Cassie tapped the phone against her hand. The house on the High Street looked interesting and she had a natural curiosity to see inside. She pictured it as being a bit old-fashioned and reserved, like its owner. Mrs Morgan had been nice to her, had baked her a cake, and now she'd invited her for coffee. It would be a shame to turn her down. She was probably a bit lonely. The world was so fast moving these days, not everyone would make time for the rather pedantic woman.

It was less than an hour to where Ben Donnelly worked. Perhaps, she could drive to Mrs Morgan's, park on the road outside, have a coffee, then head to meet him. It would work. She tapped out a reply.

I'd love that. 10ish?

Perfect. See you at 10 a.m.

Cassie was amused to have her *tenish* translated to the precise time, including the correct punctuation. The morning coffee would, no doubt, be served in fine china cups with matching saucers. There'd be home-made biscuits, or maybe freshly made scones. She hoped so. Even her poor appetite could be energised by them.

With a final glance at her phone she put it down. If Jenny Willard didn't reply, she'd think of some other way to find her.

Struggling up from the mattress, she crossed to the light switch and took a final look around the room before pressing it. She kept her finger on the switch until her eyes adjusted to the complete darkness. Although the room was still the same, it instantly felt different. It wasn't just the darkness; it wasn't even the silence.

It was the anticipation.

If the plan *was* to scare her into selling Hindon House, what was going to happen next?

28

Cassie managed to sleep for a few hours, waking when a pigeon sitting on the windowsill started his chorus of *take two coos, Taffy*. She lay listening to him for a while, wondering whether to chase him away and try to get back to sleep, or to get up and finish sorting through what was left in the attic. If she did, she could leave a note for Toby directing him where to put everything.

She wouldn't feel guilty then for taking the rest of the day off.

It was a good plan. Fifteen minutes later she was up in the attic. It didn't take long to decide about most of the stuff that had probably been there for decades. It was junk, only fit for the skip. Finally, there was one battered old suitcase to open and she was done.

Lying it on its side, she hunkered down beside it, flipped the catches and pulled the lid open. Half-expecting it to be empty, it took a few seconds to register what she was seeing, the surprise... shock... making her sway, her vision blur. She shut her eyes, took deep breaths. She was not going to faint.

When she opened her eyes again, seconds later, the contents of the case were still the same. Tiny baby clothes. Her fingers trembled as she picked up a white hand-knitted cardigan. So incredibly soft. She held it to her face and inhaled, stupidly expecting a baby smell, grimacing at the stink of camphor that had protected the garment for years, maybe decades.

Holding the cardigan in one hand, she looked through the other clothes. All white and so very, very heartbreakingly small. Cassie felt a lump in her throat as she picked up one after the other. They'd never been worn. Had the mother knitted them in anticipation, and then lost the child?

Cassie's pregnancies, those little scraps that had found her womb so toxic, had ended after only a couple of months so she'd never made any preparation for a baby's arrival. It had been Richie who had desperately wanted a child; she hadn't really cared. That's what she'd told everyone. *She hadn't cared.* She buried her face in the tiny cardigan she still held, used it to dam the tears that insisted on falling, held it to her mouth when she started to sob. Tears for herself, for the babies she'd lost, for this unknown baby and its mother.

It was as if she'd saved up all the tears she'd denied herself at each miscarriage, and it was several minutes before she stopped with a final gulp. It would have been nice to have had a name for the mother who'd made such loving preparations, but despite emptying the case, she found no indication of who it belonged to. Almost regretfully, she packed everything back inside. The cardigan she'd held was damp from her tears. She smoothed it out, placed it on top and shut the lid. Her friend Toni volunteered for the charity Baby Basics; she'd give the case to her.

She scribbled a note for Toby asking him to dump everything else, then headed back to her bedroom and put the case safely to one side.

She did minimum ablutions, pulled on fresh clothes, and made a brave attempt at covering the remainder of the bruising to her face. A glance in her small mirror told her she'd been marginally successful; it would have to do.

The discovery of the baby clothes had left her feeling on the verge of tears and as she descended the stairway to the kitchen, she felt her mood sink further. The light was working, but the room still gave her the chills. As she stood in the doorway, she came to a decision. The suite in the attic could wait, she'd ask Cody to start on the kitchen next. Get rid of all those tiny waste-of-space rooms, knock the walls down to create one big open space. It would make all the difference. Make it feel bright, airy, welcoming.

Until then, she'd spend as little time there as possible. She took a bowl of cereal and a mug of coffee to the table outside. It was a few minutes to nine, soon the peace would be interrupted by the arrival of the workmen. And Cody. He was always there first thing, giving orders, checking everyone knew their roles for the day. To get the work done as soon as possible so he could swoop in and steal it from her.

She jabbed her spoon into the cereal with more energy than was needed, sending Rice Krispies flying over the edge. An opportunistic robin immediately swooped in, grabbed one and beat a hasty retreat. 'There's no need to rush,' Cassie told him. 'I'll leave them for you.'

She managed to eat what remained in her bowl without sharing any more with her feathered friend and was hugging her mug of coffee, when a rather battered van came through the gate. It parked on the far side of the yard, near the outbuildings and two men she recognised, but whose names she couldn't remember, climbed out and strolled over.

'Morning, the kettle has just boiled,' she said.

'We're good, ta,' one replied with a smile. 'Maybe a bit later.'

Then they were gone. She had to admit, they didn't hang

around wasting time. Over the next ten minutes, three more cars appeared. Cody's wasn't among them. Maybe he was having a morning off. Maybe he was holed up somewhere making plans for her downfall. If he'd driven in at that moment, in the mood she was in, she might have punched him.

Unfortunately, or maybe fortunately, it was Toby who appeared, riding his pushbike as he did every morning. When he'd propped it against the house, Cassie waved him over. 'I've finished going through all that stuff in the attic. It can all be skipped.'

'Good job,' he said. 'I'll get it done.'

He was as good as his word, and several minutes later, Cassie was startled by a box landing with a crash into the skip only a few feet away from her. It was time to move.

It was too early to leave for her coffee with Mrs Morgan, but Cassie didn't want to get her clothes dirty by doing any of the work that needed to be done. Nor was there anywhere in the house she could simply sit and wait. Her car was the best bet. Grabbing her bag, she headed out.

Hindon was a small village. She'd already walked up and down the High Street, but she hadn't yet investigated the church. That morning she was in luck and the door stood ajar. She pushed open the inner door and smiled in pleasure. Such a pretty church. Obviously well-loved too; there were two stunningly beautiful flower arrangements.

Cassie sat in a pew. This was the kind of silence she liked, peaceful and comforting. She felt tense shoulders relax, some of the weight of her worries float away. This was a *good* place. She'd like to have stayed there. If only she could bottle the atmosphere, take it with her, release it into the Hindon House kitchen so it could ooze into every dark nook and cranny, waft along the corridor and into those cells to disperse all the ill-will that seemed to cling to the walls. If only it were that easy.

Since it wasn't possible, she did what she could, she said a prayer for the owner of the baby clothes, for the mother and her child. And then one for herself, and the babies she'd lost.

Almost twenty minutes later, with the time ticking towards ten, she left the sanctuary of the church, the sense of calm dissipating as she walked through the door. Leaving the car where it was, she walked the short distance to Mrs Morgan's house.

Only after she'd pressed the doorbell did she realise she'd come empty-handed. Shouldn't she be bringing a gift of some sort? What was the correct etiquette? She had a good idea that her hostess would know. Too late now, through the glass panes of the front door, she could see her approaching. Perhaps Cassie would gain brownie points for arriving on the dot of ten.

'Good morning,' Mrs Morgan said. 'How lovely to see you.'

Almost as if Cassie weren't expected. 'It was kind of you to invite me.'

Mrs Morgan was dressed in what Cassie was beginning to think of as her uniform: navy trousers, navy shirt buttoned to the top. Both had the sheen of man-made fabric and must have been uncomfortably warm in the recent heatwave, but the woman looked as cool as ever. 'Do come in,' she said.

Cassie hid a smile when the room she was shown into was almost exactly as she'd expected. Neat, of course; dull... definitely. White antimacassars, something she hadn't seen for years, lay on the headrest of each of the brown velvet sofas. Two small mahogany tables, a matching coffee table, and a bookshelf made up the rest of the furniture. There were no lamps, just the one central light with a fringed shade. The carpet was a floral pattern that hurt her eyes. And everything was spotlessly clean.

'Please, have a seat,' Mrs Morgan said. 'I'll go and pop the kettle on.' She waited till Cassie had sat before asking, 'I have coffee, or tea if you'd prefer?'

'Coffee would be lovely, thank you.' Cassie held a smile till the woman had left, then dropped it and collapsed back. Why had she come? How soon could she politely leave? An hour of polite stilted conversation and she'd be exhausted. The door had been left open; the sound of humming carried through making her smile again. A genuine one this time. She was being an ungrateful cow. Sitting up, she looked around the room. So neat and tidy, she wondered if it was often used or simply kept for company. For best, as her long-dead grandmother used to say.

Cassie had grown up in a two-up two-down council house that didn't have an inch of space to be kept as best. The day after she'd left to go to university, her mother, tired of her father's snoring, had moved into Cassie's old bedroom thus removing any place for her to stay if she returned. She hadn't wanted to – of course she hadn't – she was out in the big, bad world, free as a bird, ready for life's adventures.

Free as a bird? She'd had to work weekends to make ends meet. The course she'd chosen proved to be far tougher than she'd expected, which meant she'd had to study every spare minute leaving little time for socialising. But then she'd met Richie, and everything had seemed okay.

'And look how that turned out,' she muttered. Putting him as far out of her mind as she was ever able, she looked around for something to interest her. But the few ornaments were cheap figurines of little interest and no great age. It surprised her. She'd have expected old family antiques, the odd heirloom. There was one photograph in a frame on the far end of the mantelpiece. It was too far to get more than an impression of two people standing side by side. Perhaps the Morgan's wedding photograph? Approaching footsteps stopped Cassie rising to investigate further.

'Here we are.' Mrs Morgan placed a large tray gently down on the low coffee table, then stood for a moment to check that she'd brought everything necessary before she sat with a satisfied sigh.

Cassie had been right about the china. Dainty cups and saucers, a matching sugar bowl and jug. She was suddenly sorry she hadn't asked for tea; she'd have bet money there was a matching teapot. Instead, there was a rather functional cafetière. Unfortunately, she was wrong about the scones and the hand-made biscuits. There was a china plate holding garibaldi. Squashed fly biscuits her mother used to call them. The memory made her smile. 'I didn't realise they still made them,' she said, pointing to the plate. 'They were my grandmother's favourite.'

'They're also mine.' Mrs Morgan smiled as she reached for the cafetière and poured into each cup. 'Help yourself to milk and sugar.'

Cassie added milk, then picked up the cup and saucer. She waited until the plate of biscuits was held towards her before taking one. They were a good choice of biscuit; they didn't crumb when she took a small bite. The coffee was good, strong, and hot. 'Nice coffee,' she said.

'Thank you.'

No further information. If that had been Cassie, she'd have been eager to share the brand, to tell where she'd bought it. Perhaps it was unmannerly to do so. As if it was boasting about it or something.

Mrs Morgan sat back with her coffee. 'I hope the renovation work is all going well.'

On much safer ground, away from manners and antiquated

etiquette, Cassie relaxed. 'It is, thank you.' She took another bite of the biscuit, washed it down with a mouthful of coffee. 'They've almost finished making the en suite rooms. They were going to start on the attic next, but I've had a change of mind.' She smiled. 'Just this morning, actually. I've decided to get the kitchen done next. It's such a depressing space.'

'The kitchen.' Mrs Morgan nodded. 'The heart of a house, I've always thought. What are you planning to do again?'

'Well, if you remember, there's that corridor of small rooms which provide no function. I'm going to have all those walls removed, so it'll be one enormous bright open-plan room.'

'It'll be a huge space.'

Cassie wasn't sure from the facial expression or the tone of voice whether the comment was designed to be a compliment or criticism. Perhaps Mrs Morgan didn't approve of the house being turned into a B&B. Change was harder to accept when you got older. 'It'll be lovely when it's done. Brighter and airier.' There was no point in saying less scary, Mrs Morgan wouldn't understand. Cassie wasn't sure she did, but she knew the layout of the room, the lack of light, the bars on those windows, were all contributing to the bad feeling. Once it was gutted, and those walls knocked down, she'd follow Toni's feng shui advice and restore harmony to the room. It might not be as beautifully peaceful as a church, but it could be a pleasant place to spend time.

Mrs Morgan put her cup and saucer down and picked up the cafetière. 'Some more?'

Cassie held her cup forward. 'Thank you.'

The coffee poured, Mrs Morgan sat back. 'It sounds like it's going to be a big job. Weeks, I'd have thought.'

Cassie wasn't sure. It was planned to be later in the renovation, so hadn't been discussed. The floor was going to take the most time. It was composed of flagstones set onto compacted earth – a common foundation in the early nineteenth century. It needed to be dug out and filled with concrete. The wall dividing the kitchen from the corridor was a load bearing one, so that would also take time to address. 'I don't know to be honest,' she said. 'I haven't discussed it with Cody as yet, I'll have a better idea when I do.'

'He might insist on sticking to the original schedule.'

Cassie laughed. She might not know a lot about etiquette, but she did know that she who paid the bills, called the shots. 'I don't think that'll be a problem.'

'I admire your certainty,' Mrs Morgan said with a slight inclination of her head.

As before, Cassie wasn't quite sure whether to take this as a compliment or criticism. She was going to mention finding the suitcase and ask the older woman's opinion on who might be the owner, but she suddenly felt protective of this unknown mother and didn't want her subjected to critical speculation. She finished her coffee and put the cup down. 'When it's done, you will have to come around and see it, I'd love to hear what you think. Now, I must go. Thank you so much for your hospitality.'

'It's been a pleasure.' Mrs Morgan got to her feet, her bones creaking ominously as she did so. 'I don't often have visitors.'

Cassie stood and eyed the tray. Even with the coffeepot empty, it looked a heavy load. 'May I bring it into the kitchen for you?'

'That's very kind, thank you, dear, but I can manage. I'm stronger than I look.'

She looked like she could be knocked over with a feather but Cassie didn't like to offend by insisting. At the front door, she debated offering her a kiss on the cheek, but there was something about the woman's demeanour, an almost chilly reserve, that said such familiarity wouldn't be welcome. She settled for a smile. 'Thanks again.'

Outside, a few steps away from the house, she turned to offer a final wave, and was taken aback to find the door already shut. Cassie's grandmother would have stood waving till she was out of view. Sometimes, she'd try to catch her out, and pop back around the bend in the road, but her gran was always there.

It was silly to expect Mrs Morgan to behave in the same way simply because she was a similar age.

A few minutes later, Cassie was on her way to Bath, leaving Mrs Morgan and Hindon behind.

29

The builder's supply company where Ben Donnelly worked was in the village of Midford. A few miles Cassie's side of Bath, it meant she didn't have to tackle the city's notoriously awful traffic.

There were no delays along the way and thirty-five minutes after leaving Hindon, she was pulling into the car park outside Midford Building Supplies. It was obviously a thriving business if the number of vans pulling in and out was anything to go by.

Inside, it was the usual layout, a vast warehouse-type structure, with tills along the short side, and a small currently unmanned customer service desk. Cassie looked along its length, hoping to find a bell to ring or a button to press to get attention. There was nothing. She rested her back against it, and gazed around the store, searching every face that passed.

'Can I help you?'

The voice startled her, making her turn abruptly and glare at the young woman who'd addressed her. Cassie was too on edge these days. 'Thank you, yes. I'm looking to speak to Ben Donnelly.'

'I can help you with whatever it is you need.'

The woman was simply trying to be helpful. She held her smile, even when Cassie leaned closer and said, 'It's personal, I need to speak to him.'

'Personal, right. I understand.' The assistant looked behind her, then leaned forward until she was within whispering distance. 'I'll go find him, but it's best not to talk here, it might get him into trouble.' She pointed to the back of the shop. 'I'll tell him to meet you in plumbing, the end of aisle five, okay?'

It didn't seem as if Cassie had a choice. 'Okay.' She wanted to laugh when the younger woman gave her a wink and a knowing grin. She thought she was assisting in some romantic dalliance. If she only knew!

Cassie was still smiling when she reached the plumbing section. She was looking around at the selection of pipes and fixtures with little interest, when she heard footsteps behind her and turned to see a man looking at her in puzzlement.

'Poppy said a woman was looking for me.'

Cassie smiled and extended a hand. 'I think she thought she was helping a romance.'

Donnelly looked at her hand as if expecting it to do something rather than hover in the air between them. Finally, he took it in his and shook it briefly. 'I don't know you, do I?'

'No, you don't. My name is Cassie Macreddin.' She took a deep breath. She wasn't one hundred per cent sure how he was going to take what she said next. 'I'm the new owner of Hindon House.' Although she was wary about how he might take it, the change in his expression from puzzled to angry was lightening quick and caught her off-guard. She took a step backward and held up her hands. 'I'm not here to cause trouble.'

Another change of expression. This time, his face fell into downward slopes of sadness. 'What are you here for?'

'I think someone is trying to scare me off?'

Puzzled was back. 'What?'

She shuffled, frustrated that she needed to spell it out. 'I think someone is trying to frighten me into leaving Hindon House.'

He ran a not-very-clean hand over his head, ruffling his hair. 'And you think it's me?'

Thanks to Baker, she had considered Donnelly to be a likely candidate at one stage. Now, she wasn't completely sure of anything. 'Is it?'

He laughed. 'Fuck, no! Why would I want to?' Enlightenment dawned. 'I bet it was that prick, Baker. Wasn't it? Did he tell you we'd have done anything to keep it? Is that it? He liked to paint us as losers. Mark and I were convinced Baker was responsible for everything that went wrong, just because he lost out on Hindon House for a second time.'

'I don't understand.' She didn't like Baker, it would be too easy to believe the worst of him, but she needed facts not vague and biased assumptions. 'What do you mean "he lost out on Hindon House for the second time"?'

'Just that. The house had been on the market for years and Baker had hoped to get it cheap. He might have done, but his timing was crap because the Willards were looking for a place and made an offer that he couldn't match. They said he was pretty pissed off about it, made some nasty comments to them about city-folk buying up properties and pushing locals out.'

Cassie remembered Baker saying the couple had left because they had *expectations that living in a small town couldn't possibly have met.* Perhaps that expectation had simply been that people would be welcoming.

'Mark was friendly with Alan Willard and when he heard they were thinking of selling up, he asked him to give us first refusal. Only a couple of weeks later, we came to an agreement. They wanted a quick sale, so dropped the price. Baker wasn't a happy man to have missed out yet again.'

'You said he was responsible for everything that went wrong... what did you mean?' She hoped Donnelly never took up poker; his face showed every emotion. Now it was impatience that flitted quickly across his face, tightening his lips, narrowing his eyes. She sighed. 'It's not idle curiosity, honestly. I've been having a few problems.' She held up a hand to show the smaller dressing that now covered her injury. He didn't need to know it was caused by her own stupidity. She saw his eyes flick to the faint bruises still visible on her face and his expression slid into sympathy.

'We didn't end up battered and bruised, mostly just pissed off.' He folded his arms and rested a shoulder against a shelf. 'It was little things. Sinks overflowing, although we'd both swear we'd turned the taps off; tools vanishing or being mysteriously broken, the lights suddenly going out for no reason. It put Mark on edge. Then our suppliers started demanding payment upfront as if they were afraid we were a bad bet. We were convinced it was Baker, spreading lies.

'All those little problems, they added up and slowed us down. It cost us both, financially and mentally. Our budget was always tight. As soon as suppliers started making demands, it was the beginning of a slippery slope that ended in bankruptcy.' He pushed away from the shelf and shoved his hands into the pockets of his cargo pants. 'So, believe me, I have nothing to do with whatever is going on in Hindon now. I'm done with all that. It was Mark who had the big dreams. Now that he's gone back to Oz, I'm happy enough plodding along, getting paid monthly, and letting someone else take the risks.' He checked his watch. 'I'd better get to work.'

Cassie's head was thumping with all she'd heard. 'You've been very helpful.'

He hesitated, as if there was more he wanted to say.

She wasn't sure she wanted to hear whatever it was, afraid that one more ugly truth would finish her. But hiding in the dark wasn't the answer. 'What is it?'

'Baker's a nasty piece of work. It looks as if he hasn't given up on owning Hindon House and is making trouble for you too. You'd better be careful.'

'Now that I know who to blame, it'll be easier. I have a good team working on it. You might know it. Cody's Building and Renovation Services.' She didn't mention that she'd suspected Daniel Cody of being behind the problems, feeling a twinge of guilt for blaming the man.

'Sure, they get some of their supplies from us. Dan's a good guy, Reliable too.'

Cassie nodded, as if she'd never been in any doubt. 'Yes, I'm lucky there.' She extended her hand. 'You've been so helpful, thank you.'

'Good luck,' he said, shaking her hand with more warmth this time. 'And stay safe.'

She left the store and sat into her car. Cody wasn't to blame for what was happening, she'd got it so wrong. It wasn't the first time.

Richie's words came back to her with such clarity, such intensity, she moaned. *I don't love you any more, I want a divorce.*

Leaning forward, she rested her forehead against the steering wheel as the memories of that day and the following morning came back to her. The heartbreak, the devastation, the overwhelming despair at the unfairness of it all. Anger had raged then, simmering and bubbling until it had exploded with such catastrophic results.

Sometimes, she could still hear the squeal of metal as their car slid along the side of the parked van before crashing into the wall. There were times too when she could hear Richie's scream. And remember the silence that followed.

She'd thought at the time that it was heartache that had stirred that level of anger, finding it hard to believe she'd be capable of such a strong emotion for any lesser reason. Either she was wrong, or the act of threatening her dream was equivalent to having her heart broken, because anger was sizzling through her now.

Heartbreak and death. To forget, she'd wanted to be totally consumed by the renovation. For every waking moment to be lost in images of beautiful rooms, lush décor, for her thoughts to be consumed by a successful business. A fresh start for her. A new life.

She'd wanted no space to think about what had happened, just the dream that Richie's death had enabled her to fulfil. The dream. Not this nightmare with yet another manipulative, selfish, conniving, hateful man. Tears of angry frustration welled. But this time, she wouldn't allow anger to take over. She'd control it and use it to prop up her determination when it wavered.

This time, she wouldn't allow anger to make her kill.

Baker had no idea who he was messing with.

30

It wasn't until Cassie heard a knock on the car window that she lifted her head from the steering wheel to see a woman peering in, eyes narrowed in concern, mouth a little open as if she was preparing to scream for help. She looked relieved and a little embarrassed to find there wasn't a problem. 'Sorry, just checking you were okay?' she said.

Unable to trust herself to speak, Cassie nodded, smiled, and raised a hand in thanks, hoping the woman would leave her alone. The smile must have appeared genuine, normal, because the woman smiled in response and nodded emphatically as if relieved not to be embroiled in some great drama. With a wave, she turned away and walked to a car parked two spaces away.

Cassie waited until her would-be rescuer left the car park, before shutting her eyes again, this time resting her head back on the headrest. Then, with a sigh that was part angry frustration, part weariness, she started the car and began the journey home. She drove slowly, going over every conversation she'd ever had with Baker, trying to remember the words, the tone of his voice. Had there been indications she'd missed? Had she been so lost in her dream that she didn't see the signs? She gave a sardonic laugh. She'd been so damn obsessed with the house from the first that he could have had horns poking through his comb-over and she wouldn't have noticed.

She was still thinking back over their few exchanges when her mobile rang. It was tempting to ignore it, but it could be Cody with a question or, God forbid, a problem. 'Not a problem, please,' she muttered. Seeing a lay-by up ahead, she indicated and pulled in.

Convinced the call was from Cody, it took a few seconds of confusion to adjust her thinking when she saw it was a missed audio call on Messenger from Jenny Willard.

Cassie stared unblinkingly at the screen until it went dead and her eyes began to prickle. She wasn't sure she could handle any more information that day.

Perhaps Jenny Willard would have something positive to say... perhaps... or maybe she'd give Cassie more of a headache, throw another name into the mix, make her life even more impossible. Unwilling to take that risk, she dropped the mobile on the passenger seat and resumed her journey home.

A cold grey miserable day would have suited her mood, but it was a lovely day, the narrow winding roads she was travelling, tree-lined and full of dappled light. By the time she was pulling into the yard behind Hindon House the energising anger had been replaced by a weary acceptance. She'd do whatever she needed to do to make her plans succeed. The thought made her smile. She sounded like a right toughie.

Her friends would be amused at the thought. Toni who constantly told her she was softer than a marshmallow would howl, and Louise would raise her eyebrows to the ceiling before patting Cassie's arm and asking if she was quite all right.

Thinking of her friends did what nothing else did, it righted her world, made her remember she was a good person who'd done one awful thing, not an awful person who pretended to be nice.

All she needed to do was to stand her ground. Baker would get the message eventually that she wasn't going anywhere.

There was the usual crush of vehicles in the yard. The only one she recognised was Cody's. Parking her car, she grabbed her bag and phone and climbed out. The skip, she noticed, had been replaced and was waiting to be filled again. Now that she'd decided to do the kitchen as a matter of urgency, she could start emptying stuff from there. She was thinking of finding a screwdriver to take the cupboard doors off as she walked into the house.

The room was empty, the usual sounds of business drifting from overhead. Realising she hadn't, as yet, discussed starting the work on the kitchen with Cody, she walked through to the front hall in search of him.

Surprised to see the front door standing open, she crossed towards it stepping over piles of timber, sacks of cement mix, boxes of tiles. It would have been an obstacle course only a clear path had been left through it all. Cody's team took health and safety seriously she was glad to see. Now that her crazy suspicions about him had been laid to rest, she was back to congratulating herself on having chosen the best team for the job.

There was no reason for the door to have been left open, the tradespeople only used the kitchen door. Her hand was on it, ready to push it shut, her mind already on the conversation she planned to have with Cody, when she heard voices coming from outside.

Cody. She was smiling when she tugged at the heavy door, the smile dropping as quickly as her hand when the second voice drifted towards her. Baker! It was impossible to make out what they were saying, but the tone of their words was clear: Baker's angry. Cody's conciliatory.

Cassie crept away and slipped into the front room. There was little left of the moth-eaten curtains that hung at the bay windows, but there was enough to give her some cover as she peered through the dirty glass to where the two men stood.

Baker was gesticulating with closed fists, the anger on his twisted face clear even from a distance. Cody had his hands shoved into his jeans' pockets. Cassie wished he'd take them out and punch the horrible man's lights out. Violence again. She sighed and was about to turn away when everything changed. Baker held his hands up, palms out, and Cody took one hand from his pocket and clapped him on the shoulder. Not a blow, or a punch, a friendly clap. Then they were both grinning like conspiratorial idiots.

Cassie's grip tightened on the tatty curtain, feeling the fabric disintegrate under her fingers. Whatever Baker was up to, it looked as if the friendly, reliable Cody was involved. Co-conspirators perhaps, each with a finger deep in the pie that was Hindon House.

Had they imagined, these two, that the poor widow with the big dream would be a pushover? Anger curled as she thought of them plotting against her. They probably thought they'd make a killing. That she'd be so desperate to sell, she'd take a pittance to move on.

If looks could kill, Cody and Baker would fall to the ground mortally wounded as Cassie stood glaring at them. She stayed where she was as they headed back into the house, flattening herself against the wall as they passed the open door deep in conversation.

It was several minutes before she felt able to move, and when she did her steps were jerky, the shock of deceit making her weak. In the doorway, she stopped and reached a hand to the doorframe, turning to look around the huge room. The one she'd dreamed of making into a fabulous dining room, picturing her guests enjoying breakfast as they admired the room and the view across the gardens. Her gardens. Her dining room. Her damn house.

She pulled herself up, lifted her chin, then took her hand away. She didn't need anything... or anyone... to lean on.

Baker, and now Cody.

Anger bubbled inside. She'd harness it to make her stronger.

And she'd beat the bastards.

31

Harnessing the anger pushed Cassie through the hallway and into the kitchen. Half-expecting to find Baker and Cody there, probably helping themselves to her coffee, she didn't know whether to be pleased or disappointed to find the room empty. More annoyingly, when she looked out the window, she saw Cody's car pulling out of the car park behind a vehicle she assumed belonged to Baker.

'Damn!' She clenched her fists in frustration. Cody must have seen her car, would know she was back, why hadn't he waited to speak to her? Too busy schmoozing with his partner in crime. They'd probably gone for a posh lunch somewhere, knocking back food and beers and laughing about manipulating her.

Doing an about-turn, she headed back upstairs to the hallway, then followed the sound of tools at work. She put her head into a couple of rooms before she found the man she was looking for, the one she'd decided was Cody's second in command. It took a panicked search in the jumble of details in her head to locate his name. *Stu.*

He was fitting tiles to the inside of the en suite, humming under his breath.

'Stu?' When he didn't answer, or stop what he was doing, she raised her voice. 'Stu, can I have a word?'

He turned, a puzzled crease on his forehead. 'Sure.'

Cassie needed to choose her words carefully. She may be paying these men's wages, but Cody was their boss. 'I'm just back and have been looking for Cody, he doesn't appear to be around.'

The puzzled crease deepened. 'He was, I spoke to him a little while ago. He may have needed to go back to the office for something.' He shrugged as if to say it wasn't his job to keep an eye on the boss's movements.

'Well, I didn't want to wait till he returned to get the work started.'

Stu looked at the tile he was holding, and then to the space on the wall it was destined for. 'I just need to get this finished. The plumber is coming tomorrow so I won't be able to get in.'

It was Cassie's turn to frown. 'Wouldn't it make more sense to tile it all when the plumber was finished.'

'Makes no odds. I can come back and tile around the piping.'

Cassie held her hands up in surrender. All she knew about tiles was the cost. 'I want to start the work on the kitchen next, okay?'

Instead of answering, Stu placed the tile on the wall and pressed it into place. He seemed surprised to see Cassie still standing there when he turned to pick up the next tile. 'Was there something else?'

'Did you hear what I said?' She struggled to keep the bite of frustration under control.

'Sure, you want us to start on the kitchen next.'

'Exactly.' That was easier than she'd expected.

'Might not work though.' He continued to work as he spoke,

his movements slow and precise. 'The trades are all booked in advance, you see. Electricians, plumbers, etcetera. Not easy to swing them around willy-nilly. Dan only uses the best, and the best get booked up way in advance.'

She wanted to stamp her feet like a child. Demand they do what she wanted. She was paying for it, and could change her mind if she wanted to. But she could see the logic in what Stu had said.

'Right,' she said. Thoughts tumbled in her head and reformed in a different order. 'But you don't need specialist trades to demolish the wall between the kitchen and the corridor behind, nor to put up an RSJ since it's a supporting wall.' She was pleased with herself for slipping that in, it made her sound like she knew what she was talking about. He didn't need to know that all she knew about rolled steel joists, she'd learned on the internet. 'I'd like that work started as soon as possible. And all the walls knocked down behind to bring those small rooms into the space, plus the bars removed from those windows.' When that was done, when it was all one big open space, it would feel so much better. 'Start first thing tomorrow, or sooner if anyone is free.' She jerked a thumb towards the doorway. 'I'm going to start emptying the cupboards and taking the doors off. If there's anyone free to join in, send them down, please.' She left him with a very lady-of-the-manor nod. It was time she started putting her foot down. She who paid the piper was entitled to call the tune. And if it didn't fit with Cody's plans, well, tough.

In the kitchen, she didn't delay. First, she needed to empty the cupboards. Most of the contents predated her arrival. Old, chipped crockery, piles of plastic containers, a weighing scale that didn't work. All was carted out and tossed into the skip. She piled anything she was keeping onto a small table. Anything edible was, for convenience, shoved on a shelf in the fridge.

She'd finished the clearing out before one of the team joined her.

He didn't look too happy. She wondered what Stu had said to him. Probably something along the lines of *just go and keep her happy*. 'Stu said I was to come to help.'

She wiped a hand over her forehead, frowning when she realised the hand wasn't particularly clean. What she wouldn't give for a very long hot shower. 'Great. Terry, isn't it?'

'Yeah.'

Stu had sent her the runt of the team by the looks of things. 'Right, I want to get these rooms gutted.' She opened one of the cupboard doors. 'I can get these off if you could give me a screwdriver. What I'd like you to do is to make a start at taking the bars off those small rooms along the corridor, okay?'

Nodding, he reached for the screwdriver hanging from his tool belt. With obvious reluctance, he handed it over. 'Don't lose it, please.'

She wanted to smack him over the head with it. 'I'm not likely to, am I?' She used the tool to point towards the doorway. 'I'm not sure how difficult getting those bars off will be. Do your best.'

Armed with the screwdriver, she started on the cupboard doors. It was easier than she expected. Most of the doors were half falling off and she didn't need to use the screwdriver at all, one tug and they came away. An hour later, they were all removed and in the skip.

There wasn't much more she could do. She looked around the room. It didn't look as if she'd made much headway, but then again, she couldn't knock down walls. Although wielding a sledgehammer might be very therapeutic, bashing a few heads with it would be too. She was smiling at the idea as she went into the corridor to find out how Terry was doing.

She found him slouched against the wall in the first of the

small rooms, his thumb frantically tapping the screen of his mobile phone. She was going to go with a heavily sarcastic *sorry to disturb you* until she realised the bars had been removed from the window. She crossed over and looked through the filthy cracked glass. There wasn't much to see, the view blocked by the mix of weeds that grew outside. 'Well done,' she said. 'Was it difficult?'

'Not with that,' he said, pointing to the power tool on the floor beside him. 'I tried to get them off by hand first, but they weren't budging.' He slipped his phone into his shirt pocket and moved to the window. 'When they replace the glass, they can plug the holes I've made.'

Cassie bent and picked up one of the bars. Cast iron, they were heavy. Ugly too. 'It's better without them already.' She smiled at him. 'It's time you were finished, isn't it?' She handed him his screwdriver. 'Thanks for the loan. Tomorrow, when you get in, will you remove the remainder of the bars, please?'

'Can do.' He bent to pick up the power tool. 'It's still a bit creepy in here though, isn't it?'

Her eyes swept over the tall, broad, well-built man. Did he really find it creepy or was this all part of the plot against her? Was he in on it too? Maybe they all were. Maybe every bloody one of them had something to gain from frightening her away. 'You think so?' She dropped the bar she held; it landed on the others with a metal-on-metal crash. 'I don't. I think there's a lovely feel in the room now, and when the walls are down this is going to be an amazing place.' Her voice had risen in pitch and volume as she spoke. When she saw Terry's eyes widen in surprise and his uncertain step backwards, she turned away. 'Thanks, see you tomorrow.' When she turned back, he was gone.

It wasn't the room that made her shiver and wrap her arms around herself, it was the awful sensation that she suddenly felt as though she couldn't trust anyone.

32

By the time she left the room, the house was silent. From outside came the sound of engines ticking over, the crush of gravel as cars rolled from the yard, the beep of a horn to make someone get a move on. Then she was alone in the quiet.

She rested her shoulder against the doorframe and sighed. What a day! There were times when she wondered if she'd taken on too much. Just what they wanted her to think, wasn't it? It was depressing to realise that maybe they were right. Even without their games, she would probably have come to the same conclusion.

It was supposed to be the two of them. She and Richie against the world. Arm in arm. Holding each other up when times got tough. What was she left with? A dubiously solid doorframe to support her. Straightening, she poked at it. Rotten wood crumbled under her finger. Nothing was dependable any more.

Wallowing again. She needed to stop. Brushing her hands together she dislodged the flakes of paint and wood and turned with thoughts of getting something to eat. The door was almost shut behind her when she saw a car pulling in to the yard. Her first thought was that it was Cody, coming to explain, maybe even to apologise, to tell her he was on her side, that his relationship with Baker had been a mistake. After all she'd been through with Richie, it angered her that she should still tend towards believing the best in people. What was it going to take to teach her?

But as the dust stirred up by the car settled around it, she saw it wasn't him. She shook off the momentary annoyance when she saw who it was. Mrs Morgan. Cassie had told her to call around any time, she hadn't expected to be taken literally. Definitely hadn't expected to see her twice in one day.

'Hello,' she called as her visitor opened the car door and climbed out.

Mrs Morgan lifted a hand in acknowledgment, then stopped to reach back into the car. When she straightened, she was holding a box. 'I made you another cake,' she said, stepping carefully across the potholed yard. 'I had hoped to have it ready to eat this morning, but I'm not as quick as I used to be.'

Cassie smiled as the box was passed over. 'That was very kind of you.' She indicated the table with her free hand. 'Why don't we have a cuppa and a slice now. Is it warm enough for you outside or would you prefer to go in?'

Mrs Morgan tilted her head as she gave the question some consideration. 'I think here would be fine.'

Cassie, whose smile had frozen in place as she waited for the answer, nodded. 'Right take a seat, I'll get us some tea.' She lifted the box. 'And a slice of what I'm sure will be delicious cake.'

Not the most nutritious of dinners, but it was food. Cassie found a space on the counter for the box, filled the kettle and switched it on. When she found the workmen had used the last of her teabags, she threw the empty box across the floor in irritation. There was another box. She remembered putting it somewhere earlier when she'd been clearing out the cupboards, but where?

It was several frustrated minutes, muttering obscenities under her breath, before she located the box hidden under a pile of teacloths. She glanced through the window and saw Mrs Morgan staring into space. Probably wishing she'd stayed at home, had a cup of tea in the comfort of her stuffy sitting room. Cassie rapped a knuckle on the glass. 'Just coming!' When there was no reaction, she muttered, 'Deaf old bat.' The glass shook as she knocked again. 'Just coming!' This time, the woman lifted a hand in acknowledgement.

'Sorry to be so long,' Cassie said, joining her visitor a moment later. There was a tray somewhere, she'd no idea where it had gone and didn't want to waste more time looking for it. Instead, she made two trips to bring everything out.

'That's it,' she said, putting the Tetra Pak of milk on the table. 'I'm afraid it's a poor contrast to the lovely tea you gave me.'

Mrs Morgan reached out and patted her hand. 'It was easy for me, my dear, I have nothing else to do. I'm pleased you made time for me.'

There was a hint of loneliness in the voice. Cassie wanted to ask if there were children, other relatives, friends. Or perhaps the lady had outlived all. It was the sad reality of age. 'I was thinking of doing afternoon tea for my guests. Setting it out as elegantly as you did for me.' She saw a flush of pleasure on the lined cheeks. 'Maybe I could even get you to make the odd cake for me. I'd pay you of course,' she hurried to add.

'I'd like that very much.'

Cassie cut them each a slice of cake. Lemon drizzle. One of her favourites. 'This is really good.'

Mrs Morgan nibbled on a piece. 'I'm rather partial to it.' She looked towards the house. 'How is it coming along?'

Cassie would have liked to have spilled her worries, to have borrowed the wisdom of the older woman's years. She wanted reassurance; to not be alone. It would have been unfair. 'It's going well,' she said, lifting the teapot and refilling both mugs.

'Did you manage to get Daniel to change the schedule as you'd wanted?'

Cassie had almost forgotten she'd discussed changing the work around. 'I'm not envisaging any problems.' Almost a lie, Stu was quite clear it might be an issue. 'I didn't manage to talk to Daniel today. He was busy with something or other.'

'It might be better to stick with the original plan. Daniel is very organised, I'm sure it's for the best.'

Yes, but Cassie no longer believed he was working in her best interest. 'When we first discussed the work, I was keen to get the public spaces done first – the bedrooms, dining room and entrance hall. Now that I'm living here, it seems important to get the kitchen space sorted.' It wasn't necessary to explain that she hoped by getting rid of those small rooms and their barred windows, she'd also get rid of the air of malevolence that seemed to lurk in the corners. Malevolence... it was the first time she'd given a name to the unsettling feeling, but she knew it was apt. 'There are a lot of walls to knock down. That'll make a lot of dust. It makes sense to get all the dirty work done first.' Didn't it make far more sense? Yet Cody had been quite happy to go along with her plan. Was that another indicator he had his own agenda? She guessed her dilemma appeared on her face when Mrs Morgan rested a thin bony hand on her arm.

'My dear, are you sure you're all right? You've gone terribly pale.'

Cassie rustled up a smile and patted the hand gently. 'I'm fine, it's just that sometimes the scale of the work gets to me.'

'There is no disgrace in admitting that you've overreached yourself. No one is going to think less of you if you give up and return to the city.'

The words were kindly said and well meant. Cassie had always believed women of Mrs Morgan's age, women who'd endured war and savage losses, were made of tough stuff, but the hand under hers was frail, the kindly expression full of sympathy but lacking understanding. Not all women were cut from the same cloth.

'You're right, of course, but I don't think I have.' She smiled to show she'd not taken offence. 'Actually, I've taken a more proactive approach and started the work on the kitchen already.' She laughed at the woman's surprise. 'You should have seen me wielding a screwdriver. I managed to get all the kitchen cupboard doors off and tossed into the skip. I roped in one of the handymen to give me a hand. He started removing the bars from the windows. A more difficult job than he expected so he only got one room done, but it was a start. He's going to get on with it tomorrow. I'll catch Cody in the morning and set him straight. By tomorrow evening, hopefully some of those walls will be gone.'

'I do admire you.' Mrs Morgan shook her head, took her hand away and reached for her tea. She stared into it for a moment before taking a sip and putting the mug down. 'I was a much more biddable woman, I'm afraid. Always did exactly what I was told.'

There was such regret in the words, Cassie felt her heart go out to the woman. It strengthened her resolve to get on with the work whatever way she decided. She'd already had her fill of regrets. She wouldn't be like this poor old soul, looking back on her life and wishing she'd done things differently.

They sat for a little while longer. The setting sun, glowing burnt orange, cast streaks across the sky, and strange shadows crept slowly towards the table. Had Cassie been alone, they'd have sent her scuttling indoors. There was something otherworldly about it all.

It didn't appear to bother Mrs Morgan, her expression

remaining calm and composed even as shadowy fingers crept closer. She may have been biddable, but she didn't appear to be nervous. Suddenly curious, Cassie asked, 'Does anything scare you?'

If Mrs Morgan thought it a strange question, she didn't say, tilting her head as if thinking of a correct reply. 'I'm almost ninety,' she said finally. 'Lots of things scared me when I was younger but I've made my peace with the world now.'

'You don't look your age,' Cassie said. It was a lie; the woman looked every day of her ninety years. There was a fragility about her too, as if one strong gust of wind would not just blow her over but lift her up and sweep her away.

Mrs Morgan smiled, pleased with the simple lie. 'You're very kind.'

Cassie's mobile rang. It was Cody. 'Sorry,' she said, 'do you mind if I take this?'

'Of course, go ahead. Would you like me to leave?'

Cassie flapped her hand in the air. 'I'll just be a sec.' She tapped the screen to accept the call. 'Hello. I thought I'd see you today, I wanted to talk to you about a change of plan.'

'Sorry, it's been one of those days. I'll be there first thing; we can have a chat.'

Cassie wanted to say she'd seen him talking to Baker, and that she was wise to his shenanigans. Perhaps she would have done, had she not been conscious of the woman opposite. It was best to keep this kind of business to herself. 'Right, but I've decided that I want the kitchen done next. In fact, we made a start on it today.'

'That's going to make things difficult.'

'Yes, I know all about the difficulty in getting the tradesmen in, but your team can knock down the walls, yes?'

'We can, but—'

'That's sorted then, I'll see you in the morning.' Cassie cut the connection and dropped the mobile on the table. 'I think I surprised him.'

'I'm sure you did.' Mrs Morgan smiled. 'I must go. Thank you for the tea. I have had a nice time.'

A nice time, sitting on a hard chair, drinking tea, and eating the cake she'd brought herself. Cassie sighed. 'It's me who should be thanking you. The cake is lovely and I'll enjoy having more of it tomorrow.'

'Good.' Mrs Morgan rested a hand on the table and rose to her feet with a creak of old, aged bones.

Cassie stood and circled around the edge of the table to join her. Shadows were hiding the potholes and bumps on the surface of the yard. It would be a disaster if her visitor fell. 'I'll walk you to your car,' she said. She'd have liked to have linked her arm, to be doubly sure of the woman's safety, but as with that morning, she thought such familiarity wouldn't be appreciated so she was taken aback, when it was Mrs Morgan who slid a hand around Cassie's elbow as they made their way slowly towards the car.

Almost there, Mrs Morgan took the key fob from her pocket and aimed it, the clunk of the car unlocking unexpectedly loud. Cassie reached for the handle and pulled the door open. For a small hatchback, the door was surprisingly heavy. Sudden concern made her ask, 'You'll be okay getting home?'

Mrs Morgan sat into the car and settled herself before looking up with a smile. 'Don't worry about me, my dear. I'm tougher than I look.'

A twig rather than a leaf. Cassie pushed the door shut and was surprised when the window slid down.

'Please take care,' Mrs Morgan said. She held a hand out and when Cassie took it, pressed it gently. 'I'm not convinced you're as tough as you think you are. Men like Daniel Cody and Chris Baker, they're used to getting their own way. They've become big fish in the small pond of Hindon, they won't like anyone making ripples, never mind waves.'

Cassie was so taken aback that the window was shut and the car moving before she was able to voice the questions she wanted to ask. Mrs Morgan had linked Baker and Cody together. A simple coincidence? They were two of the biggest businessmen in Hindon, after all. Or was it a warning? She wanted to run after the car, stop it before it negotiated the exit from the yard, stand in front, wave it down, demand answers.

Tomorrow, she'd drive into the town, call around to her to thank her for the cake, and pose the questions then. These things were always better after a few hours thought and a good night's sleep.

33

It was nice to have someone concerned about her, and Cassie felt a little lighter for it as she carried everything back into the house, putting the remainder of the cake into a container. She hadn't seen evidence of mice – she wanted to make sure it stayed that way.

The back door was locked, and double checked. She didn't know why she bothered. If anyone really wanted to gain access it wouldn't take much to kick a hole in the rotten wood. And if she barricaded it, if she dragged the table across, all an intruder would need to do was pry open one of the sash windows. Some were so rotten that a fingernail would do.

She looked around the room. The day was fading and she hurriedly reached for the switch. There was still that moment's fear when she pressed it, that instant worry that nothing would happen, and she sighed her relief when it did what it was supposed to do. The single unshaded bulb hanging off-centre lit the centre of the room, the light fading to darkness at the edges and in the corners.

The doorless cupboards added an extra quality to the darkness, gaping black holes lining the lower walls. She stared at them, imagining someone curled up inside, waiting to jump out as soon as her back was turned. Reaching for the mobile she'd shoved into the back pocket of her jeans, she opened the torch app and shone it around the room, aiming the beam into each of the cupboards. Nobody was hiding there. Seriously, had she really thought someone would have curled up inside. A very small psychopath perhaps?

Although she sneered at her stupidity, she left the light on as she left the room. It didn't penetrate the corridor running behind it and there were no lights in any of the small cell-like rooms. Malevolent... wasn't that how she'd described the atmosphere here? But like a book you read, or a movie you watch, where you know you're going to be scared, the place held a lure for her and she took a step forward, holding her breath as she did so. Her torch app was still running; she aimed it ahead, swivelled to shine it into the first room and through the now unbarred window. Had she hoped removing the bars would make a difference? So far, it didn't appear to have done so. Perhaps only removing all the walls and opening up the space was going to achieve that.

Standing outside the first room, she aimed the beam of light down the corridor. The side and end wall had been panelled, the wood disintegrating, sections where the panelling had disappeared showing the rough brick behind. She shivered when the beam lit a quabble of woodlice, sending them scurrying for cover. She didn't mind insects but hated these creepy grey creatures.

Curious if there was anything to see from the window, she entered the first room, swearing loudly when she tripped on the bars they'd stupidly left on the floor. Arms flailing, she hit the wall with her shoulder. Her mobile went flying, and as luck would always have it, it landed face down, the light immediately dying.

She remained leaning against the wall, winded, painfully

reminded she'd not completely recovered from her previous bruises. It was the thought of those creepy woodlice running over her that made her push away and brush a frantic hand down her sleeve. She needed to find her damn phone. The darkness in the room was almost absolute, the light from the kitchen fading in the corridor outside. Cassie stepped gingerly forward on the rough floor using the toe of one foot to try to locate the mobile, reluctant to feel for it with her hand, visions of insects scrambling over it making her shiver.

One careful step forward, and then she heard it, a distinct crack that made her heart sink. Bending, she lifted her foot and rescued her mobile, praying she hadn't caused serious damage. She felt for the button to turn it on. 'Please work, please work,' she muttered. It didn't. With no torch light to guide her, she stumbled blindly from the room, smacking her already bruised shoulder against the doorway. She cried out in pain, in frustration, in anger at her stupidity for going into the room, at her predicament, at Cody, Baker and Richie.

Back in the relative brightness of the kitchen, she examined her phone. Not only was the screen broken, but the crack carried through to the plastic casing of her ultra-lite mobile. Ultra-lite didn't equate to indestructible, but you were never supposed to drop it and walk on the damn thing.

She spent several minutes holding the broken edges together and pressing to turn it on. It was a futile attempt. Frustration made her grit her teeth and fling the phone from her. It hit the wall and fell to pieces.

Alone, and now isolated, she ignored the ache in her shoulder and wrapped her arms around herself. It didn't help, she could feel terror growing, a scream building in her throat.

Upstairs. She needed to get upstairs. Lock herself into the bedroom. Feel safe. Her computer was there. She could use it to message one of her friends. *And say what? That she was scared? That she was wondering if this was retribution?*

Truthfully, wasn't that her biggest fear? That she didn't deserve any of this – the house, the dream, the new life she was hoping to build. How could she, when it was all based on the lie of what had happened that night? Her part in Richie's death.

She'd believed she could put it behind her. Draw a line under it and never cross back over. Her friends, and family, took her grief at face value. Why wouldn't they – she and Richie had been together forever and were viewed as the definitively happy couple.

Nobody knew the truth.

34

Richie's words had echoed around the room and reverberated painfully in Cassie's head. 'I don't love you any more, I want a divorce.' For several seconds, neither of them had moved, each lost in their own shock – his for saying the words, hers at hearing them.

Hearing – not believing – how could she? She waited for the punchline to another of Richie's terrible jokes. He was renowned for them, but whereas they were rarely funny, they were seldom cruel. Until now. This was cruel. She tried a laugh. It died when faced with his unyieldingly hard expression. She put a hand out, wanting to touch him, because it couldn't be true, it was a nightmare from which she'd wake laughing at how crazy it was. When he backed away from her hand, she smiled. It *was* a dream, she'd fallen asleep on the sofa as she had done so many times, woken sometimes by his kiss on her cheek, or his hand gently shaking her shoulder. Once, he'd tried to lift her in his arms to take her upstairs; she'd woken as he'd slid his arms under her. She shook her head at the memory of how they'd made love right there on the sofa before running naked up the stairs, making love again on their king-size bed.

Any moment now, she'd wake. And laugh at the crazy dream. Any moment now.

'I'll buy you out of your share of the apartment. The price has risen since we bought, you should get enough to buy yourself something a bit further from the city. Maybe you should move back to Sheffield, to be near your parents.'

Such prosaic words for a dream. When she woke, she'd tell Richie. He'd laugh.

'Say something, for fuck's sake!' Richie pushed a hand through his hair.

A lock fell across his forehead. Cassie stepped closer, raised a hand to brush it back. His hand snaked up to catch her wrist in a hard grip. And it was there, in that minute, feeling his bruisingly tight grip, the pain of it, that she realised she wasn't asleep. That this nightmare was her life. 'I don't understand.'

Were there ever such pathetic words? It was all she could manage. No tears. Everything seemed to be frozen in shock.

'We haven't been happy for a long time; you must have guessed this was coming?'

We weren't happy. That cracking sound – was it her heart breaking? 'No.' Her lips curved in a wobbly smile. 'I must be very stupid, because I didn't.' Through all their endeavours to get pregnant, all the invasive examinations and tests, the one certainty was that they'd come through it all together, because they loved each other. And when she'd miscarried, each time, they'd cried together – for her, for their unborn child, for the death of the dream. His dream. Was that it? Had he resented her lack of commitment? She drew a breath. She could make this right. 'I know how much you want a child, Richie. Perhaps it's time we thought about using a surrogate. It would still be our child. We'd just be renting a womb.'

His fingers were still wrapped around her wrist. She could feel his strength and knew there'd be bruises to show the following day. She stepped closer till their arms were pressed together by their bodies. 'We can make it work. I love you.' She met his eyes, smiling gently. Poor Richie, he was confused, maybe she hadn't understood how much having a child meant to him. 'Let's go out to dinner and we can talk.'

When she felt his fingers release their grip on her wrist, she thought she'd got through to him, so the shove took her by surprise, making her stagger backward, shock freezing the smile in place.

'I don't love you, Cassie. I don't want to be with you. I want a woman whose body isn't toxic, one who can have my child.'

Toxic! In her wildest dreams she'd never thought to blame him for his low sperm count, accepting it as the luck of the draw in the strange toss-up of life. She hadn't, but he wasn't according her the same consideration, blaming her for something she had no control over. *Toxic*. She stared at him, wishing she could hate him, wanting to feel anything except despair, grinding sorrow, absolute misery.

He'd left her standing there. She didn't move until she heard the front door slam, turning then with a cry of such desolation it seemed to come from her broken heart. There was a chair nearby. Staggering backwards she sank onto it and stared blankly ahead. Despite the bruises that were already appearing on the pale flesh of her wrists, it had to be a nightmare.

Wishful thinking. The tears came then, plopping from her bent head to spatter the navy material of her T-shirt. Could a body hold enough water to wash away her pain? It seemed not because when they stopped, when she was too exhausted to cry any more, the pain lingered.

There was no sign of Richie returning. He hadn't taken the car so he'd probably walked to their local pub and was sinking pints. Perhaps it was what she should have done, alcohol wouldn't have taken away the pain but it would have numbed it a little. She could get up and follow him, maybe over a few drinks together she could make sense of what he'd said. Maybe he'd say he'd lied, that of course he still loved her, that he hadn't meant what he'd said.

Toxic. Such an ugly word. As ugly as his expression when he'd used it.

No, she wouldn't follow him. She wasn't sure she could; she felt weighed down by her sorrow and the mere act of standing seemed almost too much for her and she staggered and reached for the back of the chair to steady herself. Step by weary step she crossed the room. In the small hallway, she stared at the front door. She wanted to turn back the clock, to see Richie, the man she loved and who loved her, come through and take her in his arms and laugh at her bad dreams.

Instead, she trudged into their bedroom. Ignoring her usual nightly routine, she peeled off her clothes and climbed naked into bed. When Richie came home, when he slipped in beside her, she'd wrap herself around him and show him how much she loved him. Everything would be all right.

She was still trying to convince herself a couple of hours later when she heard the apartment door open, the clatter of keys being dropped into the drawer of the small hall table, the heavy step of Richie's shoes on the laminate floor, the flush of the toilet in the main bathroom, then, the most heartbreaking sound of all, the click of the spare room door shutting.

He hadn't even checked to see if she was all right.

More tears. More pain. Exhaustion finally shut everything down and she slept for a few hours. Her first thought on waking was that she'd had a bad nightmare, a split-second puff of hope that was quickly dispelled when she turned to see the vast emptiness beside her. Her fingers brushed over the bruises on her wrist. They didn't hurt. Nothing did. She felt completely numb.

She could hear music drifting from elsewhere in the apartment. Gratingly cheerful music that made her bury her head in the pillow, pulling it up over her ears to drown it out. It didn't work. She threw the duvet back, scrambled from the bed and pulled on a robe. Tying the belt around her waist, she took a deep breath before opening the door. Across the corridor, the spare bedroom was obviously empty, the cover that normally dressed it, a wrinkled mess on the floor.

The music was coming from the open-plan kitchen living room. The door was shut, but there had been no attempt to keep the volume down so as not to disturb her. Perhaps it was deliberate. He wanted her to join him to see how she was coping, choosing the neutral territory of the living room rather than the intimate space of their bedroom.

She brushed a hand through her hair. After a restless night, she'd look like death. Her face would be pale, there'd be dark circles under her eyes. The white robe wouldn't help. Was it better to go back, have a shower, put some make-up on to cover the ravages, and dress in her best. Show him she didn't give a fuck? Or face him as she was. A picture of devastation.

She wasn't sure it mattered. On a sigh, she pushed open the door.

Her initial thought was that this was the nightmare. The picture of perfect domestic harmony. Her husband, the man she'd loved for so long, sitting at the table, the newspaper spread out in front of him, a mug of coffee in one hand, a slice of toast in the other. A scene from any one of the weekend mornings since they'd first begun to live together.

He looked up and waved the piece of toast toward the coffee machine. 'Want me to make you your usual?'

Unable to speak, she merely nodded, her eyes widening to see him immediately leap to his feet and start the rigmarole of making her favourite cappuccino.

He set the coffee machine going, then turned to her again. 'Toast?'

'No.' She didn't think she could eat, wasn't even sure she could drink. All she seemed able to do was to walk stiff-legged to a chair and sit.

Either Richie hadn't heard her reply or, which was more likely, he hadn't listened, because as the coffee was gurgling into her mug, he slipped bread into the toaster.

'Here you go.' He placed the coffee in front of her with unnecessary care. The toast was the way she liked it, almost burnt, the slices standing to attention in the china toast rack. She was still staring at the coffee when she heard rather than saw a plate and knife being put on the table within her reach.

It was all so bizarrely normal. Maybe caffeine would help. And sugar, although she didn't normally take it. Wasn't that what they suggested for shock. And that's what this was, why everything seemed so surreal. Reaching for the spoon, she ladled sugar into her coffee – one, two, three teaspoons, stirring it noisily. Richie had moved out of her line of vision but she could hear him, his heavy breathing, his tut as she continued to stir, coffee lapping over the edge of the mug to drip to the table. It left a brown ring on the surface when she eventually lifted it. The over-sweet sickly drink was disgusting, but she drank half in two long burningly hot swallows. Pain was good, it meant she wasn't dreaming.

Richie retook his seat at the table and pulled the newspaper closer. 'We'll need to leave by twelve.'

Leave by twelve? She put the coffee down and lifted her head to look at him. He was frowning as he read, his lips moving slightly as they always did when he was reading something he considered important, as if intent on embedding the words into his head. She wanted to reach for the paper, pull it away, tear it into shreds, roll it into a ball and throw it at him. She knew what he meant. Of course she did. The naming ceremony for a friend's first baby being held at one o'clock. Did he really mean for them to go as if everything was hunky-dory? For them both to put on brave faces and pretend all was okay?

Maybe it was. She put a hand to her forehead. It was hot. She felt sick. Maybe she was coming down with something.

She wanted to speak, to ask Richie if he'd meant what he'd said. But what if he looked at her blankly, and said he'd no idea what she was talking about? It hadn't been a nightmare, but what if she'd simply imagined it all. She lifted her wrist, brushed her fingers over the bruises. Real bruises. If she'd imagined everything, how had she sustained such marks?

'You have less than an hour to get ready, Cassie.'

What? Her eyes flew to the clock on the wall. She was sure she'd woken at seven. Her hand snaked around the mug, confusion creasing her face when she discovered it was still warm. She hadn't been sitting here that long. Maybe she'd fallen back to sleep earlier following her restless night. Richie was still reading the paper, as if everything was as it usually was.

He didn't look up as she got to her feet. 'I'll go and get dressed.'

'Right.' He still didn't look up. Made no comment on the untouched toast.

She stood looking down on him for a few seconds before

turning away with a shake of her head. Her imagination. It had to have been. It was going to get her into trouble one of these days.

Back in her bedroom, she showered and washed her hair. The routine of it all, the washing, drying, application of potions and lotions, was soothing. The naming ceremony was being held in a posh hotel. Earlier in the week she'd searched for an appropriate outfit to wear. She took the dress from the wardrobe and held it up. A bright, pink, floaty number, she supposed it had suited her mood at the time. She shoved it back onto the rail and searched for something else. The dress she finally chose was a little sombre for such a joyful occasion. She looked in the full-length mirror and frowned. It was more suited to a funeral. With a grunt of frustration, she pulled it off and took out the pink dress again. Their friends had gone to a lot of trouble to organise this event, and it wasn't fair to allow her weird mood to spoil it.

Richie had finished reading the paper and was standing looking out at the view from their fifth-floor apartment when she returned to the kitchen. As was his habit, he'd left the paper neatly folded on the table. Everything was as usual.

'I'm ready,' she said.

He turned, and without looking at her crossed to where he'd hung his jacket on the back of a chair. 'Right, let's go then.'

The car keys were in the hall table drawer; he grabbed them in passing, striding ahead as Cassie set the alarm and shut the apartment door. He was hammering impatiently on the lift button when she joined him.

The lift opened into an underground car park. Richie stepped out, aiming his fob at their car as he crossed to it, the beep loud in the echoing silence. He was seated with the engine already growling, before Cassie, slowed by her stilettos, reached the passenger door.

'We need to get a move on if we're going to get there on time,' he said, releasing the handbrake.

Cassie checked her watch, surprised to see it was later than she expected, and later than they'd planned to leave. All the faffing around with the dress had delayed her more than she'd thought. 'It took me a while to choose what to wear.'

He glanced at her as the car coasted to the exit. 'You chose well. You look very lovely.'

Cassie's hand trembled as she smoothed it over the fine material of the dress. Everything was going to be all right. She'd been working too hard recently, that was all. Stress, it could play games with your mind. When they got home that night, she'd sit Richie down and tell him everything. She imagined his laugh. He'd think it was hilarious. It *was* hilarious. How very stupid she'd been.

'When we get home...'

Had he read her mind? She turned to him with a smile. He was concentrating on the busy road ahead, his lips pressed in a thin line, vertical lines between his thick eyebrows. She waited for him to finish whatever he'd been going to say. When he didn't, she prompted him. 'When we get home, what?'

'We need to sit down and discuss finances. As I said, I'd like to buy you out of your share of the apartment. I really think you'd be better moving back to Sheffield. Your parents would be happy.'

Cassie's smile froze in place. 'You were serious? You really want a divorce?'

He gave her a brief glance, then shook his head and returned his attention to the road. 'Hardly something to make jokes about, is it?'

She held a hand to her forehead again. It still felt hot, she felt unwell, nauseous. Her head was spinning. What had Richie been doing that morning? Making her coffee and toast. As if everything was as usual. Why were they going to this blasted naming ceremony when her world had been turned upside down? Were they going to be all smiles when they met their friends. Pretend to be civilised. As if it didn't matter that her heart was breaking.

In that moment, she hated him, and herself. Hated the future she could see stretching ahead. A lonely sad one.

'I don't want to go to this thing,' she said. 'Stop and let me out. I'll catch a taxi home. You can go on your own. Tell them whatever you like.'

'Don't be ridiculous,' he said, indicating to pass a parked van. 'They're our friends, they're expecting us.'

'Let me out now.' She saw the mulish expression she'd learned to dread slip over his face and knew he intended to ignore her. Wouldn't it be better to end it there? Nobody would know what he'd planned. They'd be forever remembered as a loving couple. *A loving couple!* The anger that had been simmering, boiled over and swept away every rational thought and made her willing to risk her life to take his. She reached for the steering wheel, catching him by surprise.

His instinctive response was to jerk the wheel away from her grip. His action sent the car careering into the parked van, sparks flying as metal hit metal, the impact sending the car bouncing back into passing traffic, Richie screaming as he tried to correct the trajectory, his eyes on the cars to the right, not the wall ahead. Until it was too late.

The impact tore the car in two. Richie's side almost demolished, the passenger side – Cassie's – virtually unscathed.

She'd climbed from it as passers-by rushed to help, and stood shaking, afraid to turn to see the damage.

It was hours later before she knew for sure that Richie was never going to ask for a divorce again.

35

Richie had never asked for a divorce again, but it hadn't stopped him wrecking her life. How could Cassie possibly enjoy the future they had dreamt of for so long, when the dream had been purchased with the insurance money from his death – a death she'd caused. She had murdered him. Deliberately grabbed that wheel. She hadn't cared if she'd died, as long as he had. Wasn't that it?

Maybe. Maybe not. She'd gone back to those vital seconds so many times since that day. Some days she was positive the result was exactly as she'd intended. Other times, that she'd never meant it to go so far, that she'd simply wanted him to stop the car and let her out. She'd gone over and over it all until her head ached. Again and again, until she had no idea what the truth was.

When the police had spoken to her following the accident, she'd told them that nothing out of the way had taken place, that the journey had been going smoothly until Richie had suddenly swerved. She'd been looking out of the passenger window so hadn't seen anything, but she guessed it might have been a cat or something. She must have passed out, she said. When she'd come to, she'd seen concerned faces, and someone had opened her car door, urging her to get out. She'd assumed Richie was doing the same on the other side. She couldn't believe it, she told the police, tears making her voice thick, when she heard he'd been killed.

She told the same story so many times to friends and family that eventually she began to believe it had happened that way. The coroner recorded Richie's death as accidental, reinforcing her belief that this was exactly what it had been. An accident.

Only when she was alone, did the truth inveigle its way into her head, laughing at her, sneering, pointing, coating her with a thick layer of guilt. Sometimes, she woke feeling the steering wheel between her hands.

There were times when she convinced herself she wasn't to blame, that she'd let go in time, that it had been Richie's bad-tempered response to her request to be let out that had caused the crash. Sometimes she even believed it.

Not now though. Now, she was convinced she was getting exactly what she deserved. Leaving the kitchen light on behind her, she headed up to the ground floor. She was halfway up, one step at a time, her hand pulling on the handrail like a lifeline, feeling the weight of what she'd done pressing her down, wondering if things could get any worse. The thought was barely finished when the light from the kitchen that had been illuminating her steps suddenly died.

Cassie bit back a scream and stopped, her fingers tightening on the rail, listening for any sound. But there was nothing; she forced herself to take one step into the deep black hole in front of her, then another, and another, till she reached the equally dark hallway. The fuse box wasn't far. Taking baby steps, her hands outstretched, she headed in what she hoped was the right direction. Reaching the wall, she felt along it till she got to the fuse box. Her fingers ran across the switches. With a groan of dismay, she found them all where they should be and played her fingers over them again, slowly, checking every single one. There was nothing wrong with the fuses. She looked back to the stairway. Had someone been hiding in a dark corner of the kitchen after all? Hiding there, waiting till she'd left, then sneaked out to switch out the light. Or had the bulb simply blown?

There was a light switch near the front door, but that meant crossing an obstacle course of supplies, clear in the daylight, it would be a danger in the dark. Instead, she took the shorter route to the stairway. There was a landing light – she just needed to get to the switch. The temptation was to run. To take the steps two at a time, but when she thought of falling in the darkness, with no phone to call for help, it terrified her into taking it slowly. She felt each step with her foot before moving up, then waited a few seconds with her head tilted to listen for the slightest sound from above or below.

When she finally reached the landing, she hurried across to feel along the wall, panic building until the switch was under her hand. She pressed it, and when nothing happened pushed it off, then on again, then more rapidly, on-off, on-off, on-off, as if by some magic the friction would have an effect. Nothing happened and she cried out and turned to face the dense darkness. It could be hiding anything. Anyone. Cody and Baker might both be there, waiting for their opportunity, watching to see what she'd do next. They might have seen her throw her mobile, know that she was totally at their mercy.

She needed to get to her bedroom, get her laptop powered up and send a message to her friends to tell them what was going on. At least then if anything happened to her, if she was found dead, or mysteriously vanished, someone would know. It wasn't much bloody consolation, but at least she'd have the satisfaction of knowing Cody and Baker wouldn't get away with it scot-free.

With no light, the corridor stretched ahead of her, a tunnel of solid darkness. No light or shade, no discernible difference between walls, floor, or ceiling. Her room was the second door. Inside was her computer, her only source of communication. Desperation had her try the switch again, putting more weight behind it this time, as if that was going to make a difference. It didn't. She glanced back to the stairway. Would it be better to go back down, get into her car and leave. She could drive into the village, get a room in The Lamb, and never come back to this godforsaken house.

Just as *they* wanted. Cody, Baker – even Richie – they wanted her to fail.

In the dark, with a thick blanket of silence hanging over her, she couldn't bring herself to care, and she'd possibly have taken the leave option but for one ridiculous reason – she'd no idea where she'd left her car keys. The thought of scrambling in the dark to find them made her squirm.

It was bad enough that she needed to feel her way along the wall, her hand sliding over the first door, then over more wall to reach her room. Inside, clinging desperately to the hope that the kitchen and landing lights hadn't worked because of dodgy bulbs, she felt for the switch, pressed it, and nearly cried as she faced reality. None of the lights were working.

A worse thought hit her. She scurried across the room, almost tripping over an abandoned shoe in her haste to reach her laptop. It was an old one. She'd been promising to upgrade but felt a weird kind of loyalty to the old but still serviceable machine. She was used to its quirks, knew to keep it plugged in, its battery refusing to keep more than five minutes' charge.

She pulled it from under the mattress, opened it, slid her fingers over the keyboard to reach the power button and pressed. The screen remained resolutely blank. She felt for the power lead, checked the connection, followed it down to the plug, checked that. Despite the uselessness of the attempt, she tried the power button again, stabbing it with her finger. Repeatedly. Uselessly.

It wasn't only the lights. The electricity was off completely.

No means to contact anyone. No light, no torch.

She could search for her keys – or if she couldn't find them, she could walk into the village. Pack a bag and leave.

And do what?

Go back to London, confess she'd been a failure.

Confess.

A shiver ran through her. Maybe she'd been wrong about Cody and Baker – maybe it was Richie. Haunting her. Many people believed that the spirits of dead people hung around because they had unfinished business. If it was Richie, he was doing a fine job of scaring the wits out of her.

Was it easier to believe it was the ghost of her dead husband, or two conniving men?

That was some choice.

It wasn't the only choice she had though, was it? She could allow whoever it was to scare her away, to ruin the future she'd hoped for, or she could fight back. She felt the first stirring of anger, felt it growing, welcomed it.

She might not stay in Hindon House – in fact she was pretty sure she wouldn't – but she was damned if she was going to let any man, dead or alive, chase her away before she was ready to go.

Anger gave her strength as she opened her bedroom door. She remembered seeing lengths of wood resting against the wall further along the corridor earlier that day. It took minutes to find them, her hands feeling along the wall, grimacing to feel insect life under her fingers, relieved not to be able to see what they were, guessing they were probably those damn woodlice. It wasn't her hand that found what she was looking for in the end, it was her foot.

She bent to pick one up. The weight of it in her hand was comforting. She swung it in front of her, swiping the darkness. It might not work against ghosts but Cassie was almost sure whoever was messing with her had corporeal form. *Almost sure.* She held the length of wood in both hands across her chest. One step forward made her reconsider her grip, releasing one hand to feel for the wall, swinging her makeshift weapon with the other.

At the top of the stairway, she peered down into the black pit. So dark: if there was someone down there, they were as unable to see her as she was unable to see them. It wasn't much of a consolation but it made her move slowly down. After each step, she stopped to listen. There was something in the silence – a sense of expectation. Cassie wouldn't have been surprised to have heard heavy breathing. Shocked, terrified, but not surprised. There was someone out there.

It took minutes to reach the bottom. She waved her makeshift weapon before her, wishing she could connect with something solid. It would be satisfying to cause pain, to beat the crap out of whoever was responsible for everything. Adrenaline fizzed through her veins, giving her strength. Right at that moment, she could take on anyone – Cody or Baker, or both. They'd have no chance against her rage and adrenaline-fuelled strength.

Seconds. That was all this new energy lasted. It died immediately when she heard – not the deep breathing of a foe – but the distinct sound of footsteps.

And then a high-pitched childish giggle.

36

If Cassie had been scared behind the adrenaline and anger charged bluster, she was terrified now. The giggle came again, longer, louder, a sound full of malevolent glee that rooted her to the spot. She tried to gauge where it was coming from. Impossible, it seemed to be everywhere.

She needed to get out of there because whoever – whatever – was making that awful sound sounded like they meant her harm. As if they'd tried giving her a hint – one that she hadn't taken, because she hadn't till that very moment understood how serious they were – and now they were making it crystal clear.

She regretted not ringing Jenny Willard earlier – if she had would the woman have told her about a similar campaign of horror.

When the giggle sounded once more, Cassie took a step forwards. Too hasty, she tripped over something on the floor and fell heavily, the wood flying from her hand. It landed with a clatter several feet away. She was tempted to crawl forward to retrieve it, but shook from the fall and terrified by the continuing giggle, she couldn't move. The footsteps came again. Light ones, pitter pattering in a circle around her. Any thought that it might be Cody or Baker vanished. They might be able to arrange for that hideous giggle, but neither man could be so light-footed.

Cassie didn't stir. Perhaps if they thought they'd succeeded beyond their dreams, that the fall had killed her, they'd leave her alone. The giggle, when it came again, was tinged with puzzlement. The footsteps came a little closer.

There was something under Cassie's hip. Slowly, she moved her hand to feel for whatever it was, her fingers closing over a length of piping. It was impossible to lift it free without making a sound, so she lay there, waiting for an opportunity. Her stalker might think Cassie was dead, but they also may decide to make sure.

She wasn't going to go down without a fight.

Her cheek was pressed to the wooden floor. She fancied she could feel the vibration as the footsteps moved ever closer, circling her carefully. The giggling had stopped. Perhaps they found the situation as scary as Cassie did. They seemed to be able to see in the dark. Cassie had seen *Silence of the Lambs* several times. The scene where Buffalo Bill followed Clarice through his dungeon wearing night vision glasses was terrifying. It would be nice to think she could harness her inner Clarice to fight back and win. But this wasn't a movie. She wasn't sure what it was, just that she wanted out of it.

She was keeping her breaths shallow, silent. *Please think I'm dead and leave me alone. Tomorrow, I'll leave, I swear.* She debated whether it would be better to say the words aloud or continue with her dead-man's act. There was no choice really. Nobody would believe she'd simply walk away. Even if she wanted to – she couldn't. There was too much money invested in the house for her to be able to pack her bags and leave.

It was a few seconds before she realised the footsteps had stopped. Not left, just stopped. Was the owner standing watching her? Perhaps trying to see if her chest was rising and falling? Cassie held her breath, her fingers tightening on the cold metal under her belly.

Then she heard it, coming from overhead, the distinct sound of wheezy breathing that was so at odds with the childish giggle from before. She couldn't hold her breath any longer and risked taking a shallow breath before holding it again, listening intently for any reaction.

When it came – the sharp prod of a foot to her ribs – it almost startled a yelp from her. Her grip on the pipe tightened. Wait... wait...

The prod came again – harder, with more intent, determined to cause damage.

Cassie both heard and felt a rib crack. Just the one. She'd broken one many years before, it wouldn't cause her any lasting harm – unless she was kicked again, hard enough to send the broken ends into a lung, or her heart. She wasn't waiting for it. From the angle of the kick, she was able to determine where her attacker stood.

She rose with her makeshift weapon already swinging and grunted in satisfaction when she heard the surprised yelp of pain as she hit home. The impact jarred Cassie's already damaged hand. Intense pain shot through her and made her stagger. Only the pipe, now a walking stick, prevented her from hitting the ground again.

Confused and disorientated by her injuries, and the profound darkness, Cassie took a careful step forward, hoping she'd done enough damage to her assailant to prevent them from following. It was a short-lived hope, extinguished completely as a blow caught her across the side of her head. The force of it sent her flying across the floor to land in a heap against the wall. She slid to the floor.

And then the blackness took over completely,

37

Cassie's first thought when she woke was relief that the night had passed: she was still alive, and she could see.

Every part of her seemed to hurt. She lay without moving, trying to make sense of all that had happened. Her thoughts were a jumble and it took several minutes to untangle them. She remembered hitting her tormentor with the length of piping – but she hadn't killed them, the blow to Cassie's head was proof of that.

She hadn't killed them; they hadn't killed her. Their blow had knocked her unconscious – had they assumed she was dead? She struggled to sit, each movement, no matter how slight, causing her pain. With her back against the wall, she took stock of her surroundings. Nearby, she saw the pipe she'd used to attack her stalker. Further away, the length of wood Cassie had dropped when she'd fallen.

There was no sign of her attacker.

She rested her head back. From the light, she guessed it was early. Perhaps four o'clock. She could sit there until Cody's team arrived; wait till they rode to her rescue. How pathetic she was.

It was a painful journey to get to her feet; she did it slowly, reaching for the pipe to help her, using the wall as support. She hobbled a few steps before stopping with a frown between her eyes. The dusty wooden floor was worn and stained but there was something new – a fresher stain as if something had been dragged across it recently.

Her eyes followed the trail from the hallway to the entrance to the stairs to the lower ground floor. Passing the fuse box, she glanced over the switches she'd run her fingers over the night before. They were where they should be. What was wrong was the mains switch. Set slightly apart, it had been switched off. She pushed it back up.

She could run upstairs, plug in her computer, message her friends to get help. Or the police. She shook her head: her friends were a safer bet. Knowing what she should be doing, she ignored it and started down the kitchen stairs. The stain on the floor could only be one thing – blood. If there was someone lying injured, even the monster who'd been tormenting her, Cassie had to help.

It was instinct. And a revelation. It opened eyes that had been shut since the accident. She would never have deliberately set out to hurt anyone. Would never have tried to kill herself or Richie. Yes, she had been upset, and had reached for the steering wheel that terrible day but she'd withdrawn her hand at a sharp glance from him. It had been his bad temper that had made him lose control. Not her actions. All these months trying to see through the swirling cloud of memories and now here it was, crystal clear in her head.

Clarity gave her courage. She followed the trail down the stairs and along the corridor to where it vanished into the third of the small cell-like rooms.

Wounded animals could be dangerous. So could wounded humans. Cassie was still using the pipe as a crutch. She lifted it to use as a weapon and hobbled forward. The daylight filtering through the barred window was further dimmed by the tall weeds outside. Strange shadows moved as the breeze outside shivered through the leaves and stems.

Junk was piled against the walls waiting to be taken to the skip: broken beds and chairs, boxes of rubbish. It took seconds for Cassie to make out the shape in the far corner. Partially concealed by one of the boxes, it was a jerking movement that caught her eye. She held the pipe across her chest. 'Come out of there!'

When there was no reply, she took a step closer. 'Did you hear what I said, come out where I can see you. I have a weapon, so don't try any funny stuff.' She was sounding like a bad actress in a B movie. She had a pipe; this person could have a knife, or worse, a gun.

A faint shuffling was the only answer. Cassie thought of the trail of blood and remembered the blow she'd dealt with the pipe. Had she caused a serious injury? She'd no idea what part of this person she'd hit. Another step forward didn't bring any clarity, the box still concealing most of the person behind. 'Are you hurt?' Stupid question, they had to be. 'I'm going to come closer, okay.'

Cassie stopped in front of the huddled mass on the floor. All she could tell at first glance was that her tormentor was human, not a ghost. Not a child either, despite the childish giggle she'd heard. Not Cody or Baker either. A slighter bundle. Playing dead. Cassie wasn't falling for any tricks. She poked the body with the pipe. 'Who are you? Why were you trying to frighten me away?'

'It was my duty.'

The answer was whispered. It made no sense. 'Your duty? What are you talking about?'

The bundle shifted; a pale face emerging.

Even in the poor light, it was one Cassie recognised. Staggered, she took a step backwards. *Mrs Morgan?* This couldn't be right. 'Mrs Morgan?'

The body shifted again, sitting up straighter with a groan. 'You sound horrified. Age doesn't preclude someone from taking every step to ensure duty is done.'

Perhaps it was the pain but it seemed to Cassie that the woman was speaking in riddles. She pulled one of the boxes closer and sank onto it. 'I don't understand. I thought we were friends. You baked me cakes!' Her voice thick with unshed tears, she sounded pathetic. It was all too much.

'I had to know... what you... were planning to do.' Each word seemed to take effort.

'You're hurt.' Cassie leaned forward. In the dim light, she could make out a sheen of sweat on the older woman's face.

'You were lucky, or I was unlucky. Depends... on your... point of view.'

'I can go and get help.' She'd find her car keys, drive into Hindon.

'No.' There was strength in that one word. 'It's better this way. I've failed. Let them down.'

Cassie frowned. She'd no idea what the woman was talking about, but despite everything, she felt the need to reassure her. 'I'm sure you haven't.'

'You've no idea what you're talking about, you stupid, stupid woman.'

Taken aback by the venom in the words, Cassie sat back. Everything hurt. Mrs Morgan might not want any help, but she could do with some. Sadly, it was this bloody woman Cassie would have gone to for assistance. What a terrible judge of character she was!

'It'll all come out now,' Mrs Morgan said, resignation rather than anger colouring the words.

Cassie was immediately curious. What was so important that she'd gone to such extreme measures? 'Why don't you tell me?'

'Confess so I can die with a clear conscience, you mean?'

It would teach the old bat a lesson if Cassie left her there to die alone. What an awful thought. No, she'd stay with her. Anyway, if the woman was right, if she was dying and not pretending, it seemed important to know why she'd done what she'd done. 'If you like.'

It was several minutes before Mrs Morgan spoke again and when she did, her voice was stronger. 'After the war, this house became a convent for a few years. The Sisters of Saint Joyce. Most people have forgotten about that time and I am the last of them.'

Cassie had a vague memory of reading that the house had been used as a convent. She'd dismissed the information as being of little interest. It seemed she'd been wrong, and something about that time had twisted in this poor old woman's head. 'You were a nun?'

'Not a nun, a sister. There is a subtle difference.' Mrs Morgan lifted her left hand, the gold band on her ring finger catching the light and glinting. 'People assume I'm a widow, but I was only ever married to God. I joined the convent when I was seventeen. In the fifties, when it was still regarded as a disgrace to be pregnant and unwed, the convent became a refuge for unmarried women. They came here for help...' Her voice faded and she shuffled on the ground groaning as she moved.

Cassie shifted her box closer. 'I wish you'd let me get help.'

'No.' A sigh. 'They came for help, but our mother superior felt they also needed to atone for their sin.' When she spoke again, her voice was quieter. 'They were deemed too steeped in sin to live in the main house. They slept in these cells.'

Cassie looked around the small poky room. The bars on the window. She thought of the poor frightened women who'd stayed there. 'They were locked in?'

'For their own good.'

Of course. Cassie wanted to cry.

'The mother superior considered that they needed to suffer the pain of childbirth to atone. One of the other sisters was nearby if things went wrong.'

'Nearby!' Cassie remembered the hideous cramping pains when she'd miscarried. The shock, the unbelievable sadness. Richie had been there, holding her, crying with her. And there'd been doctors, nurses, counsellors. She could only imagine the pain and terror these poor women had gone through alone.

'Unfortunately, some of the babies didn't make it. It was, the mother superior insisted, a suitable punishment for their transgressions. The mother was sent on her way, and the child was buried.'

A suitable punishment. Cassie thought of the suitcase of baby clothes. Those beautiful hand-made garments, made with such love. Had they belonged to one of these babies that hadn't made it?

'We needed to protect our work, of course, so those babies were buried here, at Hindon House.'

Cassie remembered the pet cemetery. Was there another graveyard somewhere in the grounds for the poor babies? Her eyes flicked back to the woman on the floor. She was patting the ground beside her. Cassie's eyes widened in dawning horror. 'Here? The babies are buried here?'

'Mother said it was part of the healing process for the sinful woman to bury her dead child before she left.'

The picture of a desolated, distraught woman digging a hole in the solid ground, following what was possibly a horrendous labour, made Cassie want to throw up. Mrs Morgan was still speaking, her refined voice at such odds with the ugly tale.

'I was the youngest, the rest of the sisters very elderly. Before she died, Mother made us all promise to keep our mission a secret so that the story of the Sisters of Saint Joyce would remain an honourable one. In the next few years they died and I was left alone. I was offered a home with another convent, but I chose instead to remain in Hindon. I needed to stay close, you understand, to make sure the secrets of the house were kept.' She patted the ground beside her again. 'Mostly these rooms were used for storage and our secret was safe.'

'But then the Willards wanted to do renovation, so you chased them away.'

'Being old has some advantages. People assume I'm incapable of wrong-doing, that I'm a sweet little old lady who wouldn't harm a fly. All I need to do is bake the odd cake, dress conservatively, ask the right questions. As soon as that Willard woman mentioned renovating and extending the kitchen, I knew she had to go. It didn't take long; I don't think her heart was ever really in the place.'

'You ruined those two builders, didn't you?' Cassie shook her head. How clever the woman had been. Ben Donnelly had been convinced Baker was behind his woes. She wondered if he'd believe it was all down to an innocent-looking nonagenarian.

'It wasn't hard. They had no love for the place, they simply wanted to make a quick buck by renovating and selling it on. Greed was their downfall.'

Cassie wanted to laugh at the tone of moral superiority. This from a woman who had been complicit in the appalling brutal treatment of young vulnerable women, and who had terrorised people to ensure the secret of it all was kept. 'How did you get inside; I know I locked the doors?'

'There's a trap door at the end of the corridor. There's so little light that unless you knew about it, you wouldn't see it. I could come and go as I pleased.'

'You were responsible for everything?' Cassie was still finding it difficult to reconcile the two versions of this woman – the sweet old lady and the manipulative monster. 'The trap in the attic – that was you?' Impossible, wasn't it? Maybe the woman had an accomplice. Cassie looked warily at the door, half-expecting to see someone younger and fitter suddenly appear.

The childish giggle she'd heard earlier filled the room, startling her, making her cry out. It rolled on and on, louder, more manic. A stink of fear came off Cassie in waves. It was time to get away, to run, to find her damn keys and drive away as fast as she could. Then the sound stopped as suddenly as it had begun, leaving a silence that held no comfort.

'It's a device I found on the internet,' Mrs Morgan explained quietly. 'Very effective too. When I discovered, years ago, that I could acquire whatever I needed by the mere press of a button, it was very enlightening. The circular saw I used to cut the floorboards in the attic was surprisingly easy to use.'

There was something in the calm controlled way she spoke that sent shivers of fear through Cassie. 'I could have been killed.'

'That was the idea, you stupid woman.'

38

Cassie was stunned into both silence and immobility by the venom in the harshly uttered words, unable to believe this elderly woman had wanted her dead. The light filtering through the barred window cast strange shadows on Mrs Morgan's pale face, or perhaps it was revealing what had been there all along. The nasty malevolent woman who had hidden under the little old lady guise.

'When I heard some London businesswoman had bought the house to convert into a B&B, I thought she'd be trouble. It seemed a good idea to get rid of her as quickly and efficiently as possible.' Her voice turned querulous. 'It should have worked.'

And if Cody hadn't been there to save her, it would have done. Cassie shivered when she realised how close she'd come.

'Of course, then I met you.' Mrs Morgan's sniff was audible. 'When I saw what a lightweight you were, I knew I'd have no trouble in getting rid of you.'

Cassie was tired. She'd been terrified and beaten up. Being insulted was the last straw and she lashed out. 'You didn't get rid of me though, did you? You failed. I can't believe you've done all this to protect the memory of that obviously deranged mother superior.'

Mrs Morgan shuffled closer, the anger in her words almost palpable. 'You think that's my motivation? You are even more stupid than I'd taken you for.'

This time the insult was ignored as Cassie tried to understand. 'You said it was your duty, that you promised.' Hadn't that been what Mrs Morgan had said – or at least implied? Cassie tried to rewind the conversation in her head, but too much had occurred in the last few hours, everything was a tangle.

'Yes, it is my duty, and I did promise to protect the mother superior and the Sisters of St Joyce. But there was something more important to protect. Think! All the women who buried their children here, some may be dead; some alive, but elderly; some with families who would be devastated to hear what their relative did all those years ago. It's these women I'm protecting.'

Cassie didn't believe her. These women, these poor unfortunate souls who'd trusted the Sisters of St Joyce, who'd believed they'd be helped and who'd been so dreadfully and criminally mistreated, they would never have forgotten what had happened here. If... no, when... it came out, nobody was going to judge them harshly. They'd at last be able to acknowledge their dead infants, able to grieve, get the help that they should have been given all those years before.

Mrs Morgan shuffled closer again, her foot now brushing against Cassie's. 'People always underestimate me.'

As Cassie had done – as she was still doing. She'd been lured by Mrs Morgan's breathless struggle to speak, into thinking the woman had been badly injured. That Cassie had badly injured her. Guilt and shame, she'd had a lot of that in the last few months. It had taken until today to clarify in her head what had happened all those months ago, to realise she wasn't to blame for the crash and for Richie's death. She was quicker this time, but still too late. 'I didn't hurt you at all, did I?'

A laugh bounced off the walls. 'Oh yes, you did, the blow threw me to the floor. More unfortunately, it was unexpected and painful, and I'm embarrassed to say it made me wet myself.'

The trail – it hadn't been blood at all. What a fool Cassie had been.

'I could have finished you off there and then, but although I'm strong, I didn't think I'd be able to drag your body this far, and leaving a dead body in the middle of the hallway, well, questions would be asked, wouldn't they?'

Cassie sincerely hoped so.

'It seemed a much better idea to lure you down here,' Mrs Morgan continued, satisfaction in her voice at a plan well executed. 'I knew when you came around, you'd follow my trail. You are sadly, so incredibly predictable.' She pointed to the door-way. 'From here to the trap door isn't too far. Your body will rest in peace at the bottom.'

And never be found, much like the bodies of the poor babies who lay under the floor at Cassie's feet. Unlike Richie there'd be no big funeral with friends and family mourning her loss. Instead, she'd leave behind questions and heartache. She couldn't leave it this way. Younger and fitter, she was easily a match for a nonagenarian, all she needed to do was get up and run like hell. But before she could put the thought into action and get to her feet, Mrs Morgan was on hers, something unidentifiable in her hand cutting through the dappled light and landing against the side of Cassie's head.

It might have been that her head was harder than the elderly woman had expected, or perhaps Mrs Morgan simply wasn't as strong as she believed she was, because although Cassie was felled to the ground, she wasn't knocked unconscious. Too stunned by the blow to move though, she lay face down on the ground as Mrs Morgan stepped over her body and left the room.

Too much pain and confusion. It was easier to give in to the almost comforting blackness, to give in... give up. Richie would be waiting. The thought wasn't a consolation. He hadn't wanted her in this life, she doubted he'd want her in the next. It might be better to stay and fight. If only everything didn't hurt so much.

Lying still seemed to be the best course of action. She didn't know where Mrs Morgan had gone. Perhaps she'd left, and her talk about pushing Cassie into the cellar had just been talk. Of course it had. Perhaps she wasn't a sweet little old lady, but she wasn't a monster.

It was easier to believe that, to lay still, let her body mend. She was almost lulled into relaxation, and cried out in terror when she felt hands grasp her ankles. Dust and dirt filled her eyes and mouth as she was dragged across the floor. She felt her nails breaking as she clawed helplessly, desperately seeking something, anything to grab hold of. Panic consumed her and prevented any rational thought.

Mrs Morgan's progress was slow but steady, grunts of exertion with each pull, her bony fingers biting into the flesh of Cassie's ankles.

Even if she could, there was no point in screaming, there was nobody to hear. Helplessness. Was this how those poor women had felt? Had they been left with no other choice but to do what they could to survive? Was she less a woman than they? Shouldn't she do something? She gave a yelp of pain as she was dragged through the door into the corridor outside. She knew now why Mrs Morgan had left for a few seconds; she'd gone to open the trap door. Her plan was working out just as she'd hoped and soon Cassie would be dragged to the opening and be pushed in.

Death – it would put a stop to all the pain and right at that moment, she'd have done anything, said anything to end it all. But what if the fall didn't kill her – she'd lie at the bottom for days, in agony, unable to move. Insects would scamper over her, into her mouth, her eyes. She could almost feel them, taste them. Would she be so desperate for sustenance that she'd enjoy it?

It was at that moment, when the horror of it all was cascading through her head, that she felt the grip on her ankles relax. There was no time for thought. She jerked her body around, drew back her foot and kicked. Unable to see for the dirt that stung her eyes, she kicked and kicked again before scrambling away on her hands and knees, trying to put as much distance as possible between her and the death-trap in the floor.

It was the pain in her side that brought her to a halt at the kitchen door. The morning sun was shining through the windows, lighting up the area, making everything suddenly seem so surreal. Soon, Cody's team would arrive, and the day would carry on as normal. She'd make tea and sit outside and marvel at how realistic the dream had been.

Once again, it was the pain that made her see sense. Dreams – not even nightmares – hurt this much. She needed to get to her feet, find her car keys and get out of there. Or walk, hobble, even crawl away before Mrs Morgan came for her and dragged her back. Panic surged, pushing Cassie through the door into the kitchen. She made it halfway across the floor before collapsing again, face down, tears of pain and terror dropping to the dust underneath.

Even to save her life, she couldn't move one more inch. She'd wait for Mrs Morgan to come, and this time, she'd allow herself to be dragged back and pushed through the damn trap door. There were probably steps down to the bottom, she'd bounce off them, her cracked rib would be driven through her heart or lungs, and she'd die quickly.

When she found herself wishing that Mrs Morgan would hurry up, she stopped crying. How long had it taken her to crawl to this spot? Minutes. Long enough for Mrs Morgan to follow. Perhaps one of the frantically aimed kicks had hit home and she was lying somewhere in pain. Cassie hoped so, she hoped the old bat was in agony.

This time, she wasn't going to be stupid and go to check, even if she'd been capable. This time, she was going to lie where she was and wait till the posse came to the rescue.

She must have passed out. It was the sound of wood cracking as someone broke through the back door that made her open her eyes. She raised her head to see Cody's concerned face overhead. 'I'm sorry for thinking it was you,' she muttered.

He hunkered down beside her. 'An ambulance is on the way,' he said gently. 'What the hell happened?'

Cassie winced as she turned on her side. 'I stupidly underestimated a ninety-year-old.'

39

Cassie insisted Cody help her up. He looked instantly petrified and she wondered how bad she looked. 'I think a broken rib is the worst that's wrong with me. The rest is just bruising.'

'Just bruising! You're multi-coloured. You really should wait for the ambulance.'

She needed to tell him what had happened, to warn him about Mrs Morgan – she couldn't do that from the floor. Only when he saw she wasn't going to give up, did he help her. For a big man, he was surprisingly gentle and the pain of moving from the floor to a kitchen chair wasn't too unbearable. It did, though, bring more tears.

Cody reached for a roll of kitchen paper, tore off a few sheets and handed it to her without a word. She dabbed her eyes, snuffled, and tried to speak, but when she did, emotion drowned her words. 'I'm sorry—'

'Shush. Don't waste your energy. Accidents happen.'

She wiped the paper across her eyes and nose and shook her head. 'It wasn't—'

The interruption this time came from the arrival of a Community First Responder. He bustled in, took one look at Cassie, and shook his head before attaching a tiny monitor to her finger, and asking a number of questions. 'Broken rib?'

'Yes, I've had one before so I knew what it was when it happened.'

The responder did a thorough examination, then sat back. 'There doesn't appear to be any major damage, but we take head injuries seriously. You'll need to be admitted for observation for at least twenty-four hours, okay?'

It wasn't unexpected. Only when the first responder was packing up his equipment, did Cassie point towards the doorway to the corridor. 'There's someone else who needs your help, down the end of the corridor.'

Both men looked towards the door as if expecting someone to be standing there.

'It's Mrs Morgan, Daniel. It wasn't an accident. She attacked me.'

'Mrs Morgan!' He laughed uncertainly, then looked at the responder. 'One of the women from Hindon. She's at least ninety.'

'Perhaps we should take a look.'

Obviously unwilling to argue, the two men vanished leaving Cassie sitting to await their return. When they did, the responder looked resigned as if used to dealing with confused patients and Cody looked puzzled. 'There's nobody there.'

'The stairwell. Did you check it?' Cassie remembered the frantic kicks she'd given. Had one of them hit home? Or had Mrs Morgan given up and escaped?

'I don't—'

Cassie pointed to the doorway. 'The end of the corridor, past the last door. There's a passageway down. It was hidden by a trap door. She was going to throw me down it, but I managed to escape. I kicked out...' Her voice faded.

Cody frowned and turned to the responder. 'You have a torch?'

Nodding, he turned to his equipment pack, opened it and took out a flash lamp. 'Let's go.'

They were gone for longer this time. Cassie shut her eyes and waited. What outcome was preferable? That Mrs Morgan had escaped, or that Cassie had kicked her to her death? She opened her eyes and lifted her head when she heard returning footsteps. She didn't need to ask the outcome. Their shocked pale faces told it for them. 'She's dead.'

The first responder ignored her and pulled out his phone. Cassie felt tears start again as she listened to him giving details to the call handler. She'd killed Mrs Morgan. That it was self-defence wasn't making it any easier to bear. She thought she'd been responsible for Richie's death, and she hadn't. There was no such ambiguity here. She'd kicked the woman to her death. It didn't matter that she'd been fighting for her life. *She'd kicked a woman to her death.*

Cody was shuffling from foot to foot, obviously anxious to know the truth, but afraid to ask. The tale was too long, too complicated, Cassie didn't have the strength. She'd have to tell the police, there'd be no choice then.

With Mere police station only ten minutes away, they arrived before the ambulance.

The two uniformed officers looked at Cassie with assessing eyes before following Cody down the corridor. She could hear their radios crackling, the low murmur of voices. She was almost relieved when the ambulance arrived. More relieved when the responder filled the two paramedics in, leaving her to sit quietly, floating above it all.

She must have fainted because she didn't remember moving, or being assisted onto a trolley, or being moved from the house into the ambulance. When she opened her eyes, the face looking down on her was kindly, the paramedic patting her gently on the arm. 'You'll be okay. We're taking you to Salisbury District Hospital. They'll look after you, okay?'

Cassie couldn't bring herself to speak – if she opened her mouth, she was sure a howl would be released. Tears seemed to be her fastest way of communicating. The paramedic seemed to understand, she pulled tissues from a box and folded them into Cassie's hand. 'You just hang in there, you'll be fine.'

It was a relief to see the ambulance door shutting. To not have to answer any questions. Not to be there when they took the poor broken body of Mrs Morgen from that stairwell. Cassie would have to face it all eventually. But for the moment, she was going to do what she'd wanted to do for hours and vanish into that creeping darkness.

When she woke again, she was in a bed, in a small room. An intravenous drip had been inserted into her least bruised arm. A monitor was sending out comforting regular beeps. There was nobody else there, nobody to bother her with questions. Best of all, there was no pain. Cassie shut her eyes again and vanished.

When she woke some time later, she was still in that safe, pain-free bubble. It would have been nice to have stayed there, and she might have done if she hadn't sensed a presence nearby. Reluctantly, she opened her eyes to find Cody sitting beside the bed looking tired and strained.

'Hi.'

'The doctors said you'd come around eventually, but they also said they couldn't tell me much because of patient confidentiality, so I wasn't sure they were being entirely truthful.' He offered a shaky smile. 'I'd have said I was your partner, if the nurse looking after you hadn't been the sister of a friend and would know I was lying.'

'It's kind of you to be here, you didn't have to.'

Cody sat forward and leaned his elbows on the mattress. 'The two police officers took a statement from me then said we all had to leave.' He dropped his eyes to the bed. 'They found Elsie Morgan's body exactly where you said it would be.'

Elsie Morgan. Bizarrely, Cassie had forgotten her first name. Had never asked or had been invited to use it. Odd, considering the title, Mrs, had been inaccurate for the unmarried woman. Had Mrs Morgan used it to perpetuate her harmless little old lady status? 'I thought she was a sweet little old lady who wouldn't hurt a fly.'

'She was.' He looked suddenly embarrassed, colour flushing his cheeks. 'I mean to say, I thought she was too... a sweet little old lady, I mean.' He sat back, crossed his knees, then uncrossed them again. 'I found her; you see. I took the flash lamp from the first responder and went down the stairwell, so I was the first to see her eyes. They were wide open and staring directly at me. I didn't realise she was dead till I got very close and saw how awfully twisted she was. They're doing a post-mortem, of course, but I'd say she broke her neck when she fell.'

'She dragged me from the last room and was planning to push me down, but I fought back at the last minute.' Cassie stopped, her throat thickening and those blasted tears returning. She hadn't cried this much when Richie told her he wanted a divorce. Hadn't cried nearly as much when she'd been told he'd died. 'I didn't mean to kill her, that wasn't what I'd wanted at all.'

'You don't need to explain,' Cody said. He reached for her hand and held it.

She did, she needed to make him understand why she'd done such a shocking thing. 'I didn't mean to kill her, but I did. I'm having a hard time coming to terms with that. I've no doubt the police are waiting to speak to me.'

Cody squeezed her hand gently. 'They were here about an

hour ago. The doctor who's looking after you told them you were in no fit state to talk, and asked them to come back tomorrow.'

Tomorrow. Cassie let out a long sigh of relief. 'That's good. I should feel a bit stronger by then.' She knew he was waiting for her to speak, to explain why the elderly woman had turned on her, but she wanted to wait, to allow all that had happened to settle in her head. With Mrs Morgan dead, Cassie was the only one who knew the secret of what was buried beneath the floors of those cells. She really believed it was better for the truth to come out, for those poor women to be allowed to bury their babies properly. But that was when it was Mrs Morgan's secret to keep – now it was Cassie's, and bizarrely, that changed everything.

If the truth came out, she'd have to say goodbye to her plans. The disclosure would entail a slow and painstaking excavation of the entire area. The press would descend on the place. The women, if they were still alive, would probably come, along with their relatives and legal representatives. It would be a nightmare and take weeks, months even. And afterwards? Would they accept a fancy kitchen being built on a scene of such devastation, or would they want a memorial erected in memory of their hideous shared past.

Whatever happened, weeks and months of delay would eat up her money and Cassie's dream would fail.

Maybe she should give up now, leave and take the secret with her, sell the house to Baker if he still wanted it. 'You were talking to him,' she said, shooting a suspicious glance at Cody.

He looked behind him, then back, frowning in puzzlement. 'To who?'

'Chris Baker. Outside the house.' It seemed suddenly important to know what they'd been arguing about. 'Why were you talking to him?'

Cody obviously thought it was better to humour her because

after a brief hesitation he answered. 'I don't normally talk about my business arrangements with other clients, but if you really want to know, I suppose there's no harm. Baker wants work done on the roof of the estate agent's office. He wasn't keen on the estimate I'd given him so he came to Hindon House to try to negotiate the price down.' Cody shrugged. 'We settled it amicably in the end. I'm not sure why you want to know.'

She shook her head. 'It doesn't matter.' How stupid she'd been. All the grief she'd caused herself with her suspicions.

Cody pressed her hand again. 'Everything is going to be okay.'

He had no idea. Nobody had. Cassie was now the keeper of the secret, and she hadn't the energy to decide what to do. All she seemed able to do was cry.

'As soon as the crime scene people are finished, we'll get back to work. Stu told me you wanted to get that kitchen sorted, so we'll make a start on that.'

He said it as if it was what she would want to hear, and was startled when she sat upright, a look of horror on her face. 'No, you can't.' She collapsed back and shut her eyes. 'I mean, I'm not sure... I've been rethinking what to do with those rooms... leave it, go back to the original plan and get the other rooms finished. Maybe the attic conversion, it would be good to have that done. But I think it's best to leave it for a few days.' The words came out in a torrent, leaving her exhausted. 'I'm sorry,' she said. 'It's all too much, I can't seem to think straight.' And she needed to, needed to decide what to do. Tell the police the truth, or keep the secret.

'No, it's me who should be apologising.' He rubbed a hand over his head, mussing his already untidy hair. 'I've known Elsie Morgan forever. She was as much part of the Hindon landscape as The Lamb. After you left, I called Patrick and he came over. He waited till they brought her up and gave her a last blessing.'

A last blessing! The old bat had tried to kill her.

Cody didn't seem to realise he'd offended Cassie. 'They were quite close, you see. You wouldn't guess from seeing him now, but Patrick went through difficult times in his late teens. I was away in university; my parents were always busy, so I think he ran wild for a bit. When he started to talk about the priesthood, the parents thought it was a phase, but Mrs Morgan listened to him. I think she might have even encouraged him. It was the saving of Patrick, you know, he was a changed person afterwards. He and Mrs Morgan have remained close since.'

'Priests and sisters have a lot in common.' She saw his surprise. 'You didn't know she'd been a sister?'

He laughed. 'She never!'

Cassie was tired, she didn't want to argue with him, or explain. She didn't want to talk any more and shut her eyes hoping he'd get the hint. Maybe it was the pain relief they'd given her, or sheer exhaustion, whatever the reason, shutting her eyes had a two-fold effect – it sent her to sleep and got rid of Cody.

40

The doctor reassured Cassie that she'd sustained no lasting damage, but insisted they needed to keep her for twenty-four hours because of the blow to her head. She borrowed a phone from reception and rang her parents and friends, giving as little information as she could get away with, promising them she'd fill in the details later.

She didn't sleep well. The hospital room was quiet, but there was constant foot-traffic on the corridor outside, the murmur of voices, the jangle of equipment. And enough thoughts swirling in her head to make her dizzy. One haunted her. The vision of a sad bewildered young woman being forced to bury the body of her dead baby.

Tell the police the truth or keep the secret. It would destroy her financially if it got out, but wouldn't it destroy her mentally if it didn't?

When the clock over the door ticked to five, she decided that was time served. She was tempted to use the shower, but that would have meant asking a nurse to replace the dressings that covered the multiple grazes and they might try to persuade her to stay. So she ignored the shower and pulled on the dirt-smeared clothes she'd worn on admission. Some of the stains looked to be of dubious origin. It made sense not to look at them too closely.

When she was dressed, she left the room and wandered in search of the nurses' station. It was halfway along the corridor and staffed by a bleary-eyed young nurse who looked at Cassie in puzzlement.

'I'm feeling fine, there's no repercussions from the bang to my head, so I'm going to head off, okay?'

'It's not even five thirty,' he said, checking his watch. 'You sure you don't want to wait till after breakfast?'

'Positive, thank you. I would be grateful if you could get a taxi for me though.'

'Sure.' He reached for the phone. 'Hi, can we have a taxi from Salisbury District Hospital to...?' He raised an eyebrow.

'Hindon House.'

'... Hindon House.' The nurse put the phone down. 'He said it'll be here in fifteen minutes.' He jerked a thumb to the room behind. 'The kettle's just boiled, would you like a coffee while you're waiting?'

'No, thanks, I'll head to the exit. I could do with some fresh air. Thank you for all your care.' Seeing a worried expression appear on his face, she hurried away before he could come up with rules and regulations and insist she needed to go by wheelchair, or that she should be accompanied. She was fine, she wanted to get back to Hindon House to see if she could make some sense of things before the police arrived.

The taxi came on time and she climbed in, ignoring the driver's shocked expression when he saw the state of her. She'd seen her face in the bathroom mirror, it was not a pretty sight.

It was a thirty-minute drive, and the road to Hindon wound

and twisted. Strapped into the back seat, Cassie swayed gently and before long was fast asleep.

'Here you are.'

She woke, startled and disorientated. Outside the car window, all she could see was green. It took a few seconds, and a loud throat clearing by the driver before she realised where she was. At the front gate of Hindon House. She hadn't thought to tell him to go around to the back entrance.

'That'll be twenty quid.'

There didn't appear to be a meter running, but it sounded a fair amount to Cassie. There was one big problem though, she didn't have any money. 'I need to get my bag,' she explained, and pointed further down the road. 'If you take the next turn, we'll be able to use the back gate. It's nearer to the house, I can pop in, get my bag, and pay you.'

Five minutes later, Cassie was at the back door. Only then did it hit her that the police may have locked the door behind them. The key had been in the lock: it would have been the sensible thing to do. The police would have locked it and taken the key with them. She wasn't sure how she was going to explain to the driver that she couldn't pay him.

Perhaps he could drive her to the police station in Mere. But they'd want to talk to her and she wasn't ready. She was almost crying in frustration when she twisted the doorknob, almost laughing in relief when it turned easily and the door opened. Her bag was where she'd left it a lifetime ago. Before she'd kicked an old woman to her death.

She gave the driver twenty-five and waited while he drove away before turning back to look at the house. All the hopes and dreams she'd had when she arrived, the optimism for the future, all seemed soured. If she kept the house's secret, would she be able to continue with her plans?

Did she want to?

Maybe she'd feel a little bit better after something to eat and, with a weary sigh, she headed inside. Food was the last thing on her mind though as she stood in the kitchen. The fear, the absolute terror she'd experienced, seemed to linger in the air. She shivered and wrapped her arms around herself, wincing as she pressed against the broken rib.

Maybe the stink was simply wafting from her clothes. She'd change into something clean, dump these in the skip.

The door from the kitchen was shut. Cassie was tempted to go out the back door and come in through the front to avoid having to pass by the corridor. It was silly. That bloody woman couldn't hurt her any more.

The picture of Elsie Morgan's broken body lying on the bottom of the stairwell popped into her head. In Cassie's imagination there was a look of despair on the older woman's face. Had she known she'd failed as she tumbled to her death?

Cassie took a deep breath and twisted the doorknob, pushing the door open before she changed her mind. It was several seconds before she could take a step forward. Her eyes were fixed on the stairway ahead. She should have kept them there, she most definitely shouldn't have turned to look down the corridor.

It was dark. There was nothing to see. Yet, as she continued to stare, her eyes adjusting to the lack of light, she could make out the trap door resting against the wall behind. In front of it, hidden in shadow was the huge dark maw she'd kicked the ninety-year-old woman through. An old woman who'd spent most of her life keeping the house and its secret safe from people like Cassie.

Dragging herself away, she headed up the two flights of stairs, one weary step at a time. Rather than putting clean clothes on over her stinking body, she took them down with her and strip washed at the kitchen sink. It wasn't a shower, but it was her only option and she felt better afterwards, cleaner, almost normal. She took the dirty clothes outside and tossed them into the skip.

Back in the kitchen she stood and looked around restlessly. It struck her that she had no way of contacting the police to tell them she'd come home. They'd arrive at the hospital expecting to talk to her and be miffed to find her gone. It was only a little after seven, and she guessed they wouldn't appear for hours yet.

Unable to settle, she walked back up to the hallway, wandered into the sitting room, the lounge, the dining room, trying to recover some of the excitement she'd once had. Was it all spoilt or could she recover some of the magic?

She moved to the bay window and looked at the overgrown gardens. All the plans she'd had. If she exposed the secret, she'd be left with nothing and would have to start all over. Louise or Toni would happily put her up – for a while. So would her parents, albeit more reluctantly: they didn't want a boomerang child scuppering their freedom.

And if she kept it – if she took over Mrs Morgan's role of keeper of the house and its secrets, if she built her future on the graves of babes, how could she live with herself?

She slammed a hand on the window, then rested her forehead against the cold glass. In a minute, she'd go and take a couple of painkillers, maybe when she didn't hurt, it would be easier to decide.

Her forehead was still resting on the window when she heard something she shouldn't have done. Footsteps on the floor above. She straightened in alarm. The house had been left unsecured. Maybe some opportunistic burglar was taking advantage. She glanced towards the kitchen. Her car keys hadn't been in her handbag but they were there somewhere. She'd find them, get the hell out of there. Drive to Mere police station. Tell them everything.

No time though. The footsteps were moving. Fast. The top of the stairs was hidden from view and whoever was there was descending. She'd delayed too long. Now she was trapped.

The length of wood she'd picked up to defend herself not much more than twenty-four hours earlier was lying where she dropped it. She hurried over, bent, and picked it up as the footsteps reached the hallway.

Too late to hide. Too hurt to run. She stood and waited. When the man appeared in the open doorway, she almost fainted with relief. Cody!

41

'I wasn't expecting to see you here,' Cassie said, dropping the piece of wood to the floor, embarrassed to have been so nervous. 'You startled me. I suppose I'm still on edge.' She smiled uncertainly when he stood without speaking. Was he blaming her for Elsie Morgan's death? She'd explain, then he'd understand. She took a step forward, and only then discovered her error. Like Cody, but not him.

'Patrick?' She shook her head and smiled. 'I'm sorry, in this light you look more like your brother. Are you looking for him? I wasn't expecting him today. I think I'm going to need a day or two to see where I go from here.'

'After killing Elsie, you mean.'

Cassie felt the blood drain from her face. Once the truth came out, everyone would know they'd been fooled by the old woman, like she had. Until then, she supposed she'd have to accept a similar reaction from people.

'After Mrs Morgan tried to kill me. That's the truth, Patrick. It'll all come out. The police are coming to talk to me later, everything will be clear then.' She offered him a sympathetic smile. 'I'm sorry, Daniel said you and she had been close.'

He took a step towards her. She resisted the temptation to step back. He was hurting and needed sympathy. 'When you hear it all, you'll understand, I hope. I was defending myself, but I never meant to kill her, I was simply trying to escape, to prevent her killing me. I kicked out in the dark. I don't know if it sent her into the stairwell, or whether I made her trip and then she fell—'

He held a hand up to stop her. 'Either way, you're responsible for her death. A frail ninety-year-old woman.'

'There was nothing frail about her! She did this.' Cassie brushed fingers over her bruised face. 'Then when I was lying stunned, she dragged me across the floor. She'd have thrown me down that stairwell if I hadn't managed to free myself. She was a bloody monster!'

The slap that hit her across the face shocked rather than hurt. She held a hand against her cheek and looked at him in horror. 'You must believe me. She was waging a terror campaign to frighten me from here. She'd even boobytrapped the attic, cut into the floorboards so that I'd fall through and either injure or kill myself.' She huffed a laugh of disbelief, still trying to come to terms with how Mrs Morgan had so completely fooled her. 'She admitted that the plan had been to kill me. Can you believe it?' There was no softening in Patrick's expression. She took a step closer, rested a hand on his arm. 'I'm sorry, your brother said you were close, and this must be a terrible shock for you.' She didn't seem to be getting through to him. 'She's been hiding a secret. All these years. About what's buried under the floor in the cells along the corridor behind the kitchen.'

'She told you that.'

Cassie heard the devastation in his voice and pressed his arm gently. 'I'm so sorry. It's hard when our heroes turn out to have feet of clay.'

He laid his hand over hers, then totally unexpectedly he closed his fingers around her hand and squeezed. She could feel the bones of her hand crunching and squealed in pain. 'You're hurting me.'

He didn't let go. Instead, he moved away, dragging her behind him. She tried to keep up, tripping and sliding on the floor, afraid to fall, terrified her broken rib would shoot through her heart like a spear. 'Patrick, let me go, what are you doing?'

When he stopped and turned to her, his face had darkened in anger, eyes glinting. 'Did you really think Elsie could cut through those floorboards with such precision? Are you really that fucking thick?'

The obscenity was all the more startling coming from the lips of a priest. Looking at him, feeling the pain shooting up her arm, she realised she was *exactly* that fucking thick. She'd believed every word Mrs Morgan had told her. Worse, believed that she was the only keeper of the house's secrets. 'You know about the babies.' It wasn't a question; she could see the truth on his face. 'You were the one who set that trap in the attic.'

'You bloody people with your fancy ideas of doing this place up, you couldn't just fuck off and buy a new house somewhere else and leave this place to be swallowed up by the weeds.'

Pain could focus, but the one sending shooting darts up her arm, and making sweat ping on her forehead, was crippling her mind. 'Isn't it better if it comes out, and those poor women are able to bury their babies at last? Able to grieve.'

'Those women! Who cares about them?' He laughed. 'Is that what Elsie told you, that she was doing all this to protect those stupid women?'

Cassie blinked. Was she misremembering? Or had Mrs

Morgan lied about this as she had about other things? 'Why then? Why all the lies, the intimidation, the desperate need to keep people from finding out the truth?'

Patrick reached with his free hand to touch the white collar that advertised his calling. 'I was lost, drifting, unable to meet my parents' expectations or compete with my clever older brother. I was spaced out on something one day...' He frowned, trying to remember what it had been, then shrugged. 'No matter, but I was lucky, I'd taken shelter in the church. There was a service on, and I sat in the back pew and listened.'

Cassie watched his expression change, the scary anger fading to be replaced by something she found more terrifying, an expression of religious fervour verging on – no, steeped in – fanaticism.

'Like Paul on his way to Damascus, I had an epiphany. The priest on the altar was glowing, holding his hand out to me. In that moment, I knew I'd found my home.'

He'd been high – and had switched one drug for another. The *opium of the masses* as Karl Marx had called religion. Patrick wouldn't be the first to fall under its spell. Had his parents been relieved to see their wayward son saved, or had they worried about his newfound zeal? They should have been. So much harm was done in the name of religion.

The church had been rocked by one scandal after the other for years. None was ever going to destroy it, but each had dented its moral authority. Patrick, it appeared, had taken on the role of guardian. 'So all this was done for the good of the Church?'

He touched his collar again, as if it was a talisman, as if the wearing of it gave him the authority to do whatever he considered needed doing. 'Those women,' – the dismissive sneer in his voice saying clearly what he thought of them, – 'were sent to the Sisters of St Joyce by priests in surrounding parishes. It was for their good, and for that of their families. They were different times. The sisters would have done their best.'

Cassie wondered if he knew exactly what had gone on. Perhaps Mrs Morgan had spared him the details. But then she saw it in his face, in the hardness in his eyes. He knew, he simply didn't care, only that it shouldn't reflect badly on the Church. 'So what now?'

He looked down on her. The light of fervour was gone and his eyes were filled with sympathy. 'Elsie should never have made you privy to the secret, it was unusually careless of her.'

There didn't seem to be any point in telling him that the old bat had planned to kill Cassie after her revelation. She was in enough trouble without goading him. Her hand was still being squeezed painfully; she wasn't sure she could pull it from his grasp. Anyway, in her state, she'd not be able to run far before being overtaken.

'I think you know that I have no choice, that what I do, I do for the greater good.'

Not for her good though, Cassie guessed. She was to be sacrificed for the church. Martyred. She remembered religious education classes in school and being fascinated by women who had been martyred for a cause. Fascinated – it didn't mean she wanted to take her place among their ranks.

If she couldn't escape, she needed to try reasoning with him. 'Isn't murder against the teachings of the church?'

'I have taken vows of poverty, chastity and obedience,' he intoned. 'The vow of obedience means I need to put the good of the church before my personal welfare. It is for that reason that you must die.'

'You don't want to do this. I promise, I'll keep the secret. I'm not going to proceed with the B&B idea either. I'll sell up, and you'll never see me again.' She frowned in sudden puzzlement. 'If the church was so desperate to hide what had happened here, why didn't they simply buy the place?'

His fingers tightened on her hand making her squeal. 'That was the plan but you outbid me.'

Patrick, not Daniel Cody. She'd got so many things wrong. 'I'll sell it to you now. And leave. I promise.'

'No, it's better this way.'

Panic reared its ugly head. 'They'll be suspicious... the police... they'll be here soon. When they find me dead, they'll investigate.'

His smile was feral. Cassie suddenly realised he was enjoying it all. He might believe what he was doing was for the good of the church, but it wasn't. He enjoyed the power he had over her.

'Daniel told me how guilty you felt about Elsie's death. When the police come, when they find your broken body at the bottom of the stairwell – the very stairwell where you pushed her to her death – they'll assume you couldn't handle it, that you took the easy way out.'

Cassie imagined the scene, her poor sad broken body, the police shaking their heads, the villagers thinking she'd got her just rewards for having killed Elsie Morgan. That's the way the story would go – the way it would end. She wished now she'd told Cody everything yesterday. That the truth was known, the secrets out.

If this were a movie, or even a damn book, someone would ride to the rescue – Cody, perhaps coming to see if she was okay, the police arriving efficiently early. Ride to the rescue. Gallant knights on white chargers to her victimised helpless female.

She felt a tug on her mangled hand. It was time.

As she was pulled across the hallway, she thought once again of those poor women who had been marched into the cells to sit and wait for the inevitable outcome of their sin. The unjust punishment that had been meted out to them. Had they simply accepted it, or had they railed against the unfairness of it all? And what, Cassie wondered, had happened to the babies who'd survived?

More secrets and lies.

She was going willingly to her death. Shouldn't she fight? If not for herself, for them – the babies who died, the poor mothers who'd been forced to bury them.

Even in the full of her health, physically she was no match for Patrick. It was time to use her feminine wiles. She stopped pulling against him and kept her eyes down when he glanced in her direction. Let him think she had given up. That she too had accepted her fate.

Across the hallway, down the stairs. Almost hand in hand, and side by side. When they reached the entrance to the corridor, with no space for them to continue together, he took a step forward. Her hand was relaxed in his as she allowed herself to be led, one step forward, then a second.

Patrick was humming.

Humming!

It was time, she pulled her hand free, turned and ran, through the kitchen door, across the kitchen wrenching open the back door and running, breath heaving, eyes darting in their search for a hiding place, hearing heavy footsteps in pursuit. They were closing on her.

'You're never going to get away from me!'

Perhaps, but she was damned if she was going to go like a lamb to the slaughter. She was going to make every second count in her attempt to escape. She had one advantage. She knew the garden. Ducking under branches, she ran into the pet cemetery, skipping over the rock she'd fallen over on her first visit, praying that this time, it would be he who'd trip, he who would suffer an injury. She wondered if Patrick was praying to the same god, and wondered, bizarrely, who would be listened to.

Then he was right behind her. A hand snaked forward to grab her but she darted out of reach, her lungs burning as she tried to speed up. She heard him growl, reach again, his fingers closing over her T-shirt, then slipping off as she put on another burst of speed.

If she could just make it to the other side of the cemetery, to the exit through the old wall. She was in luck. Behind her she heard Patrick stumble. It slowed him down but also seemed to re-energise him because when he regained his footing he quickly caught up.

But the opening was just ahead, and Cassie knew something about it that he didn't. Gasping, she swung through, then grabbed the heavy wrought-iron barred gate and jammed it shut. Running head first, as he was, it hit him on the forehead, the crack gunshot loud in the silence.

Then, as Cassie stared in horror, he collapsed against the gate, and slid down it, the weight of his body pushing it open. It swung back into her hand. She held it, ready to use the makeshift weapon again if he should stir, but he didn't move.

Mrs Morgan had tried the same trick; Cassie wasn't being so easily fooled this time. She stood, heart racing, and watched for several minutes, before releasing her grip on the gate and taking a step closer to him, half expecting, as in the best creepy movie, for his hand to snake out and grab her ankle. It didn't. Nothing moved.

She hunkered down beside him. His head was twisted, his neck exposed. She rested two fingers against his jugular expecting to feel a weak pulse. When she felt nothing, she pressed harder, and when there was still nothing, not the faintest trickle, she sat back, stunned.

A wave of weakness hit her, knocking her sideways so that she lay on the ground beside him, her cheek in the dirt, eyes wide and unseeing.

How long did she lie there? Later when the police asked, she was unable to answer. Minutes, an hour, a long time, she'd no idea. Had she lost consciousness? No idea. Or had she simply succumbed to an overwhelming shock at the thought she'd killed two people in the same amount of days.

Eventually, she did scramble slowly to her feet, avoiding touching the body that lay nearby, her nose crinkling at the body fluids that were already leaking from it.

Her exertions to escape had wrenched every already-aching muscle and her movements were slow and painful as she stepped over the body and made her way back to the house. There, she sank onto a chair, bent her arms, rested them on the table then lay her head on them.

And that's where the police found her some time later.

42

Within an hour of the arrival of the police, hordes of people descended on Hindon House and Cassie had told her story twice. She'd managed to hold it together, even in the face of the first two officers' disbelief when she told them she'd killed Father Patrick Cody in self-defence.

She held it together during that telling of her long and somewhat rambling tale, and the following more detailed account she gave to two other detectives whose names she instantly forgot.

It wasn't until she saw Cody's car pulling through the gate that she allowed tears to come, only briefly, pulling herself together as she watched him climb out. He didn't approach immediately, his eyes sweeping the scene, taking in the array of people who bustled about. Pale and stony-faced, he leaned on the car door as if gathering strength.

Cassie felt her lower lip tremble and pressed her lips together. She'd liked to have run away, but she owed it to Cody to face him. To try to explain; to make him understand that she hadn't meant to kill his brother. Or Mrs Morgan. She felt a wave of nausea hit her and shut her eyes. When she opened them again, she saw

Cody had pushed away from the car and was crossing towards her. He kept his head bowed, as if reluctant to meet her eyes.

When the two detectives would have prevented him getting closer, she held up a hand. 'Please, I'd like to speak to him.'

Cody hovered for a few seconds before taking the seat opposite. 'Is it true?'

That his brother was dead, or that she'd killed him? It didn't really matter; the answer was the same to both. 'Yes.' Her mouth was dry and she hurt. She wanted to go inside, get a drink, take some painkillers, hide away until everything was over, then hide away some more. Somewhere far away.

Instead, she stumbled through her tale yet again. Explaining what Elsie Morgan had told her, the secrets she'd been keeping for all the years. 'If only I'd told you when you visited me in the hospital, or if I'd spoken to the police while I was there.' There was no point in admitting that she hadn't, at that stage, been sure if she was going to expose the horrors of Hindon House or not. If she'd spoken out, Patrick would still be alive; she was going to carry that guilt with her. 'If I had revealed Mrs Morgan's secret, your brother would have had no reason to do what he did. He wanted the truth to stay hidden. I tried to convince him that I would stay quiet, but he didn't believe me. He thought he had no choice but to get rid of me.' Cassie lifted her head and took a deep breath. 'And although I never intended to kill him, I had no choice but to do what I did.' She'd caused enough pain, she wasn't going to mention the cruelty in Patrick's eyes or his feral smile. When Cody made no comment, his eyes still fixed on the length of the table between them, she spoke again, 'Mrs Morgan said she was trying to protect the women who'd buried their children here, but your brother said he wanted to protect the church. Different motives, but with one aim. To keep that secret.'

Cody still sat with his head bowed.

Cassie would have liked to have gone to him, put an arm around his shoulders, allowed the queued-up tears of sorrow for what she'd done to fall and join in with his tears of loss. But there was a deep chasm between them that was unlikely ever to be bridged. 'I'm sorry. I was only trying to stop him. I never thought...' Her voice faded away. When she'd escaped from Mrs Morgan's clutches, she'd never expected the kick to send her to her death, and when she'd slammed that gate on Patrick Cody, she hadn't planned on killing him. Yet, both were dead. By her hand.

Perhaps when they excavated the floor in the cells and found the bodies of the babies, she'd be vindicated and the corroding guilt would ease. She'd done nothing wrong – all she'd wanted to do was to take a neglected old house and breathe life into it, make it live again, give herself a future.

Even if Cody could be persuaded to forgive her – to understand she'd had no choice – she couldn't expect him to continue working for her. Not that it mattered, that boat had sailed, and her dreams for a future in Hindon had been on it.

She waited for Cody to make a comment, but when he did, she was surprised.

'I told you Patrick had run wild when he was younger but I made it sound like it was the usual teenage high jinks. It wasn't. He had serious issues with both alcohol and drugs. My parents were talking about sending him to rehab when he suddenly changed. He'd found God. I think we were all so relieved, that we refused to see that he'd simply switched one addiction for another. Nor did any of us ever question his relationship with Elsie Morgan, a woman over fifty years his senior.

'He wouldn't ever listen to a bad word said about the Church, not even when the scandals over child abuse were unfolding. He'd get a certain glint in his eyes and would, very quietly, verbally annihilate whoever dared to criticise it. After a while, we didn't bother, but we should have done, should have seen there was something a little dark under his fervour.' Cody put a hand on the table and pushed to his feet. 'I must go, be with Mum and Dad.'

'Tell them I'm sorry.' Cassie saw him hesitate, then nod, but she knew he wouldn't tell them, wouldn't mention her name. She wasn't sure she blamed him.

More people came and went. Occasionally one would fire a question at her.

'What's the foundation in the cells made from?'

'Stone and mortar,' she said. 'With a compacted clay layer on top.' She remembered reading it in the details before she bought the house. It was an old, relatively efficient process.

'How many babies did she say had been buried under it?'

Cassie wanted to scream that she didn't know. It hadn't been her secret. Except with the priest and Mrs Morgan dead, she *had* been the keeper of the secrets, the keeper of the house. And she'd spilled them all.

'You won't be able to stay here tonight, I'm afraid.' Cassie looked up to see the kindly face of the first police officer who'd arrived what felt like hours before.

Cassie didn't think she'd ever be able to stay in the house again. However many babies were buried beneath the cell floors, the house now felt more like a mausoleum, not a home. Even after they'd exhumed the bodies, when the various people had left, when the press had moved on to the next big story, she didn't think her feelings towards it would change.

When she could, she'd talk to Baker, and ask him to sell it as soon as he could. It would be at a loss, no doubt, assuming he could find a purchaser. Or maybe, at last, he'd buy it himself.

The police officer was waiting for her response. 'I understand,'

Cassie said. 'If someone would come with me, I'll gather some belongings and try to get a room in the town for a few nights.'

His face creased in sympathy. 'I can ring The Lamb, if you like, see if they have a room?'

Why not? After all, she wouldn't need to spend any further money on renovations. 'Thank you, that'd be very kind.'

So it was that forty minutes later, she was parking her car in the small car park opposite The Lamb. She'd packed a holdall with a selection of clothes, choosing willy-nilly. The couple of pills she'd taken before she'd left weren't making inroads into her many aches and pains and she bit back a groan as she climbed from the car.

She lifted the bag from the boot and crossed the quiet road to the front door of The Lamb. If the staff knew anything about what had happened, it wasn't obvious in their friendly courteous greeting, and when they asked if she wanted a hand with her bag, she handed it over with a relieved smile.

They'd only had the one room available, and she was almost amused to see it had a four-poster bed. It also had a Nespresso machine with a generous supply of pods and a tray holding little packets of biscuits. Should she have the need for something stronger than coffee, the fridge was well stocked with wine and spirits.

She didn't leave the room for the next two days. And nobody called. She rang her parents and told them the whole sorry tale before they could read about it in the national papers. She was grateful and touched when they volunteered to come down.

'No, that's fine, don't worry, Louise will come, she can be here within a couple of hours. I just need her number again, please.' Cassie scribbled the number down. The lie reassured her parents, and she hung up with a sigh. The call to Louise took longer: she wasn't so easily palmed off. 'It's in all the papers,' she said, 'I tried to ring you, several times. I was going to ring your parents, but I didn't want to worry them.'

'I'm fine, honestly. I know you have a million questions, and I promise I'll answer them all, just not now, okay? I'm going to get a new phone tomorrow; I'll ring everyone then.'

'You sure you don't want me to come down?'

'You're a sweetheart, Louise, but no, thanks, really. I'm sleeping mostly. My body's way of recovering.'

A heavy sigh drifted down the line. 'Right, I'm not sure I believe you, but you know where I am if you need me.'

'I do, and I will. I'm going to need a place to stay for a while, I can't stay in Hindon.'

'Of course not!' Louise sounded horrified at the thought. 'Come here, for as long as you want, we'd love to have you.'

Cassie hung up with a smile.

On the third day, before she could leave to shop for a new phone, she had two visitors, the first expected, the second a surprise.

43

Cassie's first visit was from the police. They came for two reasons. To get her to sign the statements she'd made, and to update her on the progress of the exhumation.

They sat opposite her in the bedroom's small seating area, knees almost touching.

'I can make coffee, if you'd like,' she said pointing to the Nespresso machine. 'It's good stuff.'

Both men shook their heads. 'I'm all coffee'd out,' one said with a smile. 'We are grateful you're giving us free rein in Hindon House and wanted to keep you in the loop.' He opened a file he was holding and handed her a photograph.

Surprised, Cassie took it, then gasped. 'How many?' she said, staring at the image of the tiny skeleton.

'It's a slow process. So far, we've only finished one room. The skeletons of two babies were found there.' He returned the photo to the file. 'You might also like to know that since it's been in the papers, we've had a couple of calls from women who say they'd given birth in Hindon House, and how they'd been forced to bury their dead infant. Each has spoken of their relief that the story is out. They've asked us to pass on their gratitude to everyone involved.' He smiled. 'That definitely means you.'

Cassie felt her eyes fill. 'It's an oft abused word, but I think getting closure is important.'

'They'll be supported, counselled, whatever they need. The Church is falling over itself with offers of assistance.'

She brushed an angry hand over her eyes. 'Taking responsibility for their crimes, eh?' There was no hiding the bitterness in her words, but then she'd been in those cells, she'd heard what those women had been through. She'd seen that suitcase packed with tiny little garments.

'There is no evidence that what occurred in Hindon House was ever common knowledge,' the officer said calmly. 'Mrs Morgan kept the secrets of the house well. We think she only involved Father Cody to ensure they were kept after her demise.' He got to his feet, the second officer following suit. 'We'll keep you abreast of the investigation as much as we can.'

* * *

Twenty minutes later, when she was thinking about doing that trip to Salisbury to replace her phone, there was another knock on her door.

Expecting it to be housekeeping, she opened it with a smile. It died quickly when she saw Daniel Cody.

'May I come in?'

She hesitated too long.

'I'm not going to hurt you,' he said with a flash of anger. 'I need to talk to you, and a hotel corridor isn't the place for it.'

'Yes, of course, sorry, come in.' She stood to one side as he passed by. 'I didn't think you were going to hurt me. I was simply puzzled to see you there.' She waved to a chair. 'Have a seat.

Would you like some coffee?' All so bloody cordial, as if she'd hadn't killed his brother only days before.

He didn't seem to see anything amiss. 'Coffee would be good.' He was dressed, appropriately, in black. It emphasised his pallor. He seemed to have lost weight in the few days since she'd last seen him. Maybe like her, he couldn't bring himself to eat.

The coffee gurgled into cups. She remembered the way he liked it and added milk and sugar. 'Here you go.' She added a drop of milk to hers and sat opposite him.

She wanted to ask how he was coping; how his parents were doing. But she'd no right to ask either. They weren't friends, and now, never would be. It seemed better to stay silent and let him get to whatever he'd come for. She sipped coffee she hadn't wanted and waited for him to speak. After all, it wasn't as if she'd anything to rush away for, no house to renovate, no dream to make come true.

Her small coffee cup was empty before he spoke. 'We – my parents and I – we want you to know we don't blame you for what happened. We were always aware that his devotion to the Church bordered on fanaticism, we simply didn't consider that it might be harmful.'

Cassie couldn't bring herself to comment. That they weren't blaming her might eventually help her to forgive herself.

Cody was still playing with the cup he held. 'I called out to the house yesterday. They'd just exhumed the first baby's skeleton.' He shook his head slowly. 'It was so tiny.'

'The police were here a little while ago. It seems some of the mothers have already come forward. They'll be given support, help, whatever they need.'

'Good.' He put the cup down. 'I've had a long conversation with the bishop. In view of... everything... the Church has decided it would be best if you'd sell the house and land to them. They're willing to give you the full amount you paid, plus your expenditure to date and compensation for all you've been put through. It means you can buy somewhere else.'

Cassie was speechless. 'I wasn't sure what I was going to do. I knew I wouldn't be able to stay around here. This will make it so much easier.'

He put the cup down on a side table and got to his feet. 'You've got a lot of vision. You'll find somewhere else and do well.'

She stood and walked with him to the door. 'Thank you. Do you know what the Church will do with the house?'

'No idea. Not sure they can do anything with it for a while. It'll be a place of pilgrimage for some people for a time, and it'll draw those who relish in the misery of others, but like most things, the attention will fade. Then maybe they'll do something with it.' He put a hand on the door and looked down at her. 'Goodbye, Cassie. Mind yourself.'

She rested her forehead against the door after he'd left, feeling stupidly weepy. They might have had a chance together. Now, she'd have to find the strength to start all over again.

That made her smile and push away from the door. She'd find the strength.

Bloody hell, she'd survived the attempts by two fanatics to kill her.

She could survive anything.

44

Eight babies were recovered from beneath the floors of the cells. For a time, it became a place of pilgrimage for mothers who had contacted the police with their sad stories. These, by now elderly women, were finally able to bury their dead babies properly, and were able to grieve. Four of the exhumed infants remained unidentified, unclaimed and were reburied with great fanfare by the Church.

Cassie stayed at The Lamb, eating in her room, having long conversations on her new phone with shocked and stunned friends. They wanted to come, to be with her, but she'd pleaded for time to come to terms with what she'd done.

She finally returned the call to Jenny Willard. 'Hi,' she said when it was answered on the first ring. 'It's Cassie Macreddin, I rang last week—'

'I've seen the papers,' Jenny interrupted her. 'You poor thing, what a nightmare you've been through. And Elsie Morgan, of all people! She was so good to me, made me cakes, invited me around for tea. I thought she was such a sweet little old lady.'

Home-made cakes and china teacups! What a disguise it had been. 'She had everyone fooled.'

'When I read about the issues you had, I was stunned. We had an almost similar experience: lights going out, taps left running, equipment disappearing. At first, we were blaming each other, you know. By the time we began to wonder if there was someone trying to cause us trouble, it didn't matter. We wanted out.' A long sigh came down the line. 'That house was so filled with sadness. Now I know why.'

Cassie remembered the suitcase of baby clothes. It was still in the bedroom where she'd left it. She was glad now she'd not brought it with her. A suitcase full of sorrow and regret. A bit like her life. Lost babies, lost love, lost dreams.

She muted the phone and gasped her pain as Jenny chatted away oblivious, and when the conversation tailed away, Cassie clicked back in to say goodbye.

Her nights were interrupted by visions of her running. Sometimes she was caught by gnarled fingers that dragged her to her death. She'd wake with a scream that bounced off the walls, reverberating as she lay in the dark with wide eyes.

Sometimes she woke with guilt squeezing her so tightly she couldn't breathe.

Once, she'd woken in a mess of guilt and confusion thinking she'd killed Richie, relieved to remember she hadn't been responsible, enjoying a moment's relief before remembering she *had* killed Elsie Morgan and Patrick Cody.

Not deliberately, and in self-defence, but no matter how many times she told herself that, the guilt didn't ease. She wasn't sure it ever would.

She never saw Daniel Cody again. It was a solemn-faced solicitor from Salisbury who handled all the legal requirements of the sale and expedited the transfer of Hindon House to the Church.

Curious to know their plans, she asked if he knew what they were, but he merely shrugged and said he wasn't aware of any.

Two weeks after Patrick Cody had tried to kill her, and before the last of the babies had been exhumed, she packed up her belongings and left The Lamb. Any personal items she'd left behind in Hindon House could be disposed of, she'd no desire to return.

A few miles from the village, she slowed down, did a U-turn and headed back. She parked where she had that first day – aeons ago – unlocked the padlock, pushed open the gate and walked a little way along the drive until she had a view of Hindon House. She'd tried to convince herself it would be a happy place, but now she realised, even then, she'd been fooling herself. She'd seen what she wanted to see, rather than what was before her eyes, that the house, even from this distance, looked to be a grim property, ivy growing from its windows like tears.

Something evil had been done inside its walls, and no amount of redecorating or renovating was going to clear away the air of malevolence that lingered, or the sadness that had wicked up from beneath the floors to seep into every corner of the house. Even without Mrs Morgan's intervention, Cassie guessed she would eventually have left as previous owners had done.

She'd have taken a financial hit if she had done so. Now, thanks to the Church's guilty generosity, she was well set up to start again somewhere else. It could almost be said that it had worked out for the best for her. If it weren't for the dead bodies she was leaving in her wake. The aching memory of those tiny baby clothes. The photograph the police had shown her of that little, little skeleton.

Tears were never far away these days; she didn't hold them in as she stood staring at the last glimpse of her dying dream.

She turned away, and this time she didn't look back.

EPILOGUE

Ivy and brambles were already creeping across the upright bars of the main gate of Hindon House. Soon, the view would be obscured and the grounds would once again be hidden from the curious eyes of those who tried to peer through.

Sycamores, laurels and elder would continue to grow undisturbed. Closer to the house, their deep roots would dry out the soil, unsettle the foundation and eventually lead to subsidence. Brambles and ivy would edge in from the shrubbery. Tendrils would slip through gaps in the brickwork, damaging the stone further as they grew. Rain, dripping from the leaves, would seep through the same cracks to the interior where they would crumble the plaster, and rot the wood.

Eventually, neglected, and past repair, the old house would come down.

And the secrets?

Some were already out.

But not all. There were others.

The Mother Superior of the Sisters of Saint Joyce kept silent about some of the deeds that were committed on those poor unfortunate women who had sought solace with the sisters. There were some things she never shared, not even on her death bed when she'd made the young Sister Elsie promise to guard the house's secrets.

Contrary to what the police and the villagers of Hindon thought, rumours about the sisters had circulated within the Church for years. There was a collective sigh of priestly relief when there were no further entrants, and the convent died organically until only Sister Elsie remained.

When she insisted on staying in Hindon, a home was acquired for her. She wanted to stay local to keep the house under observation, and it was considered a harmless pursuit.

Until it wasn't.

When the Church was dragged into an even bigger scandal than it had survived before, it offered a serene, calm, supportive countenance to the world, while it paddled furiously under the surface to provide damage control where it could.

When the babies were exhumed, and the mothers came to claim their children, the Church was there to offer support. And the Church's solicitors were there to discuss compensation.

It took weeks for the police to finish checking every room in the house, taking up floorboards, searching underneath, digging in the grounds immediately surrounding the house. When no further bodies were discovered, the police packed up, and the Church wiped its brow.

There was no point, the hierarchy said, in mentioning rumours from fifty years before. Rumours that said it wasn't only babies who had died in Hindon House. Not only babies the sisters had buried.

In the pet cemetery in the far corner of the rear garden, where

Cassie had tripped on her first exploration, where she'd run in search of sanctuary, and where Father Cody had died, there beneath bones of pets beloved of previous owners...

...there are other bones.

ACKNOWLEDGMENTS

Writing a book fit for publication is a team effort. I write the words, my wonderful editor, Emily Ruston knocks it into shape and bats it back to me, then it's sent to the patient, diligent copy-editors, and finally to the proofreaders – and a special thanks here to Shirley Khan, proofreader extraordinaire. Then, it's dressed in a striking cover, and the wonderful marketing team launch it into the world. A huge thanks to every member of the incredibly professional and supremely talented Boldwood team.

Keeping me going through it all are the usual suspects, writers Jenny O'Brien, Anita Waller, Judith Baker, Keri Beevis, Pam Lecky, Lesley Bratspis; and so many bloggers and reviewers, that I'm not going to name any in case I forget someone – you all know who you are.

I'd like to thank the staff of The Lamb Hotel in Hindon for allowing me to use their beautiful premises in my book. If you'd like to see more details of this fabulous hotel you can find them here: https://www.lambhindon.co.uk.

Grateful thanks also to the staff of the fabulous Hindon Community Shop for allowing Cassie to 'shop' there.

And of course – a huge thanks to my family. My wonderful husband, Robert, my sisters, brothers, in-laws, nieces, nephews, and grand-nieces and nephews – a wonderful family, I love them all.

I love to hear from readers, you can catch me here:

Facebook: https://www.facebook.com/valeriekeoghnovels

Twitter: https://twitter.com/ValerieKeogh1

Instagram: https://www.instagram.com/valeriekeogh2

https://www.bookbub.com/authors/valerie-keogh

Author Central: https://www.amazon.co.uk/Valerie-Keogh/e/B00LK0NMB8

ABOUT THE AUTHOR

Valerie Keogh is the internationally bestselling author of several psychological thrillers and crime series. She originally comes from Dublin but now lives in Wiltshire and worked as a nurse for many years.

Sign up to Valerie Keogh's mailing list here for news, competitions and updates on future books.

Follow Valerie on social media:

- facebook.com/valeriekeoghnovels
- twitter.com/ValerieKeogh1
- instagram.com/valeriekeogh2
- bookbub.com/authors/valerie-keogh

ALSO BY VALERIE KEOGH

The Lodger

The Widow

The Trophy Wife

The Librarian

The Nurse

The Lawyer

The Housekeeper

Printed in Great Britain
by Amazon